JONNY THOMPSON

Christmas at the Old Mill

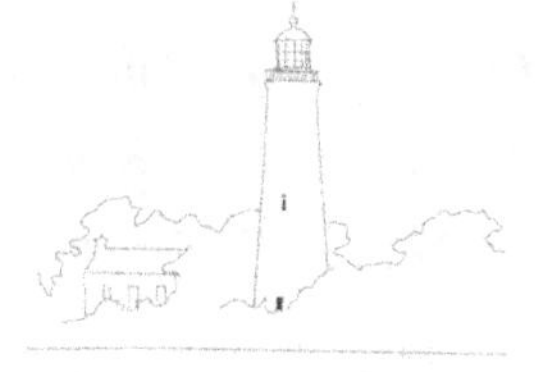

To freshly baked homemade food

up at her desk all night. She likely didn't think Noah knew, but he did. He saw the empty wine bottles the next morning despite her trying to hide them. If she was tired, it was her own fault, not his.

"I'm what?" Noah had shouted back.

"We're going up north," she'd said, looking resigned. What little fight she may have had left in her was gone, which had only made Noah even angrier.

"Why? I don't want to go up north. I want to stay here. Hang out with my friends. I don't want to go anywhere." He had just been saying words then, anything really that would put him in direct defiance of whatever Charlotte was looking for. It didn't matter if she hadn't been willing to fight, he was.

Noah had shouted out everything he could think of, his friends, Christmas, their home, how would Santa find them? He wasn't all that convinced that the big guy was real. After all, at this time of year, he could easily spot at least three of them a day around the city, and his little snitch hadn't moved from the bookshelf for months. He would have brought up school but they'd requested he not return till January, which was a little harsh, in Noah's opinion.

In the end, none of this had appeared to matter to Charlotte, who just looked weary eyed until he'd volleyed off his final outburst and simply received.

"Tough. Pack warmly, or don't and freeze. Up to you." She'd turned and walked away.

"Great parenting, Charlotte!"

"Great childing, Noah!" she'd shouted back. It had been something at least.

Noah had packed and since they'd got on the road, he'd managed to narrow down the possibilities of where they might be going to a couple of locations. He'd been holding on to some hope that it would be the place he'd been thinking about. But since it was a seasonal spot and they'd not been up there once this year, he doubted they would be going up there now to die of the cold in the middle of winter. But then again, Charlotte had been acting weird lately.

"Are you going to tell me where we're going?" Noah said, stopping the clicking of the door lock and turning to see Charlotte's shoulders relax a tiny amount. She was never truly relaxed these days.

"Does it matter? We're going there either way," Charlotte said.

"I have a right to know."

"Why?"

"Because I'm being dragged against my will to a random location. What if you plan on getting rid of me?"

"Why would I…?" Charlotte sighed.

"It's a joke, Charlotte. You remember jokes, don't you?"

"I remember. I just didn't think that it was funny."

"It was funny to me. Which is like fifty percent of the room." Noah smirked. It was something stupid his dad used to say, and he couldn't be sure, but he thought for a moment he saw the corner of Charlotte's mouth flinch. But as quickly as it had come, it was gone again, replaced with a frown.

"It wasn't funny," she said, shaking her head, her hands clutching the wheel.

"Dad would have thought it was," Noah said, crossing his arms as he switched his attention to staring out the window instead. He knew it wasn't fair but at this moment, he wasn't all too keen on playing fair. He was stuck in a car going north away from his entire life to some unknown destination. Well, not completely unknown.

"Well, he's not here," Charlotte said under her breath so softly, Noah wasn't confident she'd even said it. But he knew she had even if she'd only been thinking it. He still heard it, loud and clear. But instead of saying anything, Noah turned up the radio. It was old music, but he didn't care. He just wanted something to drown the silence in the car.

The radio played for the better part of the next hour before static kicked in, cutting out the rambling of some man praising wheat kings or something or other before Noah finally gave up and tried to find a new station.

"Have you figured out where we're going yet?" Charlotte asked as she gave a cautious glance in Noah's direction. He pretended to ignore it.

"Yes. I'm not an idiot, Charlotte." This caused her to wince. *Good. I hope it makes her feel uncomfortable,* Noah thought.

"I don't think you're an idiot."

"No?" Noah said, stopping his flipping of the music to stare at her.

"No. I just don't know… You're… I thought…"

"Thank you for your comforting words." Noah's eyes rolled dramatically.

"Dammit, Noah!" Charlottes hands smacked the wheel. "I'm trying my best here, okay."

"Maybe you need to try harder," Noah sniped.

"You're not exactly easy to deal with."

"I'm thirteen!"

"Exactly! You're a kid!" Charlotte shouted. "You should be playing with friends, not tormenting other students and damaging school property."

"You think I tormented kids at school?" Noah wanted to

scream. This was the problem with Charlotte. She was so preoccupied with herself that she never cared to learn the real story. Noah did not torment his classmates. He didn't even know anyone was in there. It was supposed to be a harmless little prank. Perhaps damaging school property was inevitable. He could be blamed for many things, but stupidity was not one of them.

"Yes. No. I mean…" She was obviously flustered. "In case you've failed to realize, we're driving to St Martins on a Tuesday. On a school day! Because you're not allowed to go back until January. Three weeks you were suspended!" Charlotte sighed, looking up at the sky for a moment as if looking to some imaginary God Noah knew she didn't believe in. "And that's if they even decide to let you back at all. I don't get it. I don't get you."

"You're right. You don't," Noah chided.

"I know!" Charlotte laughed, but it wasn't a happy laugh so much as it was painfully cruel. "I really know. Cause you're a good kid and smart and funny… but lately…"

"What?" Noah insisted.

"I don't know, Noah. Okay. Honestly, I don't know what I'm doing."

"So, is that why we're going to Nana's. So you can drop me off and leave me?" Noah replied, voicing the thought he'd been having since he'd realized where they were heading. The idea had crossed his mind and now after hearing all the things Charlotte had to say about him, he was starting to believe he'd pushed things too far and she was done with him. Well, officially done with him. Truth was, Noah felt Charlotte had been finished with him for a few months now. This was the closest thing to engagement he'd managed to receive in weeks and it all appeared to be leading up to some sort of farewell. *I hope you have a good life with your nana. I'll be in the city living my real life now without you.*

"What?" Charlotte said and to her credit, she genuinely looked confused, as if this wasn't the plan all along. Noah had to hand it to her, she could be a remarkable actor when she chose to be. "Noah. I'm not leaving you with your nana. I just thought it would be nice to get out of the city for the month, be with some family. Help Nana at the Old Mill."

"The Old Mill?" Noah asked. "You're sending me to work in the Mill?" This just kept getting better. Not only was Noah being sent away, he was going to have to work for his freedom. Pay his penance. It was hard enough to be a kid but now he would have to be a child worker in a mill.

"No. Maybe. I don't know. It will just be nice to be out of the city for a bit."

"But you already have a job," Noah protested. "Why would you work in a mill?"

"I took a leave from work for the month."

"Why?" Noah asked.

"Because I need a break. *We* needed to get away."

"I didn't need to. Definitely not to work in a mill!" Noah was shouting now.

"Noah, calm down. You know the Mill isn't an actual mill, right?" Charlotte asked.

Noah remained silent instead of stepping into any situation he wasn't prepared for. Of course he didn't know it wasn't a mill. Why on earth would he have believed the Old Mill was anything but what the name had described? It had been years since they had gone up to see Nana and for all he knew, she was owner operator of a mill, which he imagined milled...

things.

"Noah, the Old Mill is the country store your nana started. You remember those strawberry rhubarb pies she would bring?"

Noah did remember those quite well, along with some other delicious-tasting treats. But he assumed that was just Nana being Nana.

"I guess you were too young to remember it all, but you used to love it up here. Especially at Christmas."

"We used to come up here for Christmas?" Noah asked, though he vaguely remembered visiting Nana, but that felt like a long time ago.

"Occasionally. Wait, so, when I asked if you knew where we were going… and you said…" Charlotte asked gently, which only served to fuel the anger that was building within Noah. Of course she would do this.

"That's all you wanted, Charlotte! Was to catch me in a lie? Is that it? You think I'm lying to you and you have to come up with these things from my past just to catch me? Make me feel like an idiot!?" Noah shouted.

"No. That's not it at all, Noah. I wasn't trying to catch you in a lie…"

"No, you just wanted to make me feel stupid cause you're so much smarter than me. Well congratulations, Charlotte, I didn't know. Are you happy?"

"No. No that's not it at all." Charlotte looked flustered but it was clear to Noah now just how good of an actor she could be when she wanted to be. But her little games wouldn't fool him again. Not today.

"Noah please, I just wanted to know if you remembered it up here, that's all. If you had any memories about—"

"Well, I don't," Noah said, flicking to another station and turning the radio up before returning to engaging the lock on and off until even he became annoyed by the sound. All this while pretending not to notice that Charlotte clearly wanted to say something else. But she never did, she just stared at the partially plowed road, periodically glancing out her window as she tried to remove something from her eye.

2

Charlotte

"Hi, Dot." Charlotte said as the screen door shut behind her. Despite the rush of cold air following them into the little cottage, it was warm and cozy inside with the smell of cinnamon and cloves lingering in the air from the makeshift humidifier resting on top of the fire in the main room.

In that moment, all of the dread and worry Charlotte was feeling about leaving the city melted away as she was hit by an overwhelming desire to cry – not that she was going to allow herself that kind of emotion. Certainly not after the car ride she'd just had and definitely not in front of Dot, who stood, arms open, waiting to embrace Charlotte as if she were her own daughter. The last thing Charlotte needed to do was have a breakdown in front of her mother… ex-mother-in-law when she had already been so generous as to invite them up to stay for the month.

Charlotte's own parents were not the most nurturing people in the world. When they did manage to stop fighting with one another long enough to remember Charlotte was still their daughter, they were too busy trying to spend one another's money in a vain attempt to show the other who was doing better.

The only positive for Charlotte was they decided to battle it out from different parts of the world. Well, Victoria BC and Sarasota, Florida, which may as well have been Jordan for all the times Charlotte had seen either of them.

"Welcome home, my love," Dot said as she wrapped her in her embrace. The gesture still caused Charlotte to tense up slightly, as she had never grown accustomed to her husband's family's desire to hug one another when visiting. Despite being a good five inches taller than the little woman, she couldn't help but feel tiny in her arms and for a brief moment, she allowed herself to sink into the comfort.

She didn't stay there long for fear that too much sentiment would break her down past the point of no return. She'd been holding this position for months now, and she wasn't prepared to let her guard down quite yet.

"It's good to see you, Dot," Charlotte said, breaking away from the hug and taking a step back to show Noah, who was standing in the doorway holding the small suitcase he'd packed for his unexpected trip.

"Hi, Dot," Noah said absently.

"Call me Nana, love." Dot winked playfully at Noah, who barely flinched. Charlotte tried to play it off as it were nothing, giving her a weak smile but was afraid it was more of a grimace. If Dot had cared or noticed, she didn't say anything. "Wow. You've certainly gotten big." Her eye simply flicked back to Noah.

"Thanks," Noah said, and Charlotte couldn't hide her annoyance. She might have even smacked him upside the head. But that might have been seen as a little extreme, no matter how much she wanted to.

"Go and give your nana a hug," Charlotte placed a hand on his back to guide him forward, but he flinched away.

"I'm okay," Noah said, which made Charlotte's eyes go wide with fury. It was one thing to disrespect her, but this kind woman deserved none of that treatment.

Charlotte was preparing to say as much when Dot stepped in, her smile never faltering as she placed a hand on his shoulder.

"In your own time then. But it's very good to see you," Dot said. Despite being nearly fifty years his senior and barely a hairline taller than the young man, she maintained a dignity that only a person confident in themselves could hold.

"Can I go to my room?" Noah asked, glancing up to Charlotte and right past their host.

"We just—" Charlotte began but stopped when Dot placed a hand on her arm.

"Of course. You must be tired from the drive. Let's get you settled in your rooms, then maybe a tea." She said this last part to Charlotte as Noah began scanning the tiny house. "Although Bear might be having a nap in your bed at the moment."

"You still have Bear?" Charlotte asked.

"The old boy is still kicking around. Yes." Dot smiled.

Noah just looked confused. "You have a bear?"

"Bear is her dog, Noah. Why would she have a bear?" Charlotte said.

"I don't know. Why would you have a dog?"

"You really don't remember Bear?" Charlotte asked. "When you were a kid, you two used to play all the—"

"I don't," Noah said. "Can I play with my Switch now?" he

asked, though from the sound of his voice, he appeared to have an idea of what the answer was going to be. But what he couldn't have known was how tired Charlotte was from the drive up. The idea of fighting over that damned device, something she wished now she'd never given him, was just too much right now.

"Fine," she said, receiving the closest thing to a positive reaction from her son for the first time today, though it was short-lived as he waited for the compromises that were sure to follow. "Just keep it down, maybe put your headphones in."

"That's it?" Noah asked, sounding almost disappointed that there wasn't a fight at the end of it. Something they'd both begun to expect lately.

"Let me show you to your rooms," Dot said, smiling as she gestured for them to come in and for the first time Charlotte felt just how warm it was in the house. The fire crackled in the living room to their right with the kitchen off to the left. It was so lovely, all she wanted to do was lie on the couch and fall asleep until the New Year. But she knew that was never going to happen.

…

"You look exhausted, my dear," Dot said as she handed Charlotte a cup of tea.

In the twenty minutes since Charlotte had arrived, she had managed to unpack but not take a nap. Even if she had wanted to, she doubted her eyes would let her. She was all wound up from the drive, or the week, or possibly the month. If she was being honest, from life.

She didn't need a reminder of how exhausted she was, although perhaps she did, since this state had become such a constant as of late that she'd forgotten what non-exhaustion felt like. Still, she didn't love that it was so readable on her face. At the very least she wished she was able to mask it a little better.

"I'm fine," she said through a forced smile before blowing on her tea as she swivelled from side to side in one of the plush armchairs that made up the living room. Dot sat in the other chair beside her. Along with the two chairs, there was a large couch, all of which half-mooned a long, wooden table and looked at the wood stove.

It was odd, although rather nice, to be in a room where the centrepiece wasn't a TV, but rather shelves of books and a cozy fireplace. It felt comfortable, then strange as she struggled to remember the last time she'd visited.

"We both know you're not fine, my love." It wasn't a question, but a statement and one Charlotte wasn't prepared for. "And that's alright. You're allowed to not be fine."

"I am—"

"You called me, love, for the first time since… well, a year, telling me you needed to come and stay. I'm no genius but I think I can manage to put two and two together."

Charlotte let out a heavy sigh and shook her head. "I might be a little overwhelmed," she said, taking a cautious sip of her tea, which was still so hot, it burned her lips.

"I'm glad you're here," Dot said.

"You say that now." Charlotte laughed coldly.

"I'll say that always," she replied and the way she said it almost made Charlotte believe she was telling the truth.

"You don't know what he's like. He's…"

"A thirteen-year-old boy?" Dot offered.

"The school is filled with thirteen-year-old boys and they didn't all get kicked out."

"You still haven't told me what he did. Not that it matters," Dot said, raising a hand to stop Charlotte from having to answer, "I'm just saying he's young and he's been through a lot. Perhaps he just needs a little time to figure out how to deal with it all."

"It's been over a year."

"How are you coping with it?"

"Fine," Charlotte said without thinking. Even to her, it felt like an empty response. But it was something she told herself to get her through the day-to-day.

"I'm not," Dot said after a few moments of what appeared to be some minor deliberations. Charlotte wanted to smack herself for not asking her this question sooner. After all, Eli had been her son too.

"I'm so sorry. I can't believe… here I am and—"

Dot once again raised a hand mercifully to stop Charlotte's ramblings.

"I'm not trying to make you feel bad, Charlotte. I'm simply pointing out that it is alright to not be okay with all of this. What happened to Eli was a surprise to all of us and it's okay to not be okay with just moving on."

"It's my job to be okay." *Wasn't it?*

Her words hung in the air as the two women sat and sipped their tea. Charlotte was beginning to wonder if the conversation was ever going to start up again when she felt a hand rest on hers. It was soft and comforting and everything Charlotte wished she was.

There was so much love and understanding in that touch that she would be happy to exist in that feeling forever. It was a motherly connection with a woman who wasn't even her own mother and something she felt personally void of.

A part of her feared she would never have that connection with the one person in the world she was meant to feel that for—Noah.

"There is no right or wrong way to deal with loss, my love. Perhaps all you need is a little help." Dot's hand patted Charlotte's before returning to her own tea. The warmth in her touch vanished along with her hand, leaving Charlotte feeling, once again, cold and inadequate. There was truth in what Dot had said. She did need help and maybe this would be the place to get it.

3

Noah

"Are you up, Noah?" Charlotte's voice called from outside his makeshift room.

Noah called it "makeshift" because as far as he was concerned, he had never heard of a day bed but it was certainly not an actual bed. For one, it was much smaller than the one he was used to sleeping in and this one was a lot softer. Some people might enjoy the feeling of sinking into a bed, but Noah couldn't help but feel like he was trapped in it, which was likely the reason for so many of his unpleasant dreams.

It didn't help either that a large section of said bed was occupied by Bear, and the harder he tried to move the burly old dog, the deeper he sank into Noah's section and eventually, he was forced to accept his presence. Yet another distraction from his much-needed sleep.

When he'd first woken up in the night, he had completely forgotten where he was staying, which is why he didn't try to leave his room. He couldn't remember what was out in the hallway. His mind started spiralling, hopscotching from confusion, to fear, to thoughts of urinating, all while trying desperately to fall back asleep. He supposed at some point he must have since he had eventually woken up again, only to find himself repeating the process.

This was all flickering through Noah's mind when Charlotte asked him if he was up. *If only she knew.*

"Yes, I'm up," he finally called back, though from the sounds of her footsteps, she'd already started to walk away. He glanced over at the clock, now just past seven in the morning.

Noah looked around until he spotted a towel, before tossing the sheets off him and wishing he hadn't when he felt the chill of the morning air. Obviously, fires were cozy when they were on, but not when they're out. He shook his head as he ran over and gripped the towel. The sooner he got into the shower, the better.

After a hot shower and changing into some fresh clothes, Noah almost felt normal, despite constantly having to cover his mouth to fight back the yawning.

"Why do I have to get up?" he asked, approaching the island, which offered a divide between the kitchen and the living room, and was also filled with pancakes and fresh fruit.

"Look what Nana made us," Charlotte said, holding an expression of someone who desperately wanted Noah to not embarrass them by not saying something courteous, despite the fact that he'd never asked for pancakes, nor were they remotely close to his favourite breakfast. He contemplated saying nothing just to see what kind of reaction he might stir from Charlotte, but they did smell good and it would be a shame not to at least try them to make sure they were not horrible. *They certainly don't look horrible.*

"Thank you, Nana," Noah said, adding a smile for further commitment. "Everything smells incredible."

"They taste incredible too," Charlotte said, having already had two and was setting up for more. It was a strange sight for Noah considering he'd often watched her barely touch her morning cereal, choosing to stick to her morning diet of coffee and more coffee.

"So why am I up?" Noah asked again while Nana made him a plate of food that looked as though it could have fed a horse rather than a child.

"Growing boys and all that," Nana said with a wink as she placed the food down in front of him.

"I usually just stick to coffee in the morning," Noah said, which received a shake of the head from Charlotte.

"He's joking. He doesn't drink coffee."

"Do too," Noah countered.

"Do not," Charlotte snipped back. "Christ, what am I doing?" she said, shaking her head. "He doesn't drink coffee, Dot, but he is a slight pain in the ass in the morning."

"Takes one to know one."

Charlotte opened her mouth to speak but stopped, letting out a heavy sigh instead.

For a brief moment, Noah thought maybe he saw a glimpse of the old Charlotte, the one who could joke around before she became so serious about everything.

"Well, I hope you enjoy your breakfast," Nana said as she stole a glance at her watch. "But I think I need to get back into the shop."

"Back?" Charlotte asked, pausing to take a bite of her pancakes as the syrup dripped off the piece, falling back on her plate.

"I was baking for the store this morning. Usually head in for 5 a.m."

"What?" Noah nearly shouted and from the expression on Charlotte's face, she was having a similar thought. It was hard enough to get up for school at seven in the morning, he couldn't imagine getting up at five.

"You get used to it. Besides, there is nothing better than freshly cooked food."

"Sleep is better," Noah said, which received a slap to his arm from Charlotte despite the laughter it received from Nana. "Hey!" He rubbed where Charlotte had made contact.

"You don't always have to be a smartass," she chastised.

"You don't always have to be a—"

"Perhaps the two of you can come into the shop today for some lunch," Nana suggested as she moved over toward the coat rack by the door and began to bundle up for what appeared to be a light, snowy day.

Although Noah had only experienced twelve winters and perhaps six of those he could fully remember, there was a brutal understanding that all Canadians needed to accept if they were going to survive winter. Firstly, you didn't always need a jacket, but life was a lot less enjoyable without one. Secondly, if it was snowing, it always meant it would be less cold. And if it looked pleasant and sunny but the snow didn't appear to be melting, it was horrifically cold outside. Today was a category two, he would guess, and from the way Nana appeared to bundle up, his assessment was correct.

"That would be nice, thank you, Dot," Charlotte said, just as Noah cut off a piece of his pancake. He held on to little hope that he was going to enjoy it but he figured it was rude to not at least have a bite.

"Tasty?" Nana asked as she wrapped a colourful scarf around her neck.

Tasty might have been the understatement of the year. Considering Noah would have avoided pancakes nine out of ten times at a restaurant, these were arguably the best he'd ever tasted.

"Yes," was all he managed to get out between mouthfuls.

"Maybe swallow first?" Charlotte muttered.

"I take it as a compliment," Nana said, and although Noah didn't know if she was being serious or not, he chose to accept it as such.

"Syrup's good too!" He said gleefully, mouth still full, as he poured on a little more of the impressively sweet syrup.

"My God, I've raised an animal," Charlotte said, shaking her head as she cleaned the remaining syrup from off her plate with a slice of pancake.

"We sell the syrup at the shop. Bruce makes it from his farm up the road. I'll let him know you think it's good."

Noah wanted to say something, but his mouth was too full and he found himself eating as if he hadn't eaten for days. Which he supposed he hadn't. The night before, he'd not been overly hungry after the long day and chose to go to bed, which was a fruitless offering considering he hadn't managed much sleep anyway. But now, his stomach was growling and he was all too happy to feed it pancakes.

"We will see you for lunch, Dot. Thank you again," Charlotte said, her head tilting down toward the food.

"My pleasure, love. Oh, and if you leave, don't forget to put a log on the fire," Nana said with a smile. "Might be nice to have others around to keep this place warm."

"We'll do our best," Charlotte said, glancing nervously at the fire. It was clear to Noah that Charlotte was not all too keen on working on the fire, though from the determined look on her face, which might have also been stubbornness, she wasn't about to say she couldn't do it.

"No pressure, love." Nana waved and headed out the door, leaving Charlotte and Noah alone once again. Only this time in a stranger's house.

"You know it wouldn't kill you to use some manners?" Charlotte said, placing her knife and fork down on the table and giving Noah a irritable look.

"How do you know that? You a doctor now?"

"No, but I am a human being."

"And I'm not?" Noah countered.

"Sometimes, I have my doubts," Charlotte said with a small grin.

"You know I didn't ask to come here. Or get up, for that matter," Noah said. "You made me do both."

"Being here will be good for both of us," Charlotte said. "It's good to get out of the city."

"But I like the city."

"You're thirteen. You barely know what you like yet."

"So, I'm just supposed to believe that you know what's best for me?" Noah dropped his knife and fork on the plate, ignoring the last remaining pancake.

"I'm not trying to—"

"Yes, you are. Let's be honest. We're here cause you can't stand to be alone with me," Noah shouted.

"That's not it at all!" Charlotte said. "We're here because I thought it would be good for us."

"For us or for you?" Noah hit back. He wasn't sure why but all he felt right now was anger and he was ready for war.

"Us! For us. Why is it so hard for you to believe that I want anything but what's best for you? All you do is make things so difficult! I'm doing my best, Noah!" Charlotte was shouting now, her face flushed red, and it was clear to Noah that despite being somewhere different, their lives weren't different. They were just pretending things were different, but really, it was the same old problem. Charlotte didn't want him around.

"Well, do better!" Noah said, standing up so suddenly that his stool threatened to fall over. Thankfully, it didn't since it would have made his exit less powerful, though as it was, he caught a glimpse of a spectator, Nana, who must have forgotten something and was now standing at the doorway looking into the kitchen.

"Thank you for breakfast," Noah said to Nana before he turned away and stormed off to his room.

Charlotte must have seen his comment wasn't directed to her and turned to see Nana as her face turned a shade of red Noah didn't know was possible.

"Dot... I'm sorry. Noah!" she tried calling after him, but he was already heading down the hall, managing to barely catch her final question, "You don't want to finish your breakfast?"

"I'm not hungry," Noah said as he slammed the door shut and ran to jump back into his bed. He pulled the covers over him and pretended he was home in the city. At least there, he had friends he could see. Other kids in the condo building. But here, he was alone, and he had nothing to do except be stuck in this old house and play his Nintendo.

Noah hadn't even been here for twenty-four hours and already, he hated everything about this place. He would have preferred to be in school, but they had made it clear they didn't want him back. So, it would seem no matter where he was, he wasn't wanted.

He closed his eyes tightly, trying to will himself back to sleep, but he couldn't ignore the muffled sounds of dishes being cleaned up in the kitchen.

4

Dot

"Morning, Dot," Betty Penner said as she stood at the cash register, her tote bag filled with various homemade goods Dot had begun selling over the years.

"Good morning, Betty."

Dot had started the Old Mill with a simple concept of opening a store where she could sell the occasional coffee and homemade treat. However, over the years, it had slowly evolved, gaining traction in the community as the spot to go for fresh homemade goods for all occasions. Pies, cakes, tarts, quiches – basically, if you could bake it, Dot could make it. At least that was the conclusion the town seemed to have come to, and Dot wasn't going to try to refute this.

The truth was, she was always willing to try and given she'd been baking since childhood, and it was fifteen years since she'd started this little endeavour, she could more or less make whatever it was people in her little community wanted.

"Are you okay?" Betty's voice sounded distant as she stared cautiously across the counter at Dot.

"Yes, of course. Why?"

"Well, you have rung that peach chutney through three times and although I do love the stuff, I hardly think I can go through three jars of it." Betty chuckled at her own joke.

The realization of what she had done shocked Dot back to reality.

"I'm sorry. Maybe my head is a little distracted," she said, though she doubted that an apology was needed. Betty, who was a couple of years older than her, was one of the store's regular customers. Over the years, she'd been very supportive and someone Dot would consider to be a good friend, which is why she wasn't at all embarrassed to share her concerns with this woman.

"Is it the announcement?" Betty asked, her voice taking on a conspiratorial tone as she glanced around her as if someone might have been listening in on their darkest secrets.

It wasn't the announcement. Well, it wasn't entirely the announcement, since Dot would be lying to herself if she wasn't at least a little preoccupied with her upcoming news. So far, no one had heard anything, which she was grateful for, and if she had it her way, no one would until she was ready. At least no one she hadn't already told, like Betty.

"Not entirely," Dot said honestly. "My daughter-in-law and grandson are in town visiting for the holidays."

"That's wonderful… isn't it?" Betty asked, probing, as it would seem, to figure out which side of the conversation her friend needed her to be on.

"It is. I'm happy they are here. I am."

"Sounds more like you're trying to convince yourself, rather than me," Betty offered as she bagged her goods. Luckily, there weren't many people in the shop now save for her other chef, Tia, and Riley, who helped work the front of house.

"Do you have time for a coffee?" Dot asked, though she didn't wait for the answer since she knew on Wednesdays, Betty shopped in the morning, then would head home to prepare her dinner before taking her dog Coco out for a walk. It was the spoils of being retired that she had time to spare. That, and she was a big fan of coffee. So, Dot wasn't surprised when her bottom lip jetted out thoughtfully and nodded toward one of the empty tables.

"Riley, man the till. I'm going to have a chat with Betty," Dot said as she prepared two coffees.

"Of course," Riley said as she stopped folding takeout boxes and moved toward the counter. Riley was in her early twenties and had worked for Dot since she was a young girl, helping in the back in the morning and then in the front of house on the weekends. She knew the store nearly as well as Dot, though despite all of Dot's efforts, she never showed any signs of wanting to take on more responsibility.

After she returned home from university, she asked for her old summer job back while she figured things out. That had been nearly a year ago now and Riley was still content not to move on. It was great for Dot, although sooner or later, everyone needed to move forward.

Dot carried the coffees over to where Betty was sitting. She'd already lost her winter garments and looked prepared to sit for as long as was needed, or until the coffee stopped being poured, whichever came first.

"What's the problem?" she asked, not bothering with pleasantries. Betty had been a principal at the local school for years and therefore knew a thing or two about conflict resolution. She had, on more than one occasion, claimed her job to be more about placating emotions than actually teaching. Between the other teachers, students, and their parents, Betty had had her hands full trying to make sure everyone was happy. Or at the very least, not angry.

"It's not a problem. It's just, I'm worried," Dot offered. She, on the other hand, was never great with confrontation. According to her ex-husband, it was one of the reasons he was now her ex. Not that she was overly disappointed since, save for Eli, her divorce managed to give her the most fulfilling years of her life.

"Worried about what?" Betty asked, taking a sip of her coffee as she leaned in closer to Dot.

"They're fighting – a lot," Dot said.

"How old is your grandson again?"

"Thirteen."

"There you have it," Betty said, waving a hand as if this was the root cause of everything going on. Her confidence took Dot by surprise.

"That's it?"

"Of course. He's likely just trying to deal with his emotions and doesn't know how to handle them all at once," Betty said as if this was the most obvious thing in the world and perhaps to a woman who had spent her life surrounded by children, it was. But to Dot, it was all a bit confusing still.

"You really think—"

"You lost your son, Dot. How are you feeling?" Betty asked, and the abrupt turn of conversation shocked Dot a little. Although it had been over a year since Eli's death, it often felt as though there was a hole in Dot's life that, no matter what she did, she couldn't fill. Most of the time, she preferred the empty feeling since the alternative she supposed was moving on, which she wasn't prepared to do. Not yet, anyway.

"It's day by day," Dot said truthfully.

"And you're a grown woman," Betty said, her lips tightening as her hands curled around her coffee mug. "Imagine what it must feel like to not understand your emotions, to feel as though you are always sad or angry about something and not fully able to grasp the reason why. That boy has dealt with more things than any young man should. It's no surprise that he might be feeling a bit overwhelmed."

When Betty laid it out like that, it was hard to dispute her logic. It had been so long since Dot had had a child in the house, she'd almost forgotten what it was like to raise one. Having to watch on as they whittled away at all their personality traits, slowly inching their young minds forward as they carved out the foundations of who they would eventually become. It was one thing for a sixty-five-year-old woman to have to process her emotions. It was another for a thirteen-year-old still finding his footing.

"I suppose you're right," Dot admitted, feeling like the answer was so obvious now.

"You remember what you told me when you first opened this place?"

Betty's question appeared to come from nowhere, though that didn't stop Dot from trying to figure out what she might have said fifteen years ago. At that point, she was a relative stranger to her. But for the life of her, she couldn't think of it, and she shook her head.

"You told me that this place was the first step in building your life back up."

"Seems like a lot to dish out to a new friend." Dot chuckled nervously.

"Are you kidding? I was honoured," Betty said, placing a

hand on Dot's. "You were starting your life over and using the Old Mill as a way to do it. You remember this place when you first got it? I do." Betty laughed as she looked around the Old Mill.

There was no shortage of reminders in these walls of all the hardships and triumphs Dot had faced over the year building her new home. Old pictures lined the walls of what it had looked like before, where it had come from. One of those pictures hung on the wall beside her was Eli and Charlotte, who had come up to help with the initial renovation.

"This old mill was crumbling down, Dot, and you pulled it back to the studs and rebuilt it, taking care and time to keep the origins of the building but making it your own," Betty said, shaking her head. "Truth be told, the rest of us thought you were senile. No way you were ever going to get this place off the ground. Just another city person coming to disrupt our little town. But look at it now!"

Dot looked around at what was now her small country market, trying to recall what the place had looked like all those years ago when she'd first purchased it. It had been unused for decades, rundown to the point where many people, including the town council, believed the building should be condemned, thinking there was no way anyone was going to spend the money it needed to restore it. Which meant Dot was able to get it for next to nothing. That was good because she had to spend nearly everything she had fixing it up. Everything, a little sweat equity, and help.

The photos around the store didn't do the building justice—not truly, anyway. From those images, it might have looked cluttered and dirty but none of them fully grasped the scope of what Dot had to put up with. Rotten floorboards, infestations, leaking roofs—you name it, Dot was forced to cope with it all. But somewhere in all of that chaos, tear-filled nights, and a near-constant ache from physical work, Dot managed to piece herself and it back together. Stone by stone, this place transformed her and her life into the person she was now. From the exposed stone walls and timber framing, to large, rounded windows which were near impossible to replace, the oak flooring she'd sanded down herself and curved, stone archways hidden beneath years of plastered walls and rotted insulation. It was as if this building was trying to tell her something and as long as she was willing to listen, it would continue to surprise her with all of its beauty that had been covered up from the years of neglect. With a little hard work, she was able to uncover it all and share it with her new community.

Dot hadn't realized she'd begun to cry until Betty placed a tissue in her hand and wordlessly clasped it, appearing to understand what it was Dot was thinking.

"I'm being silly," Dot said quietly.

"You're not." Betty smiled.

"I still don't know what to do," Dot shook her head for a moment, trying not to think about the place she'd called home for so long. Instead, her mind wandered back to Charlotte and Noah.

"Nothing," Betty said, sounding much more optimistic than the one word of advice appeared to offer.

"Nothing?" Dot asked.

"It's Christmas. He's a kid, and she likely just needs help. Each of those things are well within your realm of kindness. When was the last time any of them were up here with you for the holidays? When else are you ever going to get the chance to have so much time with them? Enjoy it. Be there for them, and I'm sure everything will work out."

"You really think so?" Dot asked, wishing she was more hopeful like her friend, and not so pessimistic.

"Stranger things have happened at Christmas, Dot."

Dot let her words sink in as if they were some sort of wish. Because somewhere deep down, Dot knew she was right. Strange things did happen at Christmas.

5

Charlotte

"Jesus!" Charlotte said as she yet again tried to put a fresh log on the fire without burning her fingers, and once again she was unsuccessful.

"Smooth," Noah said as he walked past and into the kitchen, Bear tagging behind him, his tail wagging.

"I don't see you trying to help," Charlotte said.

"You're right." Noah opened cupboards until finding one with some glasses in it. Taking one, he filled it up with water.

"What are you doing?" Charlotte asked, locking up the fire before the flames could get her again. The fire sealed up, she took a seat in the chair next to it, enjoying the warmth from the stove.

"Getting water, Charlotte. I would have thought that was obvious," Noah said, holding the glass up and giving her a concerned look. "Are you okay?"

"I don't mean lit—" she huffed, hating that talking to her son felt like pulling teeth. "I mean right now. Should we take Bear for a walk? Or something?"

The little guy's tail began to wag uncontrollably as he

waddled over to sit at her feet. Obviously, she'd said some sort of magic words to this poor animal and now she would be forced to follow through with it or suffer his little eyes peering at her for the rest of the morning.

"I'm okay. But you can take Bear. He won't stop following me around."

"He's a pet, Noah."

"He's annoying. Last night, I barely got any sleep because this guy sleeps like some sort of log. It would be easier to move an actual bear."

As if in response to this, Bear sat next to Charlotte's feet and leaned into her legs, the weight of which was so unexpected, her knees buckled slightly at the act.

"Noah, he's a dog," Charlotte said.

"You sleep in his bed."

"Are you really so mad at me for bringing you up here? You would rather be in our apartment in the city being grounded?"

"So, you agree being grounded in the city is equal punishment to being *"free"* up here?" Noah said and his manipulation of her words temporarily set her back.

"No. That's not. You honestly believe that?" Charlotte asked as Noah's brows shot up and he gave her a little shrug. "You know being here isn't a punishment. Right?"

"Could have fooled me," Noah said.

"Well, it isn't," Charlotte said, her tone defensive. She was tired of feeling like the bad guy, as if Noah's feelings about things were somehow her fault. "And even if it was, I think there are worse ways to punish you than coming up to a small town where you can go outside and skate or do whatever it is kids do up here."

"You're proving my point. You don't even know what kids

do up here."

"I'm not a kid!" Charlotte shouted.

"So why don't you stop pretending like you're doing this for me then!" Noah shot back as he slammed his glass on the counter. Bear, as if sensing some sort of unease in the room, propped his head up on Charlotte's lap and looked at her. Or perhaps he was just tired of sitting on the floor and wanted to go for a walk.

"Put warm clothes on," Charlotte said, not bothering to look up from Bear's face.

"I told you, I don't—"

"This isn't a democracy. You're going to put clothes on, and you are going to go outside and walk Bear with me now," Charlotte said, her eyes flicking up toward Noah.

"And what if I don't want to?" Noah said, folding his arms.

"Then tough cookies. Because you're going. You want this to be a punishment? Fine. It's a punishment and while we are here, you are going to do what I say."

"Sounds more like a dictatorship," Noah countered.

"So be it. Call it what you want. But whatever you decide to call it, remember that we are here because of you. Because of your actions at school," Charlotte said as Noah began to chuckle to himself, which only served to make Charlotte even more angry than she was. "You think this is funny?"

"You trying to lay down the law?" Noah asked, but he must have picked up on the raw anger building up in Charlotte because he stopped whatever thought he was having and simply said, "I didn't do anything wrong."

"You didn't do anything—?" It was Charlotte's turn to laugh but it wasn't jovial in any way. It was cold and distant. "You could have hurt someone."

"But I didn't, did I?" Noah countered.

"That isn't the point. You could have and honestly, I don't think the safety of others was even on your list of things you were thinking about when you did it."

"Oh no? Then what exactly was on my list, Charlotte?" Noah said smugly.

"I don't know, Noah. That's the point." Her face was flushed red now and all she wanted to do was run out of the room and start to cry and she hated herself for feeling that way. She had no understanding of what to do with this kid. At every turn, it was as if he was primed for a fight. It left her broken and exhausted and frankly, she'd had enough.

"Just get your damn clothes on. We're going for a walk."

"You said da—"

"I know what I said, Noah! And for the record, you should get used to this because while we are here, we will be taking Bear out for a walk every day, twice a day, the two of us."

"That's not fai—"

"I don't want to hear it. Now suit up. We're leaving."

Charlotte stood and folded her arms, waiting for the snarky comment that was sure to come, but none did.

Noah huffed slightly but turned to go to his room.

"We leave in five," Charlotte shouted and somehow managed to feel both proud of herself and a little ill in her stomach at the same time.

I'm doing the right thing.

At the very least, she had to believe she was.

*

The mid-morning air was crisp and despite the sun shining, it was still winter and therefore cold. Unlike the city, which never seemed to have snow, or at least white snow for very long, the little town of St Martins was downright covered in the stuff. She found it quite impressive how well the town had done with clearing the snow so quickly. She had known that it had snowed a little overnight, but from the looks of the sidewalks and roads, you would never have imagined it.

"It's cold," Noah shoved his hands into his pockets.

"It's December. It's supposed to be cold."

"You know this is child abuse, making me walk around in the winter. What if I get sick?"

"You think it is abuse to make you walk around a cute little town with a dog?" Charlotte asked incredulously, which received a nod from Noah. "I think you need to get a better understanding of what that word means."

"There is nothing to do in this place," Noah kicked a ball of snow down the sidewalk, and Charlotte felt guilty when she imagined how much nicer the walk had been when he'd simply been silently brooding instead of loudly.

"We've been in this town for all of a day. How can you possibly know there is nothing to do?" Charlotte asked.

"Look at it," Noah said, gesturing around as if it were obvious.

It was a funny thing, small towns. Charlotte had never lived in one. She was a city girl through and through. At least she thought she had been, until Dot had purchased the Old Mill and she and Eli had spent their weekends coming up and helping restore the old building. She hadn't admitted to it at the time, but she had enjoyed that.

"You know your dad used to say the same thing," Charlotte said, and she half-expected some snarky reply but Noah just kicked his ball of snow so Charlotte took that as a sign that she could keep talking. "He hated the small town he grew up in and always complained about there being nothing to do."

"I feel his pain," Noah said, his brows shooting up sarcastically, a motion that reminded Charlotte of Eli so much, she thought he was there, preparing for some series of jokes that no one but himself would laugh at.

"Here's the catch," she said, holding up a finger to garner more attention. "Secretly, he loved it."

"Now I know you're lying." Noah snorted, a habit he'd most definitely received from her.

"No, I'm not. He missed it more than anything. Community, home, people, who loved and knew him. He had more experiences in his small town then he ever had in the city, because they were shared by everyone. All of his triumphs and his mistakes."

"Why would anyone want to be remembered for their mistakes?"

"Accountability. The city offers anonymity. But your dad just saw that as way of making mistakes without a community holding you accountable, with people who want you to be better."

"Sounds like hell," Noah said, rolling his eyes and this time, it was Charlotte's turn to laugh, which seemed to catch both Noah and Bear by surprise as they stopped to look up at her. The latter took the small respite to sniff around a fire hydrant and have a quick pee.

"He said it was," Charlotte admitted, "you know… until it wasn't."

"I'm not sure I understand," Noah said. "Still feels like you're telling me there is nothing here."

"There are lots of things to do here, Noah, you just have to be willing to find them," Charlotte said.

"Okay fine, name one."

Charlotte looked around. It was a Wednesday afternoon in early December. Every kid in the world except for hers would be tucked into a classroom, pretending to do work while they waited for the Christmas holidays to begin, which wouldn't be for another two weeks.

It was in that moment that Charlotte began to realize exactly what she had done. Her child had to be the only kid in town who wasn't going to school, which meant he had eight hours of every day where he was unoccupied by anything other than what Charlotte could think of.

It had been such a rash decision to come up here and stay with Dot that Charlotte never thought to imagine just what that would entail. How could she have thought that being here would be any better than being home? In fact, it was just one more problem she was forced to deal with. Not just her own job she had to be worried about, but she knew if she wasn't able to come up with a solution for Noah soon, she was going to be sitting at home eating popcorn, watching her son play his Nintendo while she tried not to burn herself on every log that had to go into the fire.

"Shit." Charlotte let the word fall out without regard for her impressionable son, who was now looking up at her, open-mouthed. Even Bear appeared to judge her as he sat on the ground, unperturbed by the cold surface, and scratched behind his ear with what appeared to be great effort for the old dog.

"Wow," Noah said, shaking his head. "Now you know how I feel." His foot stomped down on the ball of snow he'd been kicking.

Charlotte needed to think of something and quickly if she

was going to stop this spiralling. She contemplated coming up with an excuse for herself, pretending as if she hadn't really said what she just said, but she knew Noah was too smart for that and so she chose, instead, to pretend like it had never happened. She started walking, taking a moment to glance at her watch before glancing back to see if Noah was following or not.

Bear, content to have sat a little longer, waddled slowly, keeping close behind Charlotte, who was walking purposefully without actual purpose until she spotted the old, familiar blue door of the Old Mill in the distance.

"Are we just going to ignore that?" Noah asked.

"Yes, we are," Charlotte said.

"What about all that accountability stuff, and small towns?"

"I was wrong, Noah. Happy?" Charlotte said, shaking her head.

"That's it? No repercussions, no grounding?"

"That's it."

"Well, how's that fair?" Noah asked and Charlotte stopped and turned to face him.

"It isn't. But one day, you will be an adult and then you can make it unfair. But until then, you are going to have to live in a world where things are not equal. We are not equal. That's the deal."

"Pretty shit deal," Noah said, and as frustrated and distracted as Charlotte was, she had to bite her lip for fear of letting the amusement slip out of her. Instead, she forced a deep breath to compose herself and turned back to look at Noah. For a second, she glared at him, her eyes narrowing. She could see the defensive walls being built up as time seemed to slow. She held up a finger and watched as her son stiffened slightly, preparing himself for the barrage of anger about to be thrown in his direction. But it never came.

"We're going to call that even," she said, tilting her head and she watched his posture relax slightly, still preparing himself for some sort of attack, but it wasn't going to come. "It's time for lunch."

6

Noah

"It's good. I promise," Nana said as she placed the bowl of soup and half a sandwich in front of Noah.

Noah didn't know what to make of the meal. In theory, he understood what it was tomato soup and a grilled cheese. But that's not what it was called on the menu. In fact, everything on the menu was a little different than what Noah was used to. He didn't know what a Florentine was, or a cronk monster. Although that last one, he was told, he was just mispronouncing. Still, why did everything thing here have to be so complicated? Even the chocolate croissants were French.

"What do you say, Noah?" Charlotte said sharing an awkward expression between herself and Nana. Charlotte had been acting weird all morning and though she hadn't yelled at him for using a swear word, something he'd felt entitled to after her outburst, she was still distant and strange. Well, more strange than usual. Perhaps she was beginning to regret coming up here, realizing that nothing in this town was worth the drive and they would simply be better off in the city where they could continue with their lives. Not that their lives were much better there. But at least there, they knew what they were.

"Thank you," Noah said as he blinked at his food. He may not have known what it was but even he had to admit it smelt good.

Charlotte, who had ordered the fluoride egg thing, was already cutting into it as if she may never eat again.

"It's delicious as always, Dot," she said, taking a deep breath, her shoulders dropping as if somehow, this food was managing to remove whatever tension had been keeping her shoulders bolted to her ears.

Noah hadn't known what had got into her lately. Surely it couldn't all be because of the incident at his school, which in his opinion was hardly anything more than a simple misunderstanding. Noah was testing a theory and after all, wasn't that what school was all about? Being able to test theories. Surely not every theory pans out positively, or else how would anyone ever learn? Only when he tried to tell his teachers this, it all appeared to make them even more upset than they already were.

What was worse was that they asked him to leave while they talked to Charlotte and he was forced to sit in the other room listening to everything they all had to say about him which was completely unfair since he wasn't provided any opportunity to give his version of the events or at the very least explain that it had nothing to do with his dad. He was simply well… being a kid. At least he thought that's what he was doing. Apparently, making mistakes is only something adults can do.

"Thank you, love," Nana said as she bit into her own

croissant sandwich and soup. "How are you two getting on this morning?"

Noah and Charlotte shared a look as if confirming that neither one of them was about to tell this woman the truth. After all, hiding the truth was what they both seemed to be good at these days.

"Good. Fire was still on when we left. And we thought Bear could use a walk," Charlotte said, forcing a smile.

If Nana thought this was a lie, she didn't say as much. She just peered under the table, handing a bit of her sandwich to the old dog who, from what Noah understood about restaurants, shouldn't be allowed in at all, though no one appeared to notice or care. Bear, on the other hand, did notice the piece of sandwich and gobbled it up greedily.

"I'm sure he's thankful for the walk." She smiled. "Nice day for it too."

"It's cold," Noah said as he lifted half of his sandwich and gave it a smell. *That smells great!*

"It's winter," Charlotte said, rolling her eyes.

"Is it?" Noah said defiantly.

"Why don't you eat? It's going to get cold," Charlotte said.

"Is that what you do with food?" Noah said sarcastically. He thought it was funny, but Charlotte just let out a heavy sigh as her shoulders reconnected with her ears.

Noah remembered a time when Charlotte loved to banter. The pair could actually joke around. But lately, she just seemed to disengage, shut down and, on occasion, yell. Noah hated all of it.

"Just eat your food, please," Charlotte said.

Noah reluctantly took a bite of his sandwich. Despite it sitting on his plate for some time, it was still hot and as he bit into it, his mouth immediately began to salivate as the buttery bread and cheese, still gooey, pulled and stretched out from the sandwich, finally breaking apart and falling down his chin.

"Holy cow!" Though the words hardly fell out of his mouth, which was still full of the cheesy, buttery goodness.

"Don't talk with your mouth full," Charlotte chastised.

Leave it to her to ruin a pleasant moment.

"Nana! This is incredible," Noah's eyes widened as he looked up at Nana.

"Why thank you."

"Seriously, what is it?"

"It's a grilled cheese."

"No, this is heaven," Noah said, taking another bite. "This is nothing like what Charlotte makes."

"Easy now," Charlotte said, "but yes, I can hardly cook like Dot."

"As I recall, you are quite the cook," Nana said, and Noah couldn't stop himself from laughing as he received a nudge in the arm from Charlotte.

"What? Clearly, Nana's memory isn't working because you don't cook anything like this."

"I don't have time to cook anything like this," Charlotte said. "What with you being a pain in my butt twenty-four hours a day."

"Hey! I sleep for eight of those hours."

"If we're lucky," Charlotte said.

"Well, your mom used to come up and help me when we first got started here. Did you know that?"

"Really?" Noah asked. He didn't know that, although there were many things about Charlotte's life that he wasn't supposed to know much about, apparently. "Charlotte doesn't really tell me things." He took a piece of the sandwich and dunked it in his soup, which was one of the most magical things he'd ever done. "This soup. It's incredible!"

"Tomato basil, with a little secret ingredient," Nana said, giving him a wink.

"What is it?" Noah asked.

"A secret. But maybe one day, I'll tell you." Nana's brows rose playfully.

"It's not love, is it? Cause I'm not sure that tastes like anything," Noah said, which caused Nana to laugh.

"No, it's not love. Though I have to disagree. I think a love for food always come out in the meal."

"Well, if this is what love tastes like, count me in." Noah professed.

"If you want true love, maybe your mom will let you have a butter tart," Nana said.

"What's that?" Noah asked, and this must have caught Nana by surprise as she glanced up at Charlotte and shook her head.

"Has this boy never had a butter tart?"

"Of course he has. But he's never had one of your butter tarts," Charlotte said, and Noah thought this was a lie since he had no recollection of having whatever this tart thing was.

"What is it?" Noah asked, and Charlotte rolled her eyes.

Nana, on the other hand, tilted her head toward the main counter. "Behind the window, love, at the end."

Noah didn't bother looking at Charlotte since she would likely just glare at him to finish his meal, something he had every intention of doing. But he was curious now about what this tart thing was and wanted to see it. Maybe he would need to save room for it. *What if it was like a small cake or something?*

Without waiting for the okay, Noah hopped up and ran over to the glass, putting his hand up to see beyond. The woman behind the counter Nana called Riley smiled at him.

"What's a butter tart?" Noah asked.

"Please!" he heard Charlotte call out from their table.

"Please," Noah groaned.

"These little things here," Riley said, gesturing to a pile of tiny, pie-like things that appeared to be filled with some form of brown goo. Though to call them small might have been a mistake considering that each one was about the size of his hand. Though he supposed when compared to a cake, they were almost bite-sized.

"Those? Oh, I've had those. They're okay," Noah said, and he must have sounded a little disappointed at the offer because Riley laughed.

"But not these, and I think you'll be pleasantly surprised," she glanced over at Nana, who must have signalled something to her because she began to place three of them on a small plate and move around to the window to hand the plate to Noah. "Think you can get these to your table without dropping them?"

Noah was thirteen—of course he could.

"I think I can manage." He smirked.

"Go on then. And let me know what you think. But be kind," Riley said. "I made these ones."

"I will," Noah said as he carefully walked back to where Charlotte and Nana were sitting.

"We will save these for dessert," Charlotte said, taking the plate and putting them beside her as if Noah was not to be trusted with them anywhere near him. He was a little insulted, like he had no self-control. He would have said as much to Charlotte, but it appeared that while he was off getting the tarts, Nana and Charlotte had started some sort of conversation which he seemed to be part of, based on the way Charlotte nervously glanced over at him.

"I just don't know what to do." She rested her utensils on her plate and ran her hands down her face. Whatever it was that was bothering her was enough to stop her from eating. This was saying something considering anything short of getting treats couldn't have stopped Noah, who happily dipped his sandwich into his soup again, as he waited to learn just what was so troubling to Charlotte.

Knowing her, it would be blown way out of proportion and surely at the root of it would be Noah, since it seemed that everything Noah did these days appeared to lead to her inevitable discomfort.

"You've only been here for a day, love. I would hardly say that now is the time to start worrying about work. Perhaps all you need is a break. Maybe you both do."

"Nana might have a point, Charlotte. A break does seem nice," Noah said with a thin smile.

"Quiet, you," Charlotte said, and Noah received a smile for his efforts. Though this time, it wasn't a joke.

"You were never very good at relaxing," Nana said, chuckling to herself, "even on those weekends you and Eli—" She stopped suddenly, her finger tapping her chin as she thought about something. Charlotte must not have known what she was thinking because she also looked puzzled as Nana began to mutter to herself. Whatever the deliberation was that lasted so long, Noah began to wonder if maybe Nana had lost her mind.

"I've seen that look before," Charlotte said. Noah had not, so he was still confused, but not so confused that he was willing to let his food go to waste, unlike Charlotte, who appeared to abandon her lunch during this bout of deliberation. He had half a mind to inform her that her food was getting cold and to *eat up*. But that would only draw attention to him and for the moment, until he understood what all of this was about, he was hoping that he could remain in the shadows.

"Well," Nana began, "December is our busiest time of year, and we are currently looking for a cook… so maybe… if you wanted to…"

"Cook? Here?" Charlotte laughed it off as if this was a great joke, though from the expression of Nana's face, she was being very serious. "I couldn't."

"You could. You have."

"You heard Noah. I'm hardly any good at this stuff anymore."

"You're out of practice. So, practice."

"Dot, this is your business. I couldn't just—"

"Exactly," Nana gestured to the space around her. "It's mine, which means I can do anything I want. You want work, I need help. It seems perfect."

"I'd be imposing," Charlotte said, and Noah, who may have only been half-listening, was beginning to see a small problem with this situation. If Charlotte was negotiating with Nana about working at the Old Mill and Noah was not going to school, where did that leave him?

As if his realization sparked the same thought in Charlotte's mind, she glanced over at him. Everyone must have been thinking the same thing. So much for Noah's attempt to remain silently in the background.

"Don't worry about Noah. He can help too." Nana grinned

as if this was somehow doing Noah a favour.

"I'm sorry, what?" Noah said. "I don't want to work here."

"He'd be happy to help. But you're sure that would be alright?" Charlotte said, ignoring Noah's protest immediately.

"Of course. I'm sure we could find tasks suited for him. Right, Riley?" Nana said over her shoulder to the young woman, who must have been listening in.

"Extra help is always welcome," Riley agreed.

"Then it's settled," Nana said.

"But I don't—"

"Dot, are you sure about this?" Charlotte jumped over Noah, who was beginning to feel as if he may not actually exist considering no one appeared to care what he thought or acknowledge him, for that matter.

"Of course. I think it would be fun. Just like old times." Nana grinned.

"Don't I get a say in this?" Noah asked.

"No," Charlotte said so quickly and directly that it left no room for interpretation or argument. But Noah was stubborn enough to try.

"You can't force me. I'm a child."

"You're right. I can't force you," Charlotte said, though the smile she held didn't appear to imply the victory that Noah was hoping for. "But since you've managed to get yourself expelled from school and you can't stay home on your own—"

"I can too. I'm thirteen, Charlotte."

"Sorry, you're right. Let me rephrase this. Since I will not be letting you stay at the house on your own, you don't have to work but I can promise you, working here will be a lot more fun than sitting around and doing nothing in the corner. Every day."

"You're going to make me come in—"

"Every day."

"But if you work, you'll be paid," Nana offered, and this clearly shocked Charlotte by the surprised look on her face, though she didn't say anything. Apparently, Charlotte felt like it was perfectly acceptable to make him work without being paid.

"Interesting," Noah said, rubbing his hand along his chin. "Like as in money or free treats?"

"Money. But the treats are certainly a perk," Nana said, sliding the plate of butter tarts toward him. He took one cautiously.

"Noah, don't be a fool. Take the deal," Charlotte said, picking up her own butter tart. "Who knows, maybe you'll learn something."

"What do you say? Both of you," Nana asked as she too picked up her own butter tart. "We have a deal?"

"I'm in," Charlotte said taking a bite of her butter tart. Her eyes closed as she made some odd sounds of delight Noah had never heard before.

"Noah?" Nana asked.

Noah wanted to say yes, though he still didn't love the idea that he was trading his school for a job, something he didn't think was even legal for a kid to do. Nor did he like that he was once again being set up by Charlotte to do what she wanted him to do. He was still being punished for something he felt wasn't his fault. But this was the hand he was dealt and from what he could tell, his options were to either come in and work or come in and do nothing. Neither of those options appealed to him. But at least one came with a butter tart.

"Fine," he said, taking a bite of the tart and holy schnikes if it wasn't the best thing he'd ever tasted.

7

Dot

"Morning," Dot said as she placed a cup of coffee down on the island for Charlotte, who was clearly not someone used to getting up early. It hadn't been Dot's idea to get up so early. It had been Charlotte's, but from the stifling yawns, Dot thought perhaps she was starting to regret the decision.

Dot, who was used to the early mornings after fifteen years of them, could still sympathize. It was never easy to start getting up at four thirty, but fresh homemade food took time.

"Morning," Charlotte wrapped her hands around the warm cup of coffee. The house was chilly since Dot had only just managed to get the fire on to help warm it up. It was an unfortunate side effect of using a wood stove in the winter.

"Thank you for the coffee," Charlotte said, her blinks slow and long, as if her eyelids struggled to stay up.

"Not a problem, love. You sure you don't want to sleep in? We can find work for you later in the day. That's not a problem," Dot suggested.

"No, no. If we're going to help, we're going to help," Charlotte said, posturing up in her high stool to appear more alert. "It will be good for both of us." She looked around for Noah. "Is he not up?"

"The shower, love. Best to give him a minute," Dot winked as she tossed a piece of her peanut butter toast into Bear's dog bowl, though the old dog's head barely lifted from his bed as he stared at it for a moment. He must have decided it would be there for a while, opting to leave it instead of eating it.

It had only been a few days with Charlotte and Noah in the house, but Dot was already beginning to remember what it was like to have other occupants. She'd been so used to being on her own, with the exception of Bear, that she was a little nervous about sharing her space. But it didn't take long for her to realize just how nice it was to have people around.

Up till now, Dot had been working at the shop while Charlotte and Noah were at home, which from what she had gathered from her evening chats with Charlotte, was becoming a struggle. Finding ways to entertain a thirteen-year-old boy all day was no easy feat and despite having come up with the plan to have them come work for her, it took Dot a couple of days to figure out just what she was allowed to do legally.

"And you're sure everything's okay?" Charlotte asked for the tenth time since Dot had told her she'd sorted it all out the night before.

"Charlotte, I'm going to need you to stop asking that. I promise that if I have issues, I will tell you. Deal?"

"I just don't—"

"I know. And you're not. I promise," Dot said, walking over to give Charlotte a pat on the back.

Charlotte, from what Dot knew, was never great at trusting people at face value. Eli had told her once it was because

Charlotte always felt as though people were only telling her just what she wanted to hear and that it was up to her to decipher if it was an actual problem or not. This felt exhausting to Dot, and in her world, it was easier to be honest about your actions. That way, there was never any confusion.

She supposed this was why Charlotte was not all that convinced that hiring Noah wasn't the real issue, rather than Dot just trying to sort out how she was planning to pay them both. Which she did. Still, it took explaining how Riley's younger sister Cally also worked on the weekends and she was thirteen, before Charlotte finally believed it wasn't an age thing.

"We should get moving." Dot looked at her watch, now reading 4.45 a.m.

"Noah!" Charlotte said, standing up and heading toward the bedrooms, but she barely got out of the kitchen when Noah stepped out, his eyes dropping well below halfway as he let out a loud yawn.

"This is punishment," he said softly.

"This is character-building," Charlotte said, "for both of us." This last part seemed more for herself than the room.

"Well, I for one am proud of you both. It will be fun, I promise!" Dot clapped her hands.

*

In hindsight, fun may not have been the word Dot would have used to describe the morning, although she wouldn't go as far as to say difficult. As it turned out a thirteen-year-old's attention span at five in the morning was comparable to a goldfish. Still, there were always little things that needed doing around the shop that Dot didn't mind putting Noah in charge of.

For starters, she had him fold up boxes, a task that no matter how efficient any of them became, there was always a need for more. It was not the worst problem they could face considering it meant that more people were picking up and taking food.

"That's it?" Noah said after Dot finished showing him what he needed to do.

"That's it. Do you have any questions?"

"I think I can handle putting stickers on and folding things." Noah yawned, not bothering to cover his mouth, something Dot had to fight to not correct. Perhaps she was just of a different generation, the one that insisted kids have minor manners. Also, that may be something she mentioned another day. For now, she figured she should start small.

"Simple tasks done well are the difference between a successful business and a failing one," Dot said, remembering the words of advice her father had told her when she was young.

Noah yawned again, giving her a thumbs up in reply as he slid one of the boxes over and began folding it.

"If you need any help, Bear isn't your dog," Dot joked as she peered under the table to find the old dog curled up at Noah's feet. She remembered a time when he would be curled up at her feet, but in the last few days, despite Noah not being all that fond of him, Bear had been like a shadow to Noah.

"He's a dog, Nana," Noah said.

"Which is why he is no help." Dot mused. "Despite my best efforts to train him otherwise, he remains a dog."

"You're too awake for this early in the morning." Noah blinked.

"Give it time. You'll get used to it," Dot said.

"Why would I want to get used to it? It's dark and cold… and cold." Noah shivered despite the warmth of the building.

"There is a beauty in the mornings, my love. You just have to look for it."

"Sounds like something someone would say when they are trying to trick themselves into liking something they don't like."

"That's life." Dot chuckled to herself as Noah gave her a strange look. "Maybe one day, you will understand. Or maybe you won't. But if you can, I promise, your life will be a lot more rewarding."

"Did I mention it's early?" Noah said, shaking his head, and Dot placed a hand on his back and gave it a pat.

"I'll leave you to it."

Dot, not wanting to hover over him, walked away, keeping half an eye on what he was doing and though it wasn't the way she would have done it, for efficiency's sake, he appeared to be doing it, which was something. Dot didn't really need him to be the fastest, just busy.

"How are we doing back here?" Dot said to Tia and Charlotte as she pushed through the old oak doors, which she had painstakingly restored, leading back into the kitchen.

Tia, who had been Dot's saving grace over the years, was suited up in her black chefs, her hair tightly braided and held back with a royal-blue bandana. She had been with Dot now for nine years since graduating from chef's school. Dot had lucked out, knowing that Tia was talented enough to work anywhere she wanted and that any kitchen would be very grateful to have her and yet she stayed on with Dot. It was something that Dot was thankful for.

"Just showing her round the kitchen," Tia said, her infectious smile radiating the room. It was a rare treat to find someone who could manage such early mornings and long days so well. But given that the alternative for many chefs was long nights with no mornings, this may have been the reason Tia had stayed so long.

"How are you feeling, Charlotte?" Dot asked.

Her daughter-in-law looked flustered as she tied an apron around her back.

"Nervous, apprehensive, scared… would be a few of the words I would use," Charlotte said, taking a deep breath. *At least she was breathing.*

Dot and Tia shared a look, before laughing to one another.

"I'm glad my nervousness brings you joy," Charlotte said.

"Oh, don't be so uptight, Charlotte. This is going to be fun. We cook food and treats, and we provide comfort for people. No one is expecting you to be the world's best chef off the hop. Just do what you can and have fun."

"Right, fun." Charlotte sighed.

"We'll start you off simply. Just wash and cut up those potatoes there, then you can season and roast them in the ovens there," Dot said, gesturing to a wicker barrel filled with potatoes that Tia must have already pulled from the fridge, and a large, double-door oven.

"All of them?" Charlotte looked wide-eyed.

"No, maybe a quarter of that bin and the rest can go back in the fridge. Extra knives are in the bin there, love," Dot said, gesturing to the blue bin under the counter. "There's a honing blade in there as well. Tia, you're on quiches. I prepped the peppers for you yesterday. They're in the fridge. I'll take care of scones and croissants." Dot pulled an apron from a hook on the wall and began tying it around her waist. "Tia? Any orders?"

"Couple of loaves, lemon and a banana, some quiches, but nothing special. We're low on chocolate chip and ginger cookies as well as pecan tarts," Tia said, opening a small notebook from her back pocket, something Dot always loved about her. She was organized and direct, two things Dot needed in her life to keep things from falling apart.

Over the years, Dot had found that running a business was difficult but as long as she was able to surround herself with the right people, people who had strengths she herself did not possess, life was much simpler. It was never Dot's opinion that relying on the strengths of others somehow made her a bad leader. In fact, she believed it made her a better one. It is easy to pretend you don't have weaknesses, but it takes great strength to allow others to support you where you are weak.

"Sounds easy enough. Let's stick to the plan. We'll find a time later to get the treats finished up. Any questions?"

"No, Chef," Tia said with a broad smile while Charlotte just shook her head with nearly zero conviction.

"Just ask if you have questions." Dot put a hand on Charlotte's shoulder. "Remember, we're cooking food, not sending a person to Mars."

"Right," Charlotte said, though Dot could feel and see the tension in her shoulders. But there was nothing she could do now. All Charlotte needed was to dust off the cobwebs, even if it happened that these particular webs had been built up pretty thickly over the years.

*

"Is something burning?" Tia asked, not bothering to look up from the mountain of onions she was chopping up.

"Shit! Shit! Shit!" Charlotte panicked as she laid down her

knife, abandoning the potatoes she had been cutting to run over to the oven. Charlotte pulled on the doors, letting out a billow of smoke. "My timer didn't go off." She cringed as she pulled out the charred potatoes. "Shit."

"That's a lot of curses for potatoes, love," Dot said, coming over to have a look. "Salvage what you can, toss the rest," she said, though her mind was busy calculating what this would cost her. Not that she was angry about the error, after all, there was a cost to learning.

If that had been the only issue for the day, Dot would have been content with her new employees. As it was, between the nerves and the teenager, a typical day at the Mill had disintegrated into mismeasurements, mislabeling and one dropped quiche, courtesy of one poorly assembled box. It had all helped to convince Dot she should let her new employees out a little earlier than normal.

"I'm so sorry, Dot. I swear we can do better," Charlotte had said profusely as she dressed to go home, with Noah and Bear on his lead.

"I know, love," Dot said, giving her a pat on the back, "I just think it would be worthwhile to ease us all into it."

"Oh my God, we're horrible, aren't we? What do I owe you for everything we ruined—?"

"Hush, you. You don't owe me anything, love. We're all learning. Today was a good trial run and I have faith once you get out of your own head, make a little room up there, everything will come rushing back in," Dot said.

"What if it doesn't? What if I don't ge—?"

"Stop that. You're going to be great. Now go home. Start a fire and relax. I'll be home in a few hours," Dot said, shooing them out the door, and Charlotte nearly got all the way out before patting Noah on the back.

"And what do you say?" Charlotte said, her head tilting to the side expectantly at Noah, who looked more confused than anything.

"I love you, Nana," he said, turning to look up at Dot, who appreciated the kind words but didn't think, based on Charlotte's expression, it was what she'd been after.

"And you're…" She waved a hand, trying to guide her son toward her intentions.

"Excited to see you when—" Noah started.

"No, Noah. You're sorry for not making the box right and having it fall over the floor."

"It's not my fault the boxes are flimsy." Noah sighed. "And I cleaned it up."

"It was your mess!" Charlotte hissed.

"My mess—"

"Don't you dare—" Charlotte began but stopped.

"It's fine, love. I love you too, Noah and I'll see you both at home," she said, giving Charlotte a little nudge.

Once she knew they were on their way, she returned inside, taking a deep breath as she began to wonder if she'd just made the biggest mistake of her life.

8

Charlotte

"What are you doing?" Noah asked Charlotte as he walked into the kitchen, his eyes blinking away the sleep. Unlike Charlotte, he'd been smart and went for a nap, something Charlotte had wanted to do but couldn't.

She'd felt awful since leaving the Old Mill. Every mistake she'd made replayed in her mind on a loop. It wasn't as if she was a bad cook. In her past, she had actually been quite good at it, and it really hadn't been that long since she'd helped Dot on weekends with Eli. *Had it?*

"Charlotte?" Noah asked again and she turned to face him as though she only now realized he was there.

"Sorry, what's that?" her mind was still deep in her own thoughts.

"What are you doing?" his words came out slowly.

"Thinking."

"About what? And why are you doing it in the dark?"

Charlotte looked around the room. It was much darker than it had been when she'd first sat down, and although it looked like it was nearing ten at night, in reality, it was closer to four. Winter always had a funny way of making the body feel as though you should be hibernating. Even the fire looked to be dying, despite feeling as though she'd only just put a log on. She stood and moved over to grab another from the pile.

"I hadn't noticed," Charlotte said as she carefully laid a new log on top of the embers, letting the warmth of the fire warm her up as she did.

"You didn't notice that all of the lights were out and you were sitting in the dark?" Noah asked, sounding incredulous, which was impressive for a thirteen-year-old.

"No, I didn't," Charlotte said evenly as she flicked on one of the side lamps, lighting up the room a little.

"Should I be concerned?" Noah asked, which received a genuine laugh out of Charlotte.

"Maybe," she said shaking her head. "I was just thinking about things I could have done differently."

"Why?" Noah asked.

"Because I want to be of help to Dot, not make things harder."

"We are helping." Noah shrugged. "I thought that's why we're there."

"We are. But neither of us were that helpful," Charlotte said, slumping down in her chair.

"Speak for yourself. I folded like a million boxes today."

"Easy there, kid. You maybe did thirty and in case you forgot, you didn't assemble the one well enough to hold a quiche."

"Sure, pick the one I messed up on. You don't see me calling you out on your potatoes," he shot back.

"You don't need to. I already know I messed up."

"It's just potatoes. Nana said it was fine."

"Nana was being nice," Charlotte said. "Every time one of us messes up, she loses money."

"How does she lose money?" Noah asked. "We're working for her."

"She's paying us to do a job, Noah. If we do it wrong, then she needs to pay someone else to do it right. And if we mess something up… like the potatoes, she can't use those, so she needs to use more potatoes, which costs more money."

"I don't understand."

"Who do you think paid for that quiche that fell on the floor?"

"Wow, you really can't let that go, can you?"

"I'm just trying to make a point, Noah. You asked me what I was thinking about."

"I didn't think I would be dragged into it. I feel fine, I had a nap because I was tired from the morning. Maybe you need a nap."

"Noah, your nana is doing us a favour because you can't go to school—"

"It's a favour to be working at five in the morning?"

"Yes," Charlotte said.

"Some favour," Noah said, rolling his eyes.

It was no use. Maybe trying to explain the intricacies of life as an adult was too much for someone so young. Why should he even need to learn right now that not everything was always black and white? How two things can be true at the same time. He was a kid, and Charlotte should know better than to try and make him understand.

"Never mind, Noah," Charlotte said, leaning her head back on the headrest of the chair.

"You ever think that maybe you overthink things?"

"Every day," Charlotte agreed.

"Why?"

"It's how my brain is programmed."

"So, reprogram it," Noah suggested, as if this were the easiest thing in the world to do. Charlotte knew from years of trying, and therapy, and all manner of practices that reprogramming her brain was the furthest thing from easy.

"It's more difficult than that," Charlotte said.

"Maybe if you give up," Noah said and Charlotte was beginning to get angry until she realized her frustration was directed at her son, who was attempting to help her in his own, albeit naive way.

"You're right. I'll do better." Charlotte sighed.

"You're lying to me," he said, folding his arms against his chest.

"I'm not," she said, closing her eyes, realizing that all she wanted to do was go back to sitting in the dark with her own thoughts, not getting psychoanalyzed by a child.

"You do it all the time. You don't want to listen, so you just turn off," Noah said as Bear, who must have also taken a nap, was now back up and waddling into the living room, wandering over to have a drink of water from his bowl before coming to sit in front of Charlotte, his large head resting on her foot.

"You think I do it? Have you met you?" Charlotte asked.

"I'm thirteen."

"Look, Noah. I appreciate you wanting to help, I do. But there are things that you just don't understand, okay."

"Well, maybe I could understand them if you explained them!" he shouted, standing up from his chair so that he could face her.

"What do you think I was doing?" Charlotte said. "You just don't want to listen to me. So honestly, I'm not sure what else I can do."

"I don't know. Try harder?" Noah shouted.

"Stop yelling."

"You stop yelling!"

"Hello." As if nothing could make this moment worse, Dot walked in through the front door, her puffy winter jacket making her look like a gray marshmallow.

"Enough!" Charlotte held up a hand to Noah, who did not appear to want to give up at all, but before he could say as much, Charlotte pounced. "Please! Just enough. We can talk about this later."

"Which is your way of saying we will never talk about this again."

"That's not fair, Noah."

"Isn't it?" he said, stealing the last word on the matter as he turned away and stormed back toward his room, with Bear, who had taken a moment to celebrate Dot's arrival by wagging his tail and greeting her at the door, now following him out.

"Bear really likes that boy," Dot said, half-smiling, half-concerned.

"At least someone does," Charlotte said, and she smacked her hand to her forehead. "Oh God, no. I shouldn't have said that. I'm horrible."

"You're not," Dot said, chuckling. "Trust me. I've said worse."

"But Eli was…"

"Also a thirteen-year-old boy?" Dot finished for her. "You're not the first to say that, and you won't be the last."

"I don't know what to do."

"Luckily, I do," Dot said as she walked into the kitchen, went straight for the fridge and pulled out a bottle of white wine. "You need a drink." She smiled and Charlotte in that moment could have cried because she very much did need a drink.

"Yes. Yes, I do."

Dot poured Charlotte a glass and joined her by the fire, where the pair just sat and stared for a long time, neither of them saying anything. It was peaceful for Charlotte and she giggled as a memory of Eli flooded her mind.

"What's that?" Dot asked, and Charlotte turned to notice the older woman watching her. In the dim light with the fire flickering in the room, she saw the image of Eli's smile looking back at her.

"Just thinking about Eli," Charlotte admitted. She wasn't prone to talking about Eli very much, but given the company she was with, she figured if she could ever talk about him, it would be here.

"I think about him every day," Dot gave Charlotte a look of understanding. *Of course she does.* "What were you thinking about?"

"How bad he was at silence." Charlotte laughed. "He just couldn't sit without feeling the urge to talk about something. Even if he knew it was the last thing I wanted to do."

"He got that from his father. He never shut up," and Charlotte couldn't help but clock that in all of the time she had known Dot, she had never once brought up Eli's father. Even Eli didn't enjoy bringing him up. Had he not been his father, Charlotte figured he would have been happy never discussing the man ever again. "It was endearing. Until it wasn't."

"I know what you mean."

"Eli always just needed to get his thoughts out of his own head," Dot said. "Even as a boy, he analyzed everything, trying to understand the reasons for why things were the way they were. The difference between him and his father was that Eli never needed to be right."

"I'm not sure we're talking about the same Eli. That man loved to be right."

"Did he?" Dot asked, though she didn't seem to believe it. "I just always assumed he wanted other people to prove him wrong."

"Maybe, but it was still annoying. And now I have a son who apparently does it as well." Charlotte took a big gulp of her wine, which she wasn't surprised was going down easy.

"Noah is just curious."

"Perhaps too curious sometimes," Charlotte said.

"That have anything to do with why he's not in school?" Dot asked.

Charlotte had to restrain herself from chugging the last of her wine.

All Charlotte had told Dot about the incident was that Noah had messed up and done something dangerous. That's why he wasn't allowed back. She wasn't sure why, though she imagined it was that she was embarrassed by Noah's actions and she felt as though she had failed him. She knew it was silly to blame herself. He was just a kid figuring things out, so he was bound to make mistakes. Even still, what he did was dangerous and there was a line. A line Charlotte felt he'd crossed.

"Yes," Charlotte admitted, and she was happy when Dot didn't push it further despite the fact that Charlotte was in her home, and she was offering to help and had every right to know the truth.

"I'm hungry. You hungry?" Dot asked, standing up.

"Starving," Charlotte admitted, feeling her tummy rumble at the mention of food.

"Why don't we make some pasta? I'm thinking pasta and meatballs?"

"That sounds wonderful."

"Great! We can put Noah on the pasta, I'll get started on the sauce and you're on meatball duty. I'll also get another bottle of wine ready," she said, spinning the wine in her glass around playfully.

"You sure you want us touching anymore food today?" Charlotte joked.

"Charlotte, I'll admit today wasn't your best day. But you need to lighten up. The world did not end, and no one was hurt," Dot gave her a pat on the shoulder. "Making food should be fun, not stressful, or it will taste like crap."

Charlotte took a deep breath and shook her head. "I just don't want to let you down."

"As long as you are there because you want to be there and you're enjoying yourself, you won't."

"You're just saying that to make me—"

"No. I'm not. I want you to be there. But only if you want to be there."

"I do."

"Great. Then have some fun. And," she said, raising a hand before Charlotte could say anything else, "you can start by getting the meatballs ready. Meat's in the fridge."

"Deal." Charlotte grinned. "Noah! Come here."

"You going to yell at me again!?" he called out from his room.

"Only if you don't come out here," Charlotte replied.

"Sounds ominous." Noah sounded apprehensive.

"I'm kidding. We need your help."

"What kind of help?" Noah said, sulking into the room, his eyes narrowing on Charlotte before shifting between her and Dot.

"You're making pasta," Charlotte said excitedly.

"But I don't know how to make pasta," Noah said.

"Even better," Dot added. "You get to learn how to make pasta!"

"Do I have to?" Noah asked.

"Yes," Dot and Charlotte said at the same time before cheersing their wine glasses.

9

Noah

"I thought you said I would have help today?" Noah yawned so widely, he thought his jaw might unhinge.

"Cally won't be in till later," Nana said, her head poking out from the kitchen door. There was a light in the café, which Noah was using as a guide for his boxes. He wasn't sure if he was doing them correctly or not. Despite the lecture from Charlotte, he still didn't understand why it fell on him to be perfect. After all, he was a kid being forced to work against his will. He even contemplated informing the police of his unwanted captivity but in the near week since he'd been here, he hadn't seen a single one. It was as if they'd all but fallen off the face of the earth. Unlike the city, where you couldn't go five minutes without spotting at least one police car.

"It's a cruel and unusual punishment to make a child work this early."

"I heard that, Noah!" Charlotte called out from the kitchen.

"Good!" Noah called back.

"I could always set you up in a back room and you could sleep. It would mean I save money by not paying you," Nana said with a smile.

"So be here and work or be here and not work," Noah said, using his hands as if he were weighing his options.

"Bear loves a good napping buddy." Nana mused.

Noah thought about it for a moment. On the one hand, he was already up but he didn't think he would have much trouble remedying that situation with a pillow and a blanket, and he had to admit, Bear looked pretty relaxed. However, on the other hand, the idea of making his own money for the first time in his life was also tempting.

Noah felt exhausted. It was only his second day of work and already, he was done with it. He couldn't understand why anyone would ever want to do this in a million years. He was ashamed to admit that he was beginning to miss school. At least he held regular hours there. Show up, write some things down and go home. Sure, there was occasional homework but Noah didn't bother with much of that. He understood the rules of engagement there. Do enough to not be behind but not so much that you waste your time.

He had never tried to be the best at anything, just good enough to not be the worst. It seemed an efficient way to move through school. At least it had, until last week, when he'd found a test online that seemed easy enough. All he needed were some ingredients that they had in the chemistry lab. How was he supposed to know he'd mixed up the measurements?

They'd managed to put out the very small fire, which he wouldn't have even classified as a real fire, more like light burning–hardly worth calling the fire department over. The whole thing had been blown out of proportion and now, Noah was stuck in the middle of nowhere folding boxes on a

Saturday morning.

"I choose sleep," Noah said, letting the box he'd started fall to the table.

"Sounds good," Nana walked over and placed a hand on his back. "Let's get you set up in my office.

Noah followed Nana through the kitchen. He could hear the click clack of Bear's nails on the wooden floorboards right behind him. At least he wasn't alone in wanting some more sleep.

"Where are you going?" Charlotte asked, her hands covered in flour as she appeared to be crumbling up what looked like a hundred pounds of butter into it.

"Back to bed," Noah said, not bothering to look over at her since he could already feel her glare of disappointment.

"We talked about this last night—"

"You talked about it," Noah shot back. "I was hardly given a choice."

Noah looked over, waiting for her reply, but it never came. Instead, she looked at Nana.

"I'm not here to force anyone to do anything they don't want to, love."

"Thank you, Nana," Noah said smugly.

"Fine," Charlotte said reluctantly as she added another handful of butter to her mixture. "But I would like it noted that I think you're making a bad decision."

"Your objections have been noted. I will ponder them while I sleep," Noah said as he felt a nudge in the back of his leg and he looked down to see Bear resting on him—*yet another sign I should be asleep.*

Noah was about to go into the office when he caught a whiff of something that smelled very good. He started to sniff the air in an attempt to track down where the smell was coming from. In the single day and thirty minutes that he'd worked here, he'd come to realize that at any given moment the shop smelled of something incredible. It could be cookies or quiches, weird little puffed-up treats, brownies, or any other goodies Nana decided to whip up. One of the more challenging parts of folding boxes in the front room was having to sit and smell everything.

"What is that?" Noah asked excitedly.

"Good nose on you." Nana smiled as she walked over to the oven and opened it up. Steam billowed out, revealing round, light golden-brown pastries inside. "It's pain au chocolat," she said as if Noah would understand exactly what that was.

"It's the chocolate croissant, Noah," Charlotte said, interpreting his confusion.

"I've always wondered, how do you get the chocolate inside?" Noah asked, forgetting he was supposed to be getting ready for sleep.

"Tia is making some now," Nana said, walking him over to a long, metal table that was dusted with flour. "Tia?"

"Oh right. Umm…" Tia closed her eyes as if it had been some time since she'd had to explain to anyone exactly what it was she was doing. "Well, you use a puff pastry and then—"

"Puff pastry?" Noah asked.

"Right well, umm," Tia said, tilting her head side to side as if trying to find the best way to explain it. Noah wondered if she was just bad at explaining herself or if she just wasn't used to having to explain things to a kid. "It's a kind of dough that you make." She looked intently at Noah. He hoped she wouldn't just explain 'what' dough was since he'd spent the night before making a pasta dough by hand so he liked to think he had a good handle on that already. "Right. Yeah, well, you make a dough and roll it out into a long sheet, like this." She gestured to a sheet on the table beside her. "This one already has the butter in it."

"The butter is in the dough?" Noah asked, looking at the long piece of dough, confused.

"Yeah, of course, the butter gives it the flavour and the puff."

"How?"

"Well, umm, well, you take a brick of butter." She held up a wrapped pound of butter. "Then you smash it down with a rolling pin," she said, holding up a rolling pin, "until you get a rectangle of butter."

"You mean all that butter is in there?" Noah asked.

"Oh yeah!" Tia grinned. "Then you fold the dough over the butter and roll it out. Fold it into a rectangle again. Put it in the fridge to cool and repeat."

"Why do you have to put it in the fridge?"

"It stops the butter from melting."

"Why don't you want the butter to melt?"

"Because if it melts, you don't get the lamination you need for it to rise in the oven."

"Lamination?" Noah asked, fully enthralled in this impromptu lesson. He couldn't quite understand how or why this butter was so important. But he watched as Tia cut an edge off the pastry dough and held it up for him to see. Inside, there were tiny layers of dough.

"It's a fancy way of saying layers." Tia smiled. "So when we cut this for the croissants, we put this cold piece of chocolate inside, wrap it up and while it cooks, the yeast and butter in the dough help to make it rise and keep all its layers intact. It's glorious!"

"But I don't understand."

"It's chemistry," Tia grinned. "The tastiest kind of chemistry," she added with delight.

"But I think we should let Tia and your mom get back to work. Let's get you a little bed," Nana said, resting a hand on Noah's back as she guided him away.

Noah was still looking at the pastry and the oven and trying to wrap his head around what he had just learned. Chemistry wasn't something he was technically allowed to do until he reached the ninth grade. Still being in the eighth grade, he was not supposed to be allowed in the chemistry rooms. Yet another reason for his school's anger. But that was a stupid rule since he thought he should be allowed to learn if he wanted to.

As it was, however, all the chemistry books he'd found had not once mentioned baking chocolate croissants, because if they had, he was certain he would have not only remembered it but so would many of his classmates.

"What did Tia mean it was chemistry Nana?" Noah asked as he stepped into a small office with a little desk and a couch against one wall, and filing cabinets along the other. Noah headed right for the couch and Nana pulled a pillow and a blanket out from one of the cabinets, giving Noah a wink.

"Baking is chemistry," she said, as if this were the most obvious thing in the world. She laid out a pillow for him to rest his head on.

"It's not in the books I've read," Noah said.

"Are you interested in chemistry?" Nana asked, putting a blanket over Noah as Bear jumped up and rested against his feet.

"Sure. Maybe. I don't know. I like seeing how things react,

I guess."

"Interesting," Nana said, tucking him in as he let out a big yawn.

"Why is that interesting?"

"Because so do I." She grinned and gave him a kiss. "Maybe we can talk about this another time. I can show you what I mean."

"Promise?" Noah asked but his eyes were already closing, and he barely heard her say, "Promise."

*

"Turkey and brie sandwich to go." Nana's voice sounded from the kitchen, startling Noah awake. He had no idea how long he'd slept for but from the sounds coming from the kitchen, the Old Mill was in full gear.

"You got it." It was Tia who replied, sounding just as cheerful as she had at five thirty in the morning, possibly more so. "Can you handle that, Charlotte?"

"If I can't, there is something wrong with me," Noah heard Charlotte joke as the two women began to laugh. The sound caught Noah by surprise since it had been some time since he'd heard her laugh like that and he had to admit, it was nice.

Noah kicked his legs out from the blanket that he'd been wrapped in, hitting Bear in the process as the old dog was still curled up at his feet.

"Time to get up, lazy," Noah said as Bear tilted his head to look up at him before resettling back into the couch, unperturbed by the blanket partially over him now. "Fair enough." Noah stood up to stretch, letting out a big yawn.

He peeked into a mirror, noting that one side of his hair had flared up after having slept on it. He took a minute to try and fix it before realizing the futility of the situation and abandoning his action. *Who am I trying to impress?*

Poking his head out of the doorway, he peered around the corner to find Charlotte and Tia busy working away at their stations. Charlotte was carefully putting together a sandwich on a croissant while Tia was rolling out quiche tarts.

"You look busy," he said, stepping out from the office as Charlotte met his eye first.

"We are," she said with a smile, though Noah knew her well enough to know that this smile was likely just holding the ball of emotions that she would reserve for the house and not strangers. But even he had to admit, she was covering it up well.

"Good." He yawned.

"Nice nap?" Charlotte asked.

"The greatest." Noah smiled, knowing she was just trying to make him feel bad about not wanting to work. But he wasn't about to give her the satisfaction. He hadn't been the one who wanted to work in the first place. So why should he feel bad?

"Well, you were certainly out for a while. It's nearly noon." Charlotte laughed.

"It's noon!?" Noah almost shouted. He knew he was tired, but he didn't think he was *that* tired.

"It's impressive what you can sleep through." Tia chuckled. "I've been smashing butter all morning," she added, giving him a little wink.

"Did you save me a chocolate croissant at least?" Noah asked.

"I'm afraid you'll have to be here before noon to get one of those," Tia mused, "but you always have tomorrow." That sounded more like a bumper sticker than actual advice. But Noah guessed it would have to suffice since it was unlikely he was going to get a croissant today.

"I'm surprised you all managed to get so much done without my help," Noah said, strutting through the kitchen, leaning in to get a better look at Tia, who was neatly crimping the edges of the quiche pastry. "Looks good."

"Thank you, little chef," Tia said.

"You were missed, Noah," Charlotte said as she loaded the croissant with the final brie and turkey slices before wrapping it all up in a brown paper. "But Cally is quite efficient at her job." Charlotte put a stickered label on the sandwich wrap to hold it all together as she looked up and handed it out to Noah. "You mind taking this out to Nana? Tell her it's—"

"A sandwich?" Noah said, shaking his head. "Sure. So, who is this Cally anyways?"

"I'm Cally."

The girl appeared from nowhere, though Noah guessed it was more likely she'd come from the storage room in the basement since she was carrying a stack of boxes loaded up so that they nearly covered her face, with just her dark eyes peering out.

"You mind getting out of my way?" she said, gesturing with her head as Noah turned to see an empty shelf with a small tag marked *cake boxes* on it.

"Oh, sorry. You need help?" he asked, feeling like it was the right thing to do, being a boy and all, and the boxes looked heavy in her arms. But all he got was a scoff.

"No, thank you. I think I can handle it," she said, "assuming you get out of the way," she added, waiting for him to press himself up to the table as she pushed past. "Thanks." Her eyes rolled, and Noah couldn't understand what he could have possibly done wrong in that situation, though he guessed

Charlotte might have an idea as he caught her smiling across from him.

"What?" He glared.

"Nothing." Charlotte shrugged as she went back to chopping up vegetables.

"Is that the turkey and brie?" Cally asked, turning around and gesturing toward the wrapped sandwich, and for the first time, Noah got a good look at her. She was taller than him but not by much, no more than a hand or so, but that wasn't uncommon since he was short for his age. Her long, curly hair was pulled back in a frizzled bun.

"Yes," Noah said, distracted now by this girl, whose sassiness was simultaneously charming and annoying.

"Great! I can take it out for Dot."

"So can I," Noah said, slightly taken back.

"Oh well, I wouldn't want it to get in the way of your nap time," she said with a grin.

"I'm not napping anymore." Noah had wanted the words to come out stronger but instead, they felt shaky.

"Good for you," she said, her hand outstretched, anticipating the sandwich, but Noah wasn't about to give this girl anything, not after she'd gone ahead and made fun of him. No, he was asked to do something, and he would do it.

"I can take the sandwich," Noah said, moving her aside.

"Are you sure? Because I saw the boxes you folded this morning, and I just wasn't confident about what you were capable of."

"Well, I… You… I'm just…" Noah was flustered. He wasn't used to this kind of criticism, certainly not from someone his own age. He had to wonder if this was what bullying was, not that he was about to ask her since it would likely just give her more ammo.

"If you're going to take it out, I would hurry. Mr. Henry's usually in a rush this time of day," Cally looked annoyed as she turned around to leave the kitchen without another word.

"Well, she's pleasant." Noah scoffed.

"She's a hard worker." Charlotte said.

"Whose side are you on?" Noah asked.

"No sides. But…" Her eyes dropped to the sandwich in his hand.

"I'm going!" Noah threw his empty hand in the air as he stormed out of the kitchen. He wasn't quite sure what he had done to deserve Cally's ire but he wasn't about to sit back and let this girl criticize him for being lazy. He didn't want to work at the Old Mill and was basically being forced into it. What could she possibly know about any of it? She'd just come in and assumed he was lazy because he didn't want to do his job. Did she ever think that maybe he was just trying to not do it well? If she had then she might have realized just how good of a job he was doing.

Besides, making boxes wasn't hard or difficult. He just didn't want to do it. If he really wanted to do it, he would be great at it—heck, he would probably be like a billion times better at it than stupid old Cally. He may even go as far as to say that by the end of the month, he would be so good at it that they wouldn't even want Cally working here.

"Here's the sandwich, Nana," Noah said, handing it over to her as she stood talking to a tall, slender man whose cheeks were still rosy from the cold winter air.

"Well, the offer's on the table if you ever want to come out," he said, flashing Nana a toothy grin. Noah couldn't tell how old people were, especially when they were so much older than he was. If he had to guess, Mr Henry was maybe a few years older than Nana and from the way he was looking at her and ignoring him and the sandwich, he wasn't all that concerned with the food.

"Well, thank you, Henry," Dot said gratefully as she grabbed the sandwich from Noah's hand. "We will have to see if we have time."

"Your name is Henry Henry?" Noah asked, looking confused and before anyone had a chance to say anything to him, he caught Cally snickering from the corner of his eye. *That snake!*

"Just Henry, my boy. And you are?"

"This is my grandson, Noah," Nana said proudly as she put her hands on his shoulder.

"Well, it's nice to meet you, young man," Henry said, putting a hand out for Noah, which he shook. "Well, I should get moving," Henry said, tipping an invisible hat toward Nana, and Noah thought he caught the man's face turn more red, although the action appeared to amuse Nana. After the awkward exchange, Henry turned and left, leaving Noah and Nana alone. She turned him around to look at him.

"How was your nap?" she asked, which only made Cally snicker more, for which she received a smack in the arm from Riley, who was busy at the till cashing people through.

"Good," Noah said and before he had a chance to think about it more, he glared over at Cally and then up at Nana. "I think I want to work."

10

Charlotte

"How's it going?" Tia asked as she expertly rolled puff pastry around some spiced pork, which would be the special treat for the day. Tia had told Charlotte that the sausage rolls were a real crowd-pleaser at the Old Mill, though from what Charlotte could tell, there wasn't much this little town didn't love about the shop.

This wasn't always the case and Charlotte still remembered the days when all they had was a counter with some freshly baked treats on it, some to-go coffee and the occasional sandwich. In those early days, Dot had relied so much on small catering contracts that she worked nearly every day just to keep the store going.

Now she had two full-time employees and various hands to help when she needed it, including Charlotte and Noah now. She was no longer just selling treats but she had an entire product base of local meats and seasonal produce, local suppliers for honey, soaps and all manner of goods that she was happy to sell for anyone looking to start a business. Her only rule was it had to be something she would use herself.

Still, she managed to fill up the counter spaces with various items, including some niche products she'd found on her travels, mostly to Europe during her off-season.

It was a far cry from the nights she called Eli crying because she was so concerned she'd made the wrong decision. Now she was a staple in the town as well as an advocate for the community in general, encouraging new artisan shops to open on the main strip. The thought made Charlotte want to celebrate with joy and cry because she'd not been present for that period of her life. More importantly, neither had Eli.

"Good," Charlotte said, combining the mix for the quiches which she was ready to start distributing. It had been just under a week since she'd got back in the kitchen and though she wasn't remotely close to having any major responsibilities the consistency in the kitchen was giving her a much-needed confidence boost.

After the potato fiasco, she'd wanted to give up. But later that night, Dot convinced them all to make pasta. And though she would never admit this to be her plan, Dot somehow managed to remind Charlotte that after everything, cooking was supposed to be fun. Even Noah had managed to enjoy himself, learning how to mix pasta dough and roll it out to make linguini. Each cut of the pasta not perfect by any means, but when you ate it, it all tasted incredible.

"It's not about being perfect. It's about making something that tastes great," Dot had said when they'd all finally sat down for the meal.

"I'll get these in the oven then?" Charlotte asked Tia once she'd finished filling the quiches.

"All yours," Tia said as she pinched together the pastry dough.

"Can I get a smoothie, please?" Noah asked, holding a slip of paper in his hand and putting it down on one of the tables.

"I can do that," Charlotte said, walking over to pick up the slip. "How's it going out there?"

"Good." Noah said coolly. Charlotte didn't know what exactly had changed Noah's mind about continuing to work at the Mill. Just that Dot had told her that he was keen to help out again. She wondered if it had anything to do with Cally but considering this had been the first time in months she and Noah hadn't been at each other's throats, Charlotte didn't feel like questioning him. What was important was that he was willing to help, not why. If it did happen to be because of a certain young lady, perhaps he might find a reason to ask her advice. But she wouldn't hold her breath.

"Do you need anything?" she asked.

"Nope. Nana said I could take my break soon, so I might get some food and go sit down," Noah said, and Charlotte looked at her own watch, realizing what time it was.

"I'm due for one as well. Maybe I could join you?" she asked, preparing herself for the rejection that was sure to come. But it never did.

"Sure. If you want." He turned and walked out, as Charlotte resisted the urge to fist pump or jump up, knowing that it would only cheapen the small victory.

"He's a good kid," Tia said.

"He can be." Charlotte chuckled, letting out a snort as she moved to the freezer to grab the mix for the smoothies.

"He's thirteen," Tia said. "You should have seen me at thirteen. Hated everyone and everything. And that boy certainly has a lot to deal with."

"Does he? Because he certainly doesn't tell me about it."

"He's not telling me but come on. After what he's been through," she said and paused from the pastry to look up at Charlotte, a pained expression on her face. "I'm sorry, it isn't my place—"

"No, you're fine. And you're probably right. I was never good at talking to him. That was all Eli. He was so good at opening up to him and giving him space. I just seemed to get in the way, and so I kind of stopped."

"You know you've been through a lot too, right? You're allowed to not be okay," Tia said.

"I'm not okay. In fact, I'm lost. My son got suspended from school and my first thought was how I was going to survive..." Charlotte stopped and looked around, making sure the doors to the kitchen were shut and for good measure, she dropped her voice conspiratorially. "Survive being home with only him for the month. Christmas is hard enough without... you know."

"I know. Look, I don't have kids," Tia said, "but I was the oldest of five with some very large age discrepancies. To put it simply, kids are kids. They're stupid, angry, spirited and incredible. They're everything they need to be. Imagine having all the same emotions you have now with only seven or eight cognitive years of life to understand them. No concept of mistakes, loss, or moving on. Everything is so... immediate. Just thinking about it makes me want to cry, or punch something. The fact that every kid isn't just crying or punching one hundred percent of the time is an actual miracle." Tia laughed.

"I guess I hadn't thought about it like that."

"It's why kids need to be stupid while their brains develop, because if they weren't, they would spend too much time analyzing life," Tia said. "At least that's what I tell myself to justify youth." She laughed again.

"You are a wise woman, you know that, Tia?" Charlotte said as she filled up the blender with the smoothie contents and added some milk, honey and cocoa power to it, before turning it on. "Wise!" she shouted over the machine.

*

"So," Charlotte said, sitting down to have a coffee and slice of the Quiche Lorraine she'd helped make that morning. If she hadn't known she'd been the one who made it, she would have been impressed by the quality. But she knew the real secret was the crust, which she was not up to making quite yet. Still, the filling wasn't all that bad either.

"So," Noah said, setting down his grilled cheese sandwich, a staple meal for him this past week apparently, and instead of a coffee, he was sipping on a maple water drink that was supposed to be some alternative to pop. Charlotte may not understand all of the products Dot sold, but she had to admit, they were interesting.

"How's it going?" Charlotte asked, hoping she didn't sound too interested or pushy but was hitting that sweet spot where she might get something more than a one-word reply. She did not.

"Good." Noah answered.

"Good," Charlotte nodded, stopping abruptly when she couldn't seem to stop it from bobbing and Noah began to look at her funny. "I just want to say, I've been really impressed with you this week. For coming in and everything." Charlotte sat upright and held up her hands as if to say, *That's it, that's all I wanted to say.*

"You too," Noah said with a slight shrug. "You've come a

long way from burning everything."

"I didn't burn everything…" Charlotte said, slightly embarrassed—at least she was until she caught the cheeky grin he was giving her. "But it is nice to not be the worst."

"Oh, you're still the worst, Charlotte." Noah laughed. "But Tia and Nana are really good so I wouldn't worry about it," he added patting her hand in mock-compassion.

Somewhere inside, Charlotte felt very insulted, but she also felt oddly comforted by the fact that her son was choosing to poke fun at her. It was reminiscent of Eli, who had also been quick to joke around, especially when Charlotte took things too seriously.

There was a time when Charlotte had been good at taking the loving jabs. She had even tossed some of her own out when she knew it was what Eli had needed. She had been fun and exciting and had loved to joke. Now, she felt like she always had to be on, be the one who set the tone for each of them, and this had been no fun. For her or anyone, really.

"You make a good point," Charlotte said, giving him a playful smack on the arm, "but I am better than you."

"I'm thirteen, Charlotte. If you were worse than me, I would say we had a real problem here."

This caused Charlotte to burst out laughing, something she hadn't done with Noah in a long time. It caught her off guard as she covered her mouth to make sure nothing flew out of it. Maybe it wasn't the funniest thing she'd ever heard but the fact that it had come from Noah threatened to make her laugh or cry and she was thankful for everyone in the Mill that it was the former.

Lately, Charlotte had been putting a lot of thought into life, particularly into the belief that emotions were not linear, but circular. She used to think on one side, you had sadness and on the other, you had happiness. But this past year, her emotions felt more like a pinwheel, spinning around like some crazed weathervane in the middle of a storm. It was the only reason she could fathom how she could be so happy, she would cry and so sad, she laughed. The full spectrum of her feelings muddled up, creating the perfect emotional cocktail where all of life's little magic moments happened, along with all those less magical moments—neither of which a person forgets.

"Good point," she said, taking another bite of her quiche.

The pair sat in silence for a moment, even though Charlotte's mind was racing. That was something new for her. In the past, she'd always been content with silence, but for whatever reason lately, she'd felt like she had to fill that void with something, anything really. But she resisted the urge this time and sat.

At least that was her plan until she spotted the man talking to Dot beside the register. He looked familiar but Charlotte couldn't put her finger on why.

"Do you know who that is?" Charlotte kept her voice down and leaned in, happy that Noah decided to match her conspiratorial vibes as he turned to look where Charlotte had just signalled and leaned in close.

"That's Henry. He comes in nearly every day. Buys all kinds of stuff. Food, coffee, soaps, you name it," Noah said. "I think that's why Nana always talks to him."

"Every day, huh?" Charlotte asked, her eyes narrowing in on the pair talking. It had been a long time since Charlotte had talked to a man or had one show interest in her, not that she had thought about such things. But something about the way Dot and Henry were talking made Charlotte think there was something there.

"Yeah," Noah continued. "Cally said he runs a Christmas tree farm just outside of town and makes honey in the summer. Apparently, Nana sells it."

"Does she now?" Charlotte's mind was racing with ideas.

"Yeah. Cally said she goes every year, and this year, she was the one who got to pick the tree and cut it down. I didn't believe her, but Riley said she'd done it. Sounded like it was a lot of fun," Noah said, picking away at his sandwich as he glanced up at Charlotte.

Her mind was still rolling different ideas around when she finally looked over at Noah and caught a look on his face that she hadn't seen in a long time. Suddenly, she realized what exactly was happening here. Noah was telling her something. Using his words to finally hint at what he would like to do, and here she was ignoring him. All she'd wanted was to have a conversation with him and now as he was finally doing it, she was ruining it.

"It does sound like fun," Charlotte said, not wanting to push him away.

"Yeah. Only Cally said she searched the entire farm and found the best tree. I doubt it, since Henry said his farm is really big. Like really, really big. I doubt she got the best one. I mean, I could probably find a better one."

"I think you'd find the best one," Charlotte said.

"I know! Right," Noah said, shaking his head. "And, well, Henry invited us out and, well, I mean, I know it's been a few years since we had a tree. But maybe…"

"I think that would be a great idea!" Charlotte said and she could have kissed her son for being such a genius. Somehow, he'd managed to come up with an idea that would solve two of her thoughts, getting Dot to spend time outside of work with Henry and spend time with her son.

"Really?" Noah said, sounding really excited now. "I mean, we would have to convince Nana—"

"Let me handle Nana," Charlotte said, feeling a little bit like a schemer. "We will get you the best tree in the world, Noah."

"Good. Because you know, it would just be really nice to… well, you know… rub it in Cally's face when she sees how good it is." And the conviction in his voice nearly caused Charlotte to spit out her coffee.

"Don't you worry," she said after composing herself, "you will be victorious." She winked as a broad smile crossed his face.

11

Dot

"This is going to be fun," Dot lied, her face telling a completely different story than her body and mind. But what was she supposed to do? Not go along with Noah's request of getting a Christmas tree? He was her only grandson. She couldn't do that to him. Nor was she about to make her objections known. At least no more than she already had.

Dot had made the mistake of mentioning how much time they spent at the Old Mill and all that had done was convince Noah and Charlotte that the best course of action was to pick out a second tree for the Old Mill and they would dress it.

Since Dot had somehow gone from having no tree to now having two trees that she would need to clean up after, she feared what anymore objections might get her.

"I haven't been to cut down a tree in… well, ever," Charlotte said, her smile broadening. "My parents were always the fakest tree possible kind of people. It wasn't until Eli came around that we started to get real trees." Her smile faltered for a moment.

"And we haven't had a tree in a few years," Noah said as Dot pulled into Henry's tree farm, which was much busier than any of them had imagined. Well, busy for a small town, with at least ten cars parked in the makeshift driveway, and a small trailer at the end with a sign that read—*free hot chocolate.*

"It's been some years for me too, love." Dot admitted, though she left out the part that said she'd done it on purpose since it was usually just her and Bear in the house and if she did happen to go anywhere for Christmas, it was to Toronto to visit Eli and Charlotte, and only ever for a couple of days. Both she and her staff usually took January and February off from the shop, a special treat she allowed herself to ease her busy schedule. *Although this year would be a little different.* She pushed the idea out of her mind.

"Seems like we could all use a tree," Charlotte said. "And it was really nice of Henry to offer to show us around," she added, glancing over at Dot. For her part, Dot felt as though Charlotte had been acting very strangely around her for most of the day.

"Yes. He is a nice man," Dot said.

"Is he? Do you know him well?" Charlotte asked.

"He comes into the store from time to time. So yes, we've spoken," Dot said, making her way toward the trailer as she tucked her hands into her puffy jacket. The air was cold tonight, and although it was only 5 p.m., it was pitch-dark outside. The only reason anyone could see any trees at all was because Henry had put in massive lights along the rows to help light them up.

"He seems nice," Charlotte said.

"He is," Dot said, refusing to glance over at Charlotte, though she could see from the corner of her eye that her daughter-in-law was looking directly at her.

"How long does it take to cut down a tree?" Noah asked as he pulled a pair of mitts on.

"No idea," Charlotte said. "Dot?"

"Not a clue, love. But I'm sure Henry will know."

"I'm sure he will," Charlotte said and once again, Dot noticed the cheeky smile directed her way. She stopped and turned to face Charlotte, who immediately clammed up.

"What are you doing?" Dot asked.

"Getting a tree?'"

"No Charlotte, that." Dot waved a hand around Charlotte's face. "You keep looking at me and smiling and I won't lie, it's beginning to unnerve me."

"I'm not doing anything, I swear," Charlotte said, putting a hand to her heart as if that somehow made Dot believe her more. It didn't.

"Fine," Dot said.

"Fine," Charlotte replied.

"I'm thinking a ten-foot tree would really put Cally in her place," Noah said absently. "What do you think?"

"I think we have eight-foot ceilings at the house," Dot said, "so perhaps something more full, and smaller."

"But the Old Mill has massive ceilings," Noah said.

"So, you were both serious about that tree," Dot said.

"Of course we were. You don't like the idea?" Noah asked in the way that only a child could ask, where it's near impossible to say no.

"Of course I do, I just don't think I have enough ornaments to dress two trees," Dot said and this wasn't a lie.

"I was thinking about that. And I wanted to run an idea by you," Charlotte said.

"And what would that be?"

"A tree-decorating day," Charlotte said.

"Decoration Day at the Old Mill," Noah said, spreading his hands out as if imagining a large banner hanging. All Dot saw was more work and with the preparations for the holidays, she was busy enough.

"Sounds… interesting," Dot said.

"I know what you're thinking. It's a lot of work and you're busy enough as it is," Charlotte said, and Dot prepared to tell her she was wrong but never got the chance as Charlotte pushed on. "Don't even deny it. I know you are. I've seen the order forms. So, I was thinking it could be something Noah and I organize. Maybe Cally could help."

"Well, I don't know if we need her help," Noah said with a shrug.

"Maybe," Charlotte said and from the way that she was glancing at Noah, Dot was unnerved by how Charlotte looked at Noah with the same mischievous way she did her. *What are you up to, young lady?*

"Cally knows people in town. We don't. She could help spread the word."

"When do you plan on doing this?" Dot asked.

"Well, ideally December 1st. But considering that we've missed that date, I was thinking next Friday would be good."

"You want to prepare an event for next Friday? The week before Christmas?"

"Yeah, why not? Invite the community to put a decoration on the tree, have hot cider, and treats for sale. It could be fun."

"Charlotte, I appreciate your enthusiasm, but we have a lot to do. Adding this in now… I mean, no one will probably come."

"Of course they will. People love your shop. It would be a

little farewell until the New Year," Charlotte said, and Dot's heart sank a little at the thought. She still hadn't told anyone but Riley, Tia and Betty about her decision to close the shop for good come January. She was getting older and even with the help, her schedule was just getting too busy to have a life. She was afraid that if she didn't do it now, she never would. But that didn't make it any easier. She loved the Old Mill, it was like her baby. And she had lost one of those already.

Dot had wanted to tell Charlotte about the decision since she'd arrived but couldn't find the right time. With so much on her plate, all Charlotte wanted to do was come here and forget her own problems. The last thing she needed was for Dot to burden her with problems of her own.

"If you think you can organize it, we can do it," Dot said, forcing a smile, though she could tell there was nothing forced about Noah's or Charlotte's as they both clapped enthusiastically.

"But I'd like to revisit the idea of bringing Cally in, I think it's—"

"Just take the win, kid," Charlotte said, rubbing a hand on Noah's hat, which smooshed over his eyes. He wriggled away, fixing himself.

"Dot!" Henry called as he stepped out of the trailer, his large hands managing to carry four cups of hot chocolate. His large winter jacket was unzipped, revealing a white and blue woollen sweater underneath.

"Henry," Dot said, happy for the interruption. Although this had not been her idea, she would certainly try and make the most of it. What did she have to lose anyway? She fought the urge to feel guilty, knowing that this close to Christmas, it was unlikely that anyone was going to come to the store for an event. Not unless they were picking things up for their own dinners. For now, she would put that pessimism in her back pocket.

"I'm happy to see you've finally taken me up on my offer for a tree," Henry said, handing each of them a steaming cup of hot chocolate. "Sorry, it's not nearly as good as what you brew at the Mill but it will help warm you up on the search."

Dot took a sip, and he was right, it wasn't as good, but she wasn't so snobby about her hot chocolate that she was about to offend this man.

"Delicious, thank you," Charlotte said, sipping her own. "And thank you for the trees."

"Trees?" Henry asked, looking surprised.

"Correct." Dot smiled thinly. "We are looking for two trees, apparently. As well as finding some time to decorate them," she added, trying to sound enthusiastic but doubted she was succeeding.

"One normal sized tree, about…" Noah looked at Henry. "A little taller than you should be good. And then one really big one for the Old Mill."

When Henry looked confused, Charlotte added, "We're going to have a Christmas tree decorating party at the Old Mill. Invite people to put up a decoration, maybe make some. Who knows?"

"I think that sounds like a brilliant idea," Henry said, applauding, which was made very awkward by the hot chocolate he was trying to drink.

"Right!" Charlotte said, gesturing to Dot like this was somehow the proof she needed to get on board with the idea. But Charlotte didn't know Henry like she did, and how he was able to get excited about almost everything. It was something

Dot had always found to be both annoying and charming at the same time. Perhaps that was just because she was a little envious of how carefree he was.

Henry seemed to love everything. At first, she thought it was all an act but over the eight years that he'd been coming into the shop and she'd been getting to know him around town, Dot had come to realize that he was genuinely excited by things.

"Well, in that case, I think I have the perfect tree for you. But first, let's say we find the one for Dot's house," Henry said. "I'll get the saws."

"Saws?" Charlotte and Noah said at the same time, though with clearly opposing emotions.

"Cool!" Noah said.

"I thought that was a figure of speech. You mean to tell me we have to cut down the trees?"

"Of course, that's half the fun," Henry said. "Trust me, you'll love it," he said, turning to walk back toward the small trailer.

"Having fun yet, Charlotte?" Dot looked at her daughter-in-law with a much more genuine smile plastered on her face.

"Yes. Of course. Why wouldn't I be? Letting my son chop down a tree with an axe."

"It's a saw, Charlotte, and for the record, Cally did it so how hard can it be?" Noah said.

"Cally is a very capable young woman."

"So am I!" Noah said, putting his hand on his hip, only to realize a moment too late what he'd said and attempting to back track. "I mean man. Human. I'm not sure why we need to distinguish either way. I mean capable is capable. Jeez, get with it," Noah stammered though even with the crisp evening air and minimal light, Dot saw the colour in his cheeks.

"You are absolutely right," Dot said, trying to free him of his embarrassment.

"Here you are," Henry said coming back with a rather large-looking handsaw and handing it to Noah. "But you have to be careful with that thing. It's got a sheath, but it can slip and it's sharp."

"How sharp?" Charlotte said instinctively but waved a hand away as if it was no big deal before Henry could answer. "You can handle it, right Noah?" Her brows furrowed.

"Of course. Now let's go find our tree!" he said, lifting the saw up and pointing it toward the woods.

"Maybe, just with the dark and all, we don't wave that blade around in the air right now."

"I'll be careful, Charlotte," Noah said.

As Dot glanced over, she caught Noah in the corner of her eye when he thought no one was watching. Noah pulled the sheath down slightly, pressed a finger against the blade and flinched back in pain, realizing for the first time just how sharp this blade was.

"Onward," Henry said, gesturing to the woods, which seemed to amuse Noah.

"He seems nice," Charlotte said as she pulled Dot's arm in close to her.

"So you keep saying." Dot forced a smile as she ignored the reality that soon she would need to let everyone know her plans. She just wanted to get through Christmas first, since the last thing she wanted was a big fuss before.

"He certainly comes to the shop a lot," Charlotte said, giving Dot's arm a light squeeze.

"He enjoys the lunches," Dot said, her eyes narrowing on Charlotte.

"What?" Charlotte said. "I'm just saying, he's cute for an older man."

"You're not fooling anyone, Charlotte."

"Who said I'm trying to fool anyone?" she asked, her brows shooting up as she sipped her hot chocolate.

"I have enough on my plate. You, Noah, the Mill, Bear!"

"Bear seems content."

"Bear needs a lot more care than you might think."

"Like, say… walks in the woods?" Charlotte gestured to the rows of trees.

"You're relentless. You know that?" Dot said.

"How is Bear, by the way?"

"Good. Old. But good. Why?"

"I don't know he just seems… lethargic," Charlotte said.

"Big word for a dog."

"I suppose, yeah." Charlotte laughed. "But he seems—"

"He's fine, Charlotte. He's old. He's just tired," Dot patted Charlotte's arm as if to say, *Leave it there*, and thankfully, she did. Bear had been rescued a few years after she'd opened the shop and though she didn't know his real age, he was best guess close to thirteen or fourteen years old. For a long time, it was just the two of them, and she did not need anyone else to remind her of his age. Dot saw it every day. The fact that he was currently at home in front of the fire and not with them in the woods was enough to know times had changed. But Dot couldn't think about that now.

"Here it is," Henry said, gesturing to a Douglas fir about eight feet high and from the looks of it, very fetching, by tree standards.

"That's huge," Dot said. "Is this the one you had for the shop?" she asked, praying she wouldn't have to figure out a way to get this thing into the house. But her hopes were dashed quickly.

"This one's for the house," Noah grinned as he looked back toward Dot and Charlotte.

"Then which one are we getting for the store?" Dot asked, nervous for the answer.

She was even more nervous when Henry shared a looked with Noah that screamed mischief all the way.

"You want to show them or me?" Henry asked.

"I'll do it." Noah smirked.

"Show us what?" Dot asked.

"That's the tree for the store," Noah said, gesturing over toward a tree slightly larger than the one Henry was standing beside.

Dot finally let her shoulders relax. "Oh, that's a good size tree," she said, walking over and shaking the snow off the branches.

"Oh, not that tree," Noah said, laughing as he ran over, passing her and the tree she'd just shaken to stand next to the one behind it. It was easily over eleven feet high. "This tree!"

"That is a big tree!" Charlotte said, taking a step back as if that's what she needed to see it all.

"That's too big," Dot said.

"It will look great in the corner," Henry said.

"How are we ever supposed to get these home? We only have your little car," Dot said, annoyed that all her reasons for not getting the trees were being roadblocked by everyone around her.

"I'll tie them up and drop them off tomorrow in my truck," Henry said.

"That's really kind of you, Henry," Charlotte said.

"Awesome," Noah agreed.

"Yes, great. I'm just worried about how much this is going to cost us."

"The tree for the store is a gift," Henry said. "It's too large to sell anyway, so you would be doing me a favour. Consider it a donation to the big decoration party."

"Again, that's very kind—" Dot began, feeling all notions of avoiding her inevitable outcome dash away.

"This is going to be awesome!" Noah exclaimed. "Nana, imagine how cool this is going to look in the shop. And the look on Cally's face when she sees that we got the biggest tree in the lot." Noah said this last bit under his breath.

"This is all too generous, Henry," Dot said. "Thank you." She shook her head knowing she couldn't back out now. Noah had gotten his hopes up, even if those hopes were just to best a young girl. She wasn't about to strip him of that now. Not when the universe was desperately pushing her in that direction. At a certain point, it was best to not fight the current and let the world take you where it wanted to go.

"You're welcome," he said with a smile.

"You'll have to let me treat you to a lunch at the Old Mill," Dot added.

"I could never say no to that," Henry said, tapping his saw. "Right, Noah! What do you say we cut these trees down."

"I thought you'd never ask," Noah ran over to the tree and removed the sheath from his saw, careful to not let the teeth get him as Henry began explaining what he needed to do.

"This is going to be fun," Charlotte said, taking Dot's hand.

"I'm sure it will be," Dot said, unsure if she truly believed that or not.

12

Noah

"Still happy with the trees?" Henry said from the driver's seat of his old Chevy truck. The two hand-cut trees, wrapped tightly in twine, were tied in place, their tips poking out well over the cab of the truck. Noah looked back at what should have been an accomplishment—after all, he had just chopped down his own tree for Christmas for the first time—but for some reason, he just felt guilty.

"Yeah," Noah said with a shrug.

As promised, Henry had organized getting the trees to the Old Mill. Though it became very clear that Nana had nothing to put the trees in save for an old stand in her basement that appeared to need a spike hammered into the bottom of the tree somehow. Noah doubted he had the capacity for something like that.

Even the cutting of the trees had been a miraculous triumph as he'd had to take a couple of breaks and rely a little on the assistance of Henry, especially for the tree for the Old Mill, which had a much larger trunk.

"I'm sorry to be stealing you away from the store this

morning —" Henry started but Noah simply raised his hands to stop him.

"No!" Noah said a little too aggressively. "I mean, no. The shop has been fun, but I'm happy to get out and do something else."

"Oh. Okay, good." Henry said, though Noah could tell that he wanted to say more—thankfully he didn't. When Henry had shown up at the Mill and told Nana that he was happy to help though he may need assistance, Noah was all too happy to volunteer his time and get out of folding boxes for the morning.

It was nice to be out of the shop and away from Charlotte, at least for a little while. Since they had arrived in town, they had spent nearly every moment with one another and it was starting to feel a bit smothering.

Say what you will, but Noah was beginning to wonder if school only existed to give parents and children a break from one another.

Charlotte had been apprehensive about Noah going with a man she barely knew but thankfully, Nana had been there to be the voice of reason. Noah wondered if she also sensed the need for a little separation. After all, she lived in the same house as them and something about Nana's quiet nature made Noah believe she was far more observant than she let on.

"Yeah," Noah said absently as he looked out the window at the small town he'd now been living in for the past week and a half. Even in that short time, Noah felt as though he knew this town and where everything was. The downtown, where the Old Mill was, was a single road with three traffic lights, which was impressive considering he came from a city where he wasn't sure he could even count the traffic lights.

"How have you enjoyed St Martins?" Henry asked, and Noah turned in his seat to look over at the older man. *Okay, so this is happening.*

"It's small," Noah said, "but cute, I guess, in its own way." He added not wanting to offend the older man.

"It is small." Henry chuckled. "But what we lack in size, we make up for in convenience."

"How so?" Noah asked.

"Well, for one, we're at the hardware store," Henry said, nodding to a small red and gray building with a sign that read—*Hudson's Home Supplies.*

"That was fast," Noah said.

"So, we need two stands and maybe some lights for the tree at the Mill. What do you think?"

"Sounds good." Noah should have been more excited about all of this but for some reason, his chest ached, and he felt mildly nauseous, and he had no idea why.

Henry hopped out of the truck and Noah followed suit as they entered the store, which appeared quiet, or maybe this was busy? Noah didn't know.

"Chuck," Henry said, waving to a man checking things off on a clipboard. He waved back at Henry as he came in. The same went for Kate, and Leonard, who were stacking shelves and appeared to know Henry by name.

"You come here a lot, Henry?" Noah asked.

"A few times a week." Henry admitted. "But sooner or later, you get to know everyone."

"Sounds exhausting," Noah said. If he had tried to get to know everyone at the places he visited in the city, his brain would likely explode.

"Aww, it's not so bad. Has its perks."

"Yeah? Like what? Cutting the line?" Noah mused as he gestured to the only other customer in the store.

"No, not like that. It's just nice to know people sometimes. Makes you feel welcomed. Something your Nana does really well."

"Does she?" Noah asked.

"That woman can tell you the name of nearly every person who walks through her doors, who their parents are, their kids. Her mind is like a steel trap. It's impressive."

"You seem impressed."

"I am. I don't have the same noggin," Henry said, tapping the side of his head as if Noah didn't know what a noggin was. "When you get a little older, you'll just be happy if you can remember where you put your keys."

"You do remember where you put your keys?" Noah asked jokingly and Henry made a show of pretending to pat his jacket pocket before finding them. Noah found himself pleasantly amused by this, though he thought it was rather childish.

"You think we'll find a stand for those trees?" Noah asked.

"Oh, don't you worry about that," Henry said with enthusiasm. "I'm sure we will have no problem." And as if he'd planned it, Noah turned the corner to a whole aisle filled with Christmas supplies, including a few stand options.

"You're good, Henry," Noah said giving the larger man a pat on the back.

"We all have our strengths." He clapped his hands and walked over to look at one of the stands. "So, you're not a huge fan of the town I'm guessing."

"Why do you say that?" Noah said, tapping one of the stands, as if that would somehow tell him how durable the thing was.

"Call it a hunch."

"It's not that I don't like it. It's just, well, it's not my life."

"You miss your life back in the city then?"

"Sort of. Maybe. I don't know." Noah sighed. "I guess I just wasn't expecting this, you know."

"Expecting what?" Henry said as he lifted out a large, plastic stand that Noah thought had too many parts for something that just held a tree. "This one is self-watering." Henry pointed to a little water holder.

"Cool. Looks like it will hold a tree too."

"Should do the trick," Henry said. "What do you say we get two? Surprise your nana by setting the tree up at the house as well."

"Sure!" Noah said, taking the stand from Henry. "I'll get this one, you get another."

The stand was surprisingly heavy, but Noah managed to hold it with both hands. Henry didn't appear to have the same issue, grabbing the stand and a couple sets of white tree lights as well.

"Something tells me your nana is more of a traditional white light person than a coloured light fan," Henry said.

"Why do you say that?" Noah asked.

"Clean look, simple, elegant. You've seen the way she runs the Old Mill." Henry mused.

Noah *had* seen the way Nana ran the shop, and he would have to agree, though he was the one out here picking up the stuff for the trees and not Nana.

"But a little colour never hurt anyone," Noah said, his brows shooting up as he tilted his head toward a set of colourful lights. He readjusted the tree stand, trying not to show how awkward it was for him to hold.

"Umm, you make a good point," Henry said. "What do you say we compromise. White lights for the Mill and colourful lights for the house?"

"I can live with that," Noah said with a grin.

"It's settled then," Henry said, swapping out one of the white lights for a set of colourful ones. "Should we go set up the tree at the house?"

"Sounds good to me," Noah said forcing a smile, relieved to be getting out of the store and finally putting down the stand.

After some light conversation at the front desk with Chuck, which Noah found to take more time than it needed (although he thought Henry would have been happy to stay and chat all day), they managed to get the stands into the back of the truck and head off toward Nana's house.

"You excited for Christmas?" Henry asked.

"Yeah." Noah shrugged, feeling like that was the answer he was expected to give rather than the one he wanted to give.

"Convincing," Henry said.

"What? I am. I mean, it's Christmas," Noah said, the words coming out as if he had been trying to convince himself as well as Henry of its truth.

"Just because it's Christmas doesn't mean you have to be happy," Henry said.

"Are you not happy at Christmas?" Noah asked.

"Sure. Sometimes. I like the snow, skating, the joy it brings to the town—"

"The Christmas trees."

"Yes." Henry laughed. "Of course, the Christmas trees."

"But you're not happy?"

"No, I am. Some of the time. But sometimes, it's hard."

"Hard how?" Noah asked.

"Well, I have a son and we don't always get along," Henry said.

"Why? You're so nice."

"Being nice doesn't always mean you're doing the right thing," Henry said. "I made a lot of mistakes in my life."

"Me too. Just ask Charlotte." Noah rolled his eyes.

"I'm sure your mom loves you."

Noah tilted his head thoughtfully, wondering if that were true. Somewhere inside, he knew that it was, but lately, he didn't feel it quite as much. "She is just always mad at me and never wants to hear my side of the story," Noah said, shaking his head. "It's not fair."

"Have you tried talking to her about it?"

"I have! She just gets mad."

"Keep trying. Who knows, maybe she'll surprise you?" Henry asked.

"Have you talked to your son?" Noah asked.

"It might be too late for that," Henry said. "I've made *a lot* of mistakes."

"So, you're saying I should give up?" Noah asked, feeling like this would be the easiest solution since Charlotte would only need to put up with him for a few more years and then he would leave and she could have her life back.

"No."

"But you did," Noah said.

Henry opened his mouth to speak and closed it, looking like he was at a loss for words.

"You got me there, kid," Henry chuckled. "But for what it's worth, I can tell your mom loves you."

"Is that why she dragged me out to the middle of nowhere at Christmas? Choosing to be anywhere else but alone with me?" Noah said the one thought that hadn't left his head since she'd told him they were leaving the city. In his mind, it was so obvious. All she ever wanted was to not be with him. She avoided him at every turn. Finally, the one chance that they would have had to be alone together, she upped and moved them to this place, and the first thing she did was take a job. He didn't need any more proof that she did not want to be with him.

"I think there might be more to it than that," Henry said.

"Actions speak louder than words, Henry. And I think it's obvious what her actions are saying."

Henry fell quiet for a moment and Noah took the time to stare out the window, passing the already familiar town on the way to Nana's house. He wondered if Bear would be waiting at the door for them when they arrived. At least the dog always seemed to want to be with him. Even if he did kind of smell and take up a huge portion of the tiny bed Noah slept in.

"I'm sorry, Noah," Henry finally said. "Maybe you should talk to her, tell her how you feel."

"I think I would prefer to bottle up my emotions and store them deep inside myself. You know, finally grow up."

"You think that's growing up?" Henry asked.

"Isn't it?" Noah looked over at Henry, whose face was all scrunched up as if struggling with the concept. Noah, on the other hand, didn't need to struggle with it. From what he'd seen, all adults seemed to do was internalize their problems, so why should he treat life any differently? Charlotte could hardly expect him to want to talk to her when she wouldn't talk to him. How was that fair?

"I hope not," Henry finally said, letting out a heavy breath.

"You are quite the kid, Noah." He laughed awkwardly and shook his head. "Quite the kid, indeed."

13

Dot

"It's big," was all Dot could think to say as she stared up at the eleven-foot Douglas fir that she'd had to move two tables to fit in. She wasn't quite sure how it made sense that losing seating in the dining area would lead to more business, but hey, what did she know? She'd only been running the store for fifteen years.

The only positive at present, well, two positives she could muster up, were that the tree did have a pleasant scent, and Henry had used the good sense to at least get white lights instead of the tacky coloured lights that she despised. It wasn't that she was against coloured lights, but too many on a tree always looked childish and messy while the monochromatic white offered the clean look Dot enjoyed.

"It's awesome," Noah said with a big grin as he turned to give Henry a high five, which was a little awkward since Henry was over six feet tall and Noah was not. But they managed to sort it out.

"I think you picked a good one, Noah. Likely the prettiest tree in town," he added with a nudge, which seemed to make

Noah even happier.

Dot wasn't sure if she was allowed to point out the fact that Noah clearly had a crush on Cally since there was no reason why any kid would want to go through so much effort to make a girl jealous unless of course he fancied her. But since she had already raised one boy, she knew it was best to sit back and watch this unfold.

"Thank you for doing this, Dot," Charlotte said as she looped her arm under Dot's and gave it a light squeeze. "I know you don't love it as much as we do but—"

"Don't be silly, love. I think it is a good idea," Dot lied. Charlotte, apparently, was going to organize a decoration party at the store for the following Friday and was expecting the town to come and support it.

Dot, who had been a part of the town now for fifteen years, had always found it a struggle to get people to come and support her. First, it was that everything was too expensive, then not enough food, or they weren't open enough. Whatever they decided at the time, it wasn't working for them. That's when Dot had decided that she would always do what was right for her business, regardless of what people thought. *Until now, I suppose.*

"I think it will be a good way to go out." Dot smiled, her momentary lapse in judgement receiving a curious look from Charlotte.

"What do you mean?"

"Oh, for the year, love. End the season off with a bang," Dot said with mock enthusiasm. What she really meant was the end of the store, and likely her true relationship with the community. When push came to shove, she knew that despite the support she received through her business, she would always be from away and therefore never fully accepted into the small town. When Charlotte's tree experiment failed, it would be the final push she needed to retire and leave the endless hours of work behind.

"I think so too," Charlotte said as she took a deep breath, and her eyes started to water up. "Will you excuse me a moment?" Charlotte smiled, turned and disappeared around the corner toward the restroom.

Dot didn't know if she should check on her or not, or if this was one of those times where she just needed to be alone. Dot had always liked Charlotte, although she had found her to be a little too stressed, especially during the moments of life where she had the least control. Those were the moments where Dot herself thrived because it meant there was never a wrong answer. Charlotte appeared to take the opposite direction of thinking she was always wrong. In Dot's mind, that mentality would have been exhausting, since she was the only one living her life. Why on earth would she ever let herself believe she'd lost? *Maybe I wasn't always like this?*

"Alright people, we still need to get things ready for the afternoon." Dot clapped her hands, dispersing the small gathering of people that had formed to look at the tree.

"I still can't believe you let them put a tree in here," Tia said, chewing on a pecan square as she chuckled to herself.

"If it can make them happy." Dot shrugged. "Then I'm happy to do it."

"Have you told them yet?" Tia asked, her voice dropping low.

"No," Dot said evenly. "Why ruin all of this with that kind of news?"

"Well, it is kind of big news, don't you think? You should

really talk—"

"Thank you, Tia," Dot said, putting a hand on the young woman's shoulder, "but I think I need to handle this in my own way."

"Right. Yeah. Of course," Tia said her face looking a little pink.

"Have you given anymore thought to my offer?" Dot asked.

"Yeah. I reached out to your friends. They seemed keen on having a chat to hear what I was thinking. So that's promising. Though the idea of going to the city now feels a bit daunting."

"You're young! And Toronto is such an incredible place for food. You can get anything you want whenever you want it. It's special."

"Yeah, but you have to be special to survive there," Tia said, shuddering a bit.

"You are, my dear. You're one of the most brilliant people I've ever worked with. All of this wouldn't have been possible without you."

"All of this would've been impossible without you." Tia's brows lifted slightly. "You know there are other options than just closing down."

"So you keep reminding me." Dot smiled.

"Well, it's true. Maybe we can—"

"I told you. It's not what I need right now."

"I know. It's just hard," Tia said, shoving the rest of her square in her mouth.

"There's always the third option. You take this place and turn it into whatever you want," Dot said, and Tia shook her head adamantly while she chewed frantically to finish her square. She finally managed to swallow the last bits, which to Dot, looked rather painful.

"No. This place... changing it... no," Tia said, looking around the Old Mill. "I couldn't do it. I wouldn't even know where to start."

"Neither did I. And look where that got me."

"An eleven-foot tree?" Tia joked.

"God, I know. I thought the wreath on the door and some hanging lights would be enough. But now a tree ceremony."

"It's a way for the community to show their support," Tia offered.

"I know. That's what I'm afraid of." Dot laughed. "At the very least, I'm sure we will have enough wine for us."

"Ye of little faith, Dot." Tia smiled as a timer started beeping from the back kitchen. "That's me. Break time's over."

"I'll be back in a moment, love. Just need to do something."

"I bet you do," Tia gave Dot a wink, which made her cheeks flush red involuntarily.

"I didn't... I'm not... stop, you," was all Dot managed to get out while Tia half-danced, half-laughed back to the kitchen. "Silly girl."

Dot spotted Henry talking to Noah and she was surprised to see the pair getting along so well.

"I just wanted to thank you for your help," Dot said to Henry as he and Noah turned to look at her, the smiles still fresh on their faces from some sort of joke they must have shared. Dot didn't know what this unlikely pair would have in common but whatever it was, it appeared to work. "Both of you," she added, putting an arm around Noah.

"My pleasure," Henry said.

"I wanted to go with the colourful lights, but Henry thought you'd prefer the white." Noah shrugged.

"I love the lights." She smiled, giving him a hug and using it as a cover to mouth the words, *Thank you,* to Henry.

"Where's Charlotte? I wanted to ask her something," Noah asked.

"She just ran to the back room I think, love," Dot said, wondering if she should tell him about her mood or not but then she figured if anyone could talk to her in that state, it would be Noah.

"Thanks. See you, Henry!" Noah waved and ran off, not bothering to wait for a response, though it didn't appear to bother Henry one bit.

"He's a great kid," Henry said, letting out a chuckle as he added, "A little old for his age, but hey, maybe that's a good thing."

"What do you mean?"

"Nothing, I mean, he's just… He sees things, I guess." Henry shrugged as if he had more words he wanted to say but didn't know how to say them. All Dot had ever seen was a little boy who enjoyed testing his mom, but hey, if Henry saw something else then that was great.

"He sure does," was all Dot could think of saying.

"Yeah. Oh, and fair warning. To get you the white lights here, we had to make a bit of a compromise."

"What would that be?" Dot asked, her eyes narrowing.

"Well, let's just say, your tree at home is a little more colourful," Henry said.

"Perfect," Dot said, unable to keep the sarcasm from her voice.

"But it's a cute tree."

"I'm sure it is. Thank you, Henry. You have to let me know what I owe you for the trees, and the lights, and the stands! Gosh, we were unprepared for this," Dot said, pressing her fingers to her temples as she forced out a laugh.

"You don't owe me anything. Consider it a gift."

"That's too generous. Please let me give you something."

"Well, if you must... maybe a butter tart," Henry said, pretending to think.

"And a sandwich!" Dot insisted.

"Fine, twist my arm," Henry said playfully before he began rubbing his arm nervously as he looked at Dot.

"Anything else?" she asked, her eyes narrowing suspiciously.

"No," he said quickly but seemed to regret it immediately. "*No!* I mean, yes. Yes, I have something else, but yeah, well, maybe if you have time, you want to join me?" Henry said. "You know, so I don't have to eat alone and all. But also, I know that you are running the store and I totally understand if now isn't the best time. It isn't, is it? Of course it isn't." He was rambling now and as it happened, the small bell behind the door rang out as Riley walked in.

"Riley," Dot said, thankful for the interruption, as she was starting to feel badly for the man.

"Wow that is... a big tree," Riley said, looking up at the massive thing. "I like it. Smells like Christmas," she said, turning to look at Dot. "Sorry, am I...?"

"No, you're just in time," Dot said, taking a sideways glance toward Henry, who looked as though he wanted to jump out of his own skin standing there.

"Maybe I should—" he started but Dot cut him off.

"I'm just about to have a little break. Treat Henry here to lunch to say thank you for all his hard work today. You think you can manage the counter?"

"You mean handle my one and only job?" Riley said, pretending to think about it. "I think I can manage. What do you need? I'll bring it out to you."

"You don't have—"

"It's my job Dot," she said, giving Dot a wink. "It's why you pay me the big bucks. Go on, have a seat." She waved a hand passively as she took off her jacket and mitts, hanging them up on a set of hooks beside the counter.

"I guess we should have a seat then," Dot said, turning to look at Henry.

"I guess we should," he said. "Lead the way."

14

Charlotte

What is wrong with me?

Charlotte knew deep down there was nothing actually wrong with her. But for whatever reason, she was having a difficult time keeping herself together lately. Although this was the first time she'd had a breakdown in front of anyone else. Until now, she'd been doing so well, leaving the room, giving herself space at night to let the emotions swell up and then move on. But seeing the tree and the store reminded Charlotte of the many times that she and Eli had come up for Christmas and how much he enjoyed the entire Christmas season.

It was never Charlotte's thing. Before Eli, she had liked to pretend that Christmas wasn't a big deal because in her family, it wasn't. More of a chance to get away and go on some big trip that almost always descended into her parents fighting until they decided that they'd had enough and split apart.

After that, Christmas stopped being anything more than an opportunity for her parents to use her as a tool to manipulate one another. It wasn't until Eli invited her to Dot's one year that Christmas had started to feel joyful again. Then, as if the universe was trying to remind her that her life was not put on this earth to experience joy, Eli got sick, and in a flash, all of that joy disappeared as life once again became about pretending. Only this time, it was for Noah's sake, only to have it all come crashing down on her again in tiny incremental breakdowns.

"Charlotte?" Noah said, tapping on the door. "You okay in there?"

She was not. She was sitting on a toilet seat weeping into a tissue, trying to pretend everything in her life wasn't descending toward complete chaos. She missed her partner, and the joy he gave her, she wished her son would call her Mom, and more than anything, she wished she could tell someone about the secret she'd been carrying for the past two weeks.

"I'm fine," she lied, which only served to make her feel worse. But that's what she did. She'd dug a hole. Now that hole was so deep, its walls thwarted her escape as she slowly entombed herself in with her own reluctance to tell anyone what was really going on. Worst of all, it was as if she was watching this as a spectator of her own life.

"I just need a minute, Noah."

"Okay," he said but didn't appear to leave the door, as if he wanted to say something else. Charlotte stopped breathing, trying to prevent herself from making anymore weeping sounds and giving him anymore reason to worry. She'd already managed to mess him up enough over the past year. The last thing she needed to do was let him know just how much of a failure she was. How she couldn't even manage to keep a semblance of what his life should look like.

She wasn't sure at which point she had finally managed to become her parents. Somehow Eli's death had effectively stripped away all of the good qualities he had seen in her and replaced them with her true nature. A reality of her life she'd known she was destined for even as a child. The tiny little liar who managed to destroy everyone she touched—her parents, Eli, Noah, and now Dot. The final vestiges of a life she'd always dreamed she could have had, slipped through her fingers. The best thing she could do for anyone would be to disappear, and had it not been for Eli's final favour, she may have done it. Somewhere in the back on her mind, she knew she had to try because it was what Eli wanted. Only his words were left to guide her, and she was afraid that his words were beginning to fade and soon, all she would be left with was her empty shell.

But not today.

15

Noah

"It's okay," Cally said, her arms folded as she looked up at the massive tree now occupying the main floor of the Old Mill.

"I think what you mean to say is 'impressive,'" Noah said.

"I'm not sure if 'impressive' is the right word," Cally tilted her head from side to side, "unless it was to say that I am impressed that you managed to find this tree."

"What is that supposed to mean?" though he regretted the words the moment he said them since he already knew her answer was not going to be something that he wanted to hear.

He wasn't sure why he cared so much about what this girl thought of him but since the day they had met, she had done everything in her power to make him feel inadequate and he hated every second of it. After all, who was she to say anything to him?

"I'm just saying that for someone like you to find such a nice tree is impressive," Cally said with a shrug.

"Someone like me?" Noah said, unable to hide the indignity he was feeling at her judgement.

"Yeah, you know," she gave him another shrug, which only

served to annoy him further. He didn't know what she meant, and he certainly had no idea where she got the nerve to assume things.

"You don't know anything about me," happy they were alone at this moment. Cally had come by after school to meet her sister, Riley, who was in the back with Nana, while Charlotte and Tia were cleaning up and planning for Charlotte's impromptu tree-decorating event.

Cally had played the part of excited young pupil well, telling them she would make signs and share them at the school. But now that all the adults were busy and it was just them, it was clear she was letting her true colours show. No longer the nice, happy girl everyone seemed to think she was, but a cruel and mean girl who for reasons unknown hated Noah.

"I think I know everything I need to know about you," Cally said, eyeing Noah up and down, reading him like she might a book. Which she wasn't because she was stupid and knew nothing. And Noah was going to prove it.

"Is that so?" Noah said. "Well, maybe I know everything there is to know about you."

"You know nothing about me," Cally protested.

"I know that you're mean, and that you pretend to be this goodie two-shoes but it's all an act so that you and your sister can make some money from my nana."

"How dare you," Cally said, pushing Noah, which caught him off guard and he fell to the floor. Not that this deterred Cally in any way as she stepped over him and pointed. "Don't you dare say anything about me or my sister," Cally said, her voice low now. "Dot, your Nana has been there for the two of us for as long as I can remember. I would do anything for her."

"So would I!" Noah said, but Cally only laughed.

"Please, you show up here having been kicked out of school for God knows what and then on your first day here, you cry about not wanting to work and you do a terrible job. I mean, what kind of child can't put a box together?" Cally said, shaking her head and when Noah tried to retort, she waved a hand in his face, not allowing it. "No, don't even speak. I heard what you were like and I saw what you did. But this building and this store mean so much to me and my sister and I will do everything in my power to make sure that not you or anyone comes into this place and ruins it. Not now."

"You think I'm trying to ruin this place?" Noah asked.

"I don't think you even care about it. You don't realize what this place has meant to so many of us. To me. You just come in from your big city, probably thinking that a place like this is one of many. But it isn't, it is the only one and when it's gone, we may not get it ever again."

"What do you mean, when it's gone?" Noah asked, which seemed to shake Cally a little but only for a split second as she ignored him.

"Yes, I work here. So do Riley and Tia. Your nana gave us a chance to be a part of something special. She taught me about food and what it can do for people, how it can bring a community together. Then you come here, and you don't care. You just think it's a big joke," Cally said, shaking her head.

"I don't think it is a joke, Cally."

"Really? Is that why you slack off, ignoring everything in this place besides your strange pursuit to make me feel small?" This took Noah aback, but not Cally, "That's right, I have eyes, Noah. But I have news for you. I'm not small, and there's nothing you could ever do to me that's going to make me feel like I'm not good enough. You know why?"

Noah didn't know what to say, but he thought that this would be a good time to say nothing since it appeared that Cally was willing to rip his head off if he so much as breathed in her direction. So, he opted for silence.

"Because Dot has given me the opportunity to learn, and grow and challenge myself to be better than I am. And now it's all going away." Cally was in tears, and she wiped them away on the sleeve of her jacket.

Noah, still on the ground, felt terrible, but he didn't know why. After all, he had just been playing around and now this girl was yelling at him for no reason. All he wanted was for her to see that he picked out a good tree. Something he didn't think she believed he could do. Now she was critiquing him on all manner of things he didn't think that was fair. Once again, she said it was going away. He wanted to ask her about what she meant. But she didn't look like she wanted to talk to him.

She wiped her eyes again and turned to walk back into the kitchen.

"Wait!" Noah said, scrambling to his feet and taking a few steps toward her. But Cally turned sharply on him, ready for a fight, and Noah instinctively raised his hands in protection.

"What?" she eyed him cautiously.

"I'm sorry," Noah was surprised that he meant the words as he said them. He still wasn't entirely sure what he had done to offend her, but he could see that whatever it was had caused her real pain. Why his actions, someone who she clearly didn't even appear to like, could create that sort of reaction was beyond him. All he knew was that he didn't enjoy seeing her in pain. "I'm not trying to make you mad," Noah said.

"I know. You just do," Cally said, folding her arms against her chest. "Because you don't see how lucky you are."

"You think I'm lucky?" Noah said, letting out a hollow laugh. "I had to watch my dad die."

"I know you did," Cally said, her anger vanishing for a moment as she looked at him with something akin to pity.

"Stop that!" he said, jabbing a finger in her direction.

"What?" she asked.

"That. That look. I don't need you to pity me. I don't need more people in my life looking at me as if they feel sorry for me."

"What do you want then, Noah?" she said, catching him off guard.

"What?"

"You don't want pity and you don't want to feel lucky… So what? Anger? Because fine, I can do that too," she said, taking a step closer to him. "I'm sorry about your dad, I am. But your nana lost a son, and your mom lost her husband, and they're supposed to just get on with their lives, not letting people see how much pain they are in while you go around doing whatever you want, because hey, you're sad," she said mockingly. "I've heard about you. And now I've seen it firsthand. You want people to see you're in pain, but you don't want people to do anything about it. You just want them to accept it."

"I do not!" Noah wanted to shout at this girl who was really starting to annoy him now. After all, what did she know about his loss?

"Yes, you do." Her words had such conviction, Noah felt

himself take an involuntary step back. "Let me ask you this. Why did you get kicked out of school?"

"It was a misunderstanding," Noah sneered.

"Really? Your school just happened to get so upset that they kicked you out the month before Christmas?"

"Yes!" he hissed. "I saw an experiment online and I thought it would be fun to try. I didn't realize it would be that big of a deal."

"What did you do?" she asked curiously.

"I may have put a mentos in a pop bottle and let it loose inside one of the older year's chemistry labs. I didn't expect it to *explode* explode," Noah said, remembering the mix of emotions he'd felt at the time. He'd been waiting in the hallway, giggling, but after the pop and the screaming, things had just gotten a little out of hand. He didn't know exactly what had happened. All he knew was that in the chaos, someone had knocked over a vial of alcohol, which had caught fire on a Bunsen burner, starting a small fire. He'd realized something had gone wrong when all of the kids had begun filing out of the room, screaming, and he peered in to see Mr Lee standing there with an extinguisher in his hands, his face covered in sweat or tears as he managed to put out the small fire before finally turning to glare out at Noah, his expression a mix of anger and fear.

"You started a fire at your school?" Cally's eyes were wide.

"Technically, no. I didn't start the fire," Noah said, "but I did get blamed for it." He shook his head. "I just thought people would get wet."

Cally looked at him for a long moment before she started to snicker, which eventually turned into a big laugh.

"Why are you laughing?" Noah asked, as he started to laugh

as well, though he didn't feel like it was something to laugh about. At least that was what all of his teachers had told him.

"You just thought they would get wet," she repeated. "Wow. What a terrible plan."

"I didn't really think about it too much," Noah said.

"Clearly," Cally said, laughing loudly now. Noah couldn't help himself from laughing along with her. The pair began to laugh so hard that Riley and Charlotte even poked their heads out to look at them, although they didn't feel the need to ask them why. That was probably a good thing since Charlotte was unlikely to find the same humour in the story. At least she hadn't found it funny at all when she'd been forced to pick him up from the school and told that he wasn't allowed back.

Noah's stomach began to hurt before he finally managed to subdue his laughter. Cally had been gripping her own stomach as well, before she turned back to make sure that the pair were back to being alone.

"I get it," she said, letting out a heavy sigh.

"Get what?" Noah asked, unsure what she could possibly be talking about now.

"The desire to want people to see you on your terms. Not the way they think they should," Cally said, and Noah couldn't help but begin to feel annoyed again. That wasn't what he was trying to do. He thought it would be fun. It was, until it wasn't. He didn't expect people to get hurt or scared. That was his only mistake. Not that he was trying to control the way people looked at him.

"That wasn't what I was doing," Noah said. The laughter dissipated fully now.

"Sure." Cally clearly did not believe Noah at all, but before Noah could say anything, she shrugged. "But I'm going to let you in on a little secret. Something Dot taught me." She walked up to him and poked his chest. He fought the urge to swat it away. "Only you get to decide how people perceive you, and it's not by what you say, but what you do."

"What do you know about anything?" Noah said, hating the fact that this girl his own age was trying to give him advice. She had already made it clear that she didn't like him and all he had done was show up. Now he was supposed to believe that the reason she didn't like him was because of what he did.

"More than you know," Cally said, cutting Noah's thoughts off as he saw a new look on her face and it wasn't one he was used to seeing. In fact, he didn't even know what he would call it. Despite their conversation and everything she had just said to him, he couldn't help but feel the look had nothing to do with him. But he didn't have the chance to ask as Riley walked in, breaking up whatever connection the two kids were sharing.

"Ready to go?" Riley said, coming up and putting a hand on Cally's back.

"Yeah," she said softly, and they turned to leave through the back room, but before Cally left, she stopped and turned to face Noah. "It is a really nice tree," she said, giving Noah a shrug and a smile before walking out.

"I do not understand that girl," Noah said as he slumped down in a chair and ran the conversation over in his mind, attempting to figure out what in the world had just happened.

16

Charlotte

"Perhaps it is a bit of overkill," Charlotte said, looking at the bowls of popcorn and boxes of Christmas ornaments that were laid out on the floor of Dot's living room in front of the tree.

"You think?" Noah said, lifting one of the boxes and pretending it was a struggle for him.

"Don't be so dramatic," Charlotte said, swatting a hand playfully in his direction.

"You realize we just have the one tree, right?" Noah said, looking around the room.

"I'm not planning on putting everything on," Charlotte explained. "I just didn't know what to bring, so I brought everything."

"You certainly did," Dot said, pouring some hot water into a teapot.

"Look, we all don't have to do this. I just—"

"No, no, no," Dot said, "we're just poking fun at you. This will be good for all of us. It's been some time since I set up a tree. Probably good to go through it all."

"I know it's ridiculous. But after last year, I just—"

"You don't have to explain yourself, love," Dot said, grabbing three mugs and setting them down on the island which separated the living room and the kitchen. The wood stove was all warmed up and between the heat of the stove and the boiling kettle, the windows to the tiny cottage were steamed up. It was the first time that Charlotte had felt like it was Christmas since they had arrived.

Eli on the other hand, had always loved setting up trees and making the most of the holidays and a part of Charlotte didn't want to let that tradition fall away now that he was gone. But she struggled to make it as effortless as he always had.

"So, what's with the popcorn?" Noah asked, sticking his hand in and taking a scoop. "It could use some butter, if I'm honest."

"It's for stringing up. Don't you remember you and Dad would spend hours threading popcorn, making strings of it to put on the tree?"

"Sort of," Noah said, looking guilty.

"It was a while ago," Charlotte said, not wanting Noah to feel badly about not remembering. She wanted this to be fun, not become mournful which, if she was being honest with herself, was feeling a bit impossible. Noah may not remember what Christmas had been like, but Charlotte did, and she was confident that Dot would have memories as well.

"I used to do the same thing with Eli when he was a boy," Dot said thoughtfully. "Gosh, all I remember was the mess that it made afterwards." She chuckled to herself. "I would be fishing popcorn out of the furniture for weeks."

"If it makes you happy, he never got any better at it," Charlotte said. "Noah was the responsible one, making small piles and neatly threading the popcorn through, careful not to poke himself."

"So, I have always been like this?" Noah asked, looking down at the organized piles in front of him.

"Yes."

Charlotte and Dot both laughed as Noah shrugged.

"Nothing wrong with enjoying a little structure, Noah," Dot said, and Charlotte couldn't help but giggle as she looked over at the older woman, who had consciously or subconsciously neatly lined the mugs up, each of their handles pointing out to the right, each one perfectly positioned for Dot to handle and divvy up.

"What?" Dot began looking down to see what Charlotte could have been laughing at. "Oh. I see it." She laughed. "We're just working with what we have."

"Oh great, so I'm Nana?" Noah tossed his arms up in mock-protest.

"There are worse people to be like, Noah. Trust me," Charlotte said, trying to remember her own parents who, like Dot, liked things to be organized but, unlike Dot, refused to allow anything that wasn't perfectly structured to exist in their presence. She began to recall some of her many Christmases where she was asked to rewrap her presents because, as her mother put it, they looked like a child had done them. When Charlotte had informed her that she was a child, her mother had reminded her that she was their child and no child of theirs was going to fail at such a simple task as wrapping gifts.

After that, Charlotte had stopped enjoying Christmas so much. At least that was until Eli had come along and reminded her that there could be fun in life's imperfections.

"Here you go," Dot said, handing Charlotte a cup of tea,

bringing her out of the memories she found herself wrapped up in.

"Thank you," Charlotte said with a thin smile. She'd not felt like herself all day and she was really hoping that she might be able to find a small piece of herself in decorating the tree. Now she was beginning to feel as though it was all a big waste of time. She wasn't sure anyone else wanted to do it either.

"So, what's first?" Noah said, directing her feelings toward the tree-decorating endeavour.

Maybe this is all just a stupid idea?

"Perhaps we should open them up, see what we got. Plan an attack so to speak," Dot said, rubbing her hands together. It wasn't a singing endorsement, but at least she wasn't suggesting giving it all up entirely.

"Sure," Noah said, opening one of the boxes.

"We also don't have to do it at all. I'm sorry, I just thought…" Charlotte said, feeling a little uneasy about saying what she wanted out loud. Last Christmas had been awful since it was the first year without Eli and Charlotte hadn't handled it all that well. She'd not refused to set up anything Christmassy but neither had she gone out of her way to make it happen. Mostly, all she'd wanted to do was sleep, which was more or less all she had done for the months after his death.

It had been the beginning of the end for her and, as it would happen, her job. They'd been very considerate after Eli's death but as the year progressed and Charlotte hadn't seemed to move on, they had finally had enough. Now she had a few months of savings to help get them through the winter, then she wasn't sure she'd be able to make condo payments. She shared none of these problems with anyone.

"Nonsense," Dot said, gesturing to the boxes. "We have

come this far, the least we can do is set some of it up."

"Maybe not all of them?" Noah said, pulling out a small, clay ornament with a child's foot on it.

"Aww," Charlotte moved in to grab it from Noah's hand. "We have to put this one up. It's the first one we ever gave you."

"So, your first Christmas gift was a cast of my own foot?" Noah said, his eyes rolling at the thought. "Bit of a let-down, if you ask me."

"Oh come on, you were thrilled at the time. Making all those gurgling sounds."

"Still, my own foot?"

"You were nine months old, Noah. It wasn't like you did much," Charlotte joked. "It's not like we were going to give you anything big. I mean, for the first three or four years, you were more interested in the box a gift came in than the gift itself." Charlotte laughed as a memory flashed through her mind of Eli making a small tunnel out of large boxes that zigzagged through their first tiny apartment.

Eli had insisted that he go through first to make sure it was safe, only to get stuck, which resulted in a rescue mission for Noah and Charlotte. She doubted Noah had any memories at all of that, but she did.

"That's because boxes are awesome. You can make forts out of boxes." Noah chuckled.

"Yes, you can!" Charlotte said cheerfully as Christmas music began to fill the tiny cottage. Charlotte looked over at Dot, who was fiddling with her phone.

"I figure if we are going to do it, let's do it right." She shrugged.

"Fair enough," Charlotte said, gesturing to a stack of boxes.

"Noah, you take those, I'll take these and Dot, you handle those ones there." Charlotte signalled to a small stack she'd put near Dot's chair. "Bear, you just keep warm by the fire!"

Bear's head poked up to look at Charlotte before rolling back down on his bed.

"What are we looking for?"

"Anything you want on the tree goes up." Charlotte hadn't thought it all through, nor had she ever thought either Noah or Dot would let her get this far so she would be happy with anything at this point.

"Even these?" Noah said, pulling up a set up of three crystal cherubs that had their names engraved on the wings. Charlotte remembered her mom giving them to their family after Noah was born. She didn't much like them then and continued to dislike them now. Why she would want three tiny, naked babies on the tree was beyond her.

"Maybe not those," Charlotte said thinking about it before getting up. "Well, maybe this one." She walked over and grabbed the one with Eli's name on it. "But only because I know how much he would have loved us putting it up."

"Dad hated these," Noah said, which caused Dot to laugh.

"You're right, he would love that." Dot smiled.

"I'm sorry, am I missing something here?" Noah asked.

"One day, you'll understand," Charlotte mused as she put the little naked baby up on the tree. "Perfect."

The next hour or so, the three of them rifled through their boxes, picking out various ornaments and listening to music as they decorated the tree. It was a lot longer than Charlotte had thought any of them would last. She'd managed to only let herself cry five times in the process as various memories struck her. Despite the fact that this had been her idea, she hadn't quite realized how hard it would be. So, it wasn't surprising after Charlotte had started sniffling over a homemade ornament Noah had made when he was eight for Eli that Dot stood from her seat and exclaimed, "I think we need cookies!"

"Yes, please!" Noah said and the distraction was just enough for Charlotte to get over her small bout of sadness and join in what was supposed to be a fun evening.

"Great, you can help me."

"You want to make cookies?" Noah said.

"Yes, of course. I hear you're quite the chemist," Dot gave Noah a wink as his face flushed red and he turned to glare at Charlotte, who raised her hands up in defence.

"Don't look at me."

"Then—Cally! It was a mistake—"

"Oh come on! It's a good story. No one was hurt and you got to hang out with me for the month," Dot said and though Charlotte didn't really want to encourage her son's desire to cause destruction and potential harm to his fellow students, she had to admit one good thing had come from it all. The idea of being at home in their apartment right now was agonizing.

"Well, maybe not a great idea to toss an explosive bottle into a room full of kids," Charlotte said, unable to help herself from being a mom.

"Fair point," Dot said. "You know there are better ways of using chemistry."

"Oh yeah? Like what?" Noah asked, getting up from the floor when Dot curled a finger to have him come over. "And for the record, I wasn't trying to hurt anyone. I just thought it would be funny."

"And was it?" Charlotte asked, her tone even.

"It had potential," Noah said after thinking about it for far too long. "That's a cookbook." Noah said when he finally reached the island, hopping up on a chair to meet Dot's eye.

"This is not just a cookbook, my dear. It is the science of cooking. The best part of being a chemist lies right in here," Dot said.

"Sure," Noah said, pushing the book away as Dot feigned shock.

"But hey, what do I know… I'm just a baker."

"The nerve of this kid." Charlotte joked as she rummaged through one of the boxes. Inside, she found a set of folded stockings. The top one was Noah's and under that was Eli's. She held it for a moment, letting her finger run over the handstitched name that Dot herself had sewn on when he was a boy.

In the back of her mind, she could hear Dot telling Noah about her past life, the one where she'd been a pharmaceutical major and how her journey through chemistry had always led her to food. Charlotte had heard the speech before. But Noah, she was pleased, appeared to enjoy it. She gripped the stocking in her hands, feeling the tears fall down her cheeks and onto her hands before she even realized she'd been crying.

It wasn't the first time since Eli's death that Charlotte had thought the universe had done it all wrong. That it should have been her to leave first. It was unfair that she would be here in Eli's mother's house with their son, a child she'd never been sure she'd wanted. But she knew she wanted one with Eli, and where did that leave her now?

She'd never felt like she'd been put on this earth to care for anyone else. She'd barely managed to take care of herself. But now within two years of being on her own, with no Eli to help, she'd already destroyed the world they had created together. She'd lost her job, her relationship with her son, and soon, they would lose their apartment. All things Eli would have managed to keep together. Without him, she was doomed to fail. Worst of all, she knew it.

Charlotte resisted the urge to run away and cry in the bathroom, something that was becoming a painful hobby of hers. Instead, she wiped the tears away and pretended to laugh at Dot's story of running off to open the Mill. Surprised to see Noah interested in the story as well, having even pulled the cookbook back to flip through the pages. She was impressed Dot could manage to keep him engaged at all. But given that some part of her was Eli, maybe that wasn't all that hard to believe.

Charlotte folded Eli's stocking back up and set it aside, feeling guilty as she laid it on her do not use pile. She quickly returned to rummaging through her box, trying to push the feelings she had down. As she pulled out her own stocking, she was surprised that there was something in it. She reached in, pulling out a card with her name on it.

She turned it over in her hand. The back had been sealed with the words, *For Christmas morning*, written in marker across the back in Eli's handwriting. The words were accompanied by an absolutely terribly drawn broken heart beside it. *Definitely Eli's.*

In the year since Eli's death, Charlotte had found letters written by Eli for her to open on various occasions. They had been incredibly difficult to read. At first, she'd avoided them, not wanting to be rid of the last things Eli had left for her. Finally, she'd managed to open one, then two and soon enough, she'd got through what she thought was the last one.

Something that marked both a sad and happy day for her. But it would appear she had missed one. The last note Eli had written her. The gesture had meant a lot to Charlotte since she knew Eli was never a big fan of letters. He'd only ever written them for Charlotte because she'd mentioned how much she loved them once. It was just one of the many ways Eli had chosen to express his love. *For Christmas morning.*

Charlotte read the back again, feeling for the first time in her life that she would be grateful to wait.

17

Dot

"Dot, your timer," Tia said as the soft beeping sound filled the room, causing Dot to finally look up from the pastry dough she'd been mixing.

"What's that, love?" Dot said, giving her head a shake.

"Your tourtières, they're done, I think," Tia said, nodding toward the timer and then over to the ovens.

"Right, of course," Dot said, pulling her hands out from the dough and wiping them down on the towel hooked at her waist around her apron.

"You alright this morning? You seem a little distracted," Tia said as she chopped up mountains of mushrooms for the breakfast tarts.

"Do I?" Dot asked absently. Her brain was still not following the conversation. "Never mind." She shook her head, opening the ovens and checking the meat pies. Luckily, Tia had been paying attention as they were very nearly overcooked. "Maybe I am a little distracted this morning." Dot made room on one of the tables for the pies to let them cool before being boxed up.

"Anything I can help with?" Tia asked, looking at Dot a little too closely, as if she were some sort of wounded animal as she pulled out the pies, realizing only now that she had accidentally put in five pies instead of the four that were ordered.

"Shoot."

"It's just, I'm not used to… this," Tia said, waving a hand in Dot's general direction. "Normally you're… not this." Her tone attempted to remain as neutral as possible, trying to say what she wanted without actually saying, *You're off today.*

"I suppose I am a little off this morning," Dot admitted, choosing to ignore the pie. She would just have to find something else to do with it later. Her mind was a little preoccupied with the events of last night. It had been a wonderful night getting to spend time with just Charlotte and Noah. She was also keen on the prospect of finally finding a shared interest with her grandson that they both enjoyed. It was a delight to discover that even just the process of making cookies appealed to him.

Secretly, she relished the possibility of passing on a little bit about what she knew. His interest in chemistry, albeit a little misguided, filled Dot with a sense of pride. Dot really wanted to build on that connection, and last night had been the perfect introduction. She had even decided to bring him into the kitchens later in the day to try out some other recipes.

Science and food were two things Dot loved. Being able to share that love with her grandson would be one of the greatest gifts she could receive. After all, food had been her passion for as long as she could remember.

"Eli wrote Charlotte a letter. She found it last night in her stocking," Dot said evenly. There was no great way to explain it, or how she felt about it, so the facts felt safe.

"I see. And you're upset he didn't write you one?" Tia asked.

"No. No, nothing like that. I did get a card, after he passed, and I cherished every word. This is different."

"How so?"

"I feel terrible for Charlotte. She has so much going on right now, and then this. She set it in the tree and didn't talk about it. Just left it there. Like this massive looming presence in the house."

"And you want her to open it?"

"I don't know what I want, Tia." Dot shrugged. "Honestly. I suppose I just wouldn't want it sitting there if it was me. It said to open it on Christmas Day."

"Well then, there you go."

"Right! But it's been less then twelve hours and the suspense and stress are killing me and it's not even my card." Dot shook her head.

"You're right, it isn't yours," Tia said flatly, and Dot went to open her mouth but the way Tia was looking at her, she knew she was in the wrong here and Tia was right. It wasn't Dot's card, nor was it her place to hold on to any feeling about how Charlotte handled it. No matter how painful it was for her.

"I finished the boxes, Nana," Noah said, coming in from the front room and letting out a big yawn.

"And I got everything you needed from that supplier." Charlotte sounded much more chipper than Dot would have imagined. Although, she had her suspicions it was all just an act she was putting on for all their sakes.

"What can I do now?" Charlotte and Noah asked at the same time. Dot wanted to say, go home, open that letter and then tell her what was in it, but that wasn't helpful. So instead, she smiled at the pair and tapped the counter while she thought.

"Umm… Charlotte, I'll get you on quiches. We have a list, just there," she pointed to a list attached to a magnet on the fridge, "for pick-up. Get those sorted first, then make a few for the shop. Not sure how today is going to look, what with the weather and all," Dot said, glancing toward the back door where puddles had formed from all the snow being dragged in.

"The roads were not great," Charlotte admitted.

"I figured as much. I thought about telling Riley and Cally not to come in. Save them both the misery," Dot said, amused when she caught the look of disappointment on Noah's face at the mention of this. A part of her was happy that Noah and Cally seemed to finally be getting along, or at least they were no longer bickering endlessly with one another. She wasn't sure what changed but she was happy, and admittedly a little sad, since she knew where this unlikely friendship was heading. With Noah and his mom going back to Toronto. But she would be damned if she was going to be the one to let the harsh reality of life ruin something so nice.

"But they told me they were keen on coming in anyway," Dot said with a grin, looking away so as to not let Noah realize she'd been watching his enthused expression.

"Wouldn't want to tell her how lazy she is," Noah said in a bad attempt to look nonchalant about the whole thing.

"Well, at least we can avoid that," Dot said, watching both Tia and Charlotte smile knowingly. "Maybe this would be a good time to get prepped on next week's orders. I'm going to look them over and see what we can do today. With any luck, none of us will need to come in to prep next Tuesday."

"That would be something of a Christmas miracle," Tia said

as she cracked an egg into her pastry.

"Wouldn't it just." Dot smiled. "Right, everyone know what they're doing?" Dot asked, and Noah looked around, confused.

"No. What am I doing?" Noah asked.

"You, my boy," Dot said enthusiastically, having thought of an extra-special project for Noah to work on, one she thought he might enjoy rather than endlessly folding and stickering the boxes, "you are going to help me go through these orders and see what we need to do."

"Oh, fun," Noah said, doing his best and failing to sound enthusiastic about the whole thing. "Paperwork."

This got a laugh out of Charlotte and Tia, who were both moving around prepping their area of the kitchen.

"We're just going to give your mom and Tia some space to work for a bit. Once we know what we need to do, I thought you and I could take care of cookies and croissants," Dot said, moving over to pull out the stack of order forms attached to the large industrial fridge, pretending not to notice Noah's building excitement. "I mean, you did such a good job with them last night, I thought you might like to try it again. Not to mention, you have no idea how cool lamination is, and what it does to your pastries." Dot shrugged.

"And your cholesterol." Tia laughed as she mixed a batch of shortcrust pastry.

"That too," Dot mused. "But, I mean, if you would rather—"

"I'm in!" Noah said, walking over and grabbing the stack of papers. "Where do we start?"

It was a good hour later before Dot had managed to organize the order forms and get her totals for the week. This morning had been particularly rough since she'd found her brain not working at full capacity. She'd hoped the change of task would help her, but it had not. And after reading the numbers wrong on two forms, she had decided it best to triple check her work. Which meant by the time she'd finished organizing, the enthusiasm Noah had felt at preparing cookies had all but faded into obscurity as he struggled to keep his eyes open reading the forms.

"Two banana loaves and two vegetarian quiches," Noah read aloud, his eyes watering as he stifled a yawn.

"Perfect," Dot said, looking at the final document. She had her list ready, and she felt mildly optimistic that they might not need anyone to come into work on Tuesday, which would mean a full two days off for the whole staff, something everyone needed leading up to the final week before Christmas.

Dot still wasn't sure what Charlotte was thinking about the tree-decorating party, which was still happening at the end of the week. She hoped it wouldn't require too much effort since Dot was already feeling ready for a long rest. If it wasn't for the fact that she knew that after this Christmas, she would get that break, she might have felt a little frustrated by the new addition of this Old Mill Christmas celebration. Or whatever it was Charlotte had decided to call the night.

As it was, Dot had decided to make the most of the situation, realizing it would be the best opportunity to share with the community, or at least the dozen or so people who showed up, that after the New Year, she would be shutting the doors to the Old Mill for good. It was a reality that made her both sad and excited at the same time. She knew this little store had pulled her out of one of the darkest moments of her life, but after Eli passed away, something had changed. And now the whole endeavour felt different, like she owed it to herself to take some time to try something new, not stay stuck in yet another pattern.

"Does this mean we get to do cookies now?" Noah asked, glancing up at the clock on the wall. "Because I think it would be nice to have them finished before Cally arrives, you know, so I could rub it in her face."

"You have a very strange relationship with that girl." Dot grinned, amused by the sight of young love, even if they didn't understand what it was.

"She started it." Noah shrugged. "Besides, you never explained to me what the purpose of the baking soda was in the cookies. All you said was that it created a chemical reaction, and honestly, I don't understand."

"Oh, you will! It's simple. The baking soda is sodium bicarbonate, and when it mixes with an acid, it creates carbon dioxide and—"

Dot stopped, despite having Noah's full attention, because of a knock at the front door. She turned to see a man standing there, covered in snow and waving, though it was hard to tell who it was with the fogged-up windows. Dot looked up at the clock, they didn't open for another forty minutes. "Just a sec," Dot said, standing up to check the door as Noah's eyes rolled and he dropped his head to the table.

"Just when we were getting to the good stuff!" he whimpered.

"I'll just be a second, love," she said as she moved to the door, slid the bolt latch, and opened the door slightly, trying her best to not let the frigid air and snow in. "We don't open— Henry?" Dot said, chuckling to herself as she opened the door and rushed the big man inside. "What are you doing here?"

"Sorry, I know I'm early," he said, stepping inside as Dot closed the door behind him and began patting him down, wiping the snow off him.

"I don't want to drag this mess inside," Henry said, looking down at the pile of snow.

"Gosh, it is bad out there."

"It's winter, that's for sure." Henry chuckled. "Sorry to barge in."

"Apology accepted, Henry," Noah said from the table, smiling at the big man.

"Working hard, Noah?" he asked.

"Trying to." Noah shrugged.

"Well, I won't keep you long. I was just wondering if you by any chance had anything made? I didn't get a chance to make anything this morning and I have twenty-five trees I got to chop down by this afternoon for pick-up. It was poor planning, I know."

"Today? In this?" Dot said, gesturing to the snow falling outside which was both beautiful and scary depending on how you looked at it. For Dot, the idea of being in a vehicle would be the latter.

"No rest for the wicked," Henry said. "Besides, it should slow down by pick-up time this afternoon. It's supposed to be a beautiful evening."

"We just have to get there. I think we have something—actually!" Dot said, running into the back room, picking a box off the shelf as she did. A few moments later, she returned with a box containing a full tourtière. "How about this?" she said, passing it to him. "My brain wasn't working this morning and I made an extra one. Perhaps I knew you would need it."

"This is a lot for one person," Henry said.

"Nonsense. I'm sure you can handle it." Dot smiled.

"How much do I—"

"It's on the house. You just have to tell me what you think," she said, giving him a pat on the arm.

Henry smiled broadly as he shook his head. "You're too good to me, Dot."

"You're my best customer."

"I doubt that very much. Oh, by the way," Henry said, unzipping his jacket and pulling out a small piece of paper a little damp from the snow. "I've been letting everyone know about the decorating party here this Friday. People are excited."

"You're doing what now?" Dot said, taking the paper from him and examining the handmade flyer. "Who did this?"

Noah coughed behind her. "Well, Cally and I thought it would be good for spreading the word, so Mom helped us out and we made it. I thought it could have used more gusto, but Cally is a difficult person to work with." He said, as if recalling a memory. "Do you like it?"

"I love it," Dot said, since it was the only reaction she could have with something like this. Personally, she thought it was a waste of time but if it made Cally and Noah work together and Henry wanted to waste his time handing them out, so be it. "Thank you... all of you." She said this last bit to Henry.

"I should get going. Umm, thank you for the pie... tourt... pie." He chuckled and perhaps it was the cold air from outside, but Dot could have sworn he looked embarrassed.

"You're welcome," Dot said.

Henry turned to leave but paused, his hand on the door.

"Sorry, I put the latch—"

"Do you want to have dinner with me tonight?" Henry said, the words falling out of him like an opened dam, causing Dot to take an involuntary step backward, which appeared to startle both of them.

"I'm sorry. I was just—"

"Tonight?" Dot asked, surprised by the shift in the mood.

"Yes. I mean, if you're free," Henry said, and suddenly, Dot began to feel like a little girl being asked to a school dance. But she was a grown woman with things to do and she couldn't just go for dinner with this man. *Could I?*

"Well Noah and—"

"We'll be fine, Nana. You should go," Noah said, giving Henry a not-so-subtle thumbs up.

"The weather, it's—"

"I can pick you up. If you want. No pressure. I just thought—"

"Sure," Dot answered before her brain had a chance to catch up with her emotions. Logically, this was a ridiculous idea. She was busy working and didn't have time for this, but she was also getting ready for a new chapter and maybe this was it. Maybe the universe was trying to tell her something and if she ignored it, then what? She couldn't simply ignore the universe. Besides, it was just a dinner. Maybe it would be nothing.

"Really? I mean… great. Yeah. I'll see you tonight," Henry said, turning and walking into the door. "The lock." He smiled, sliding it to the side.

"Smooth," Noah said under his breath, which caused Dot to chuckle, though she didn't know if Henry heard it or not with all his layers on.

"See you… later," he said, opening the door and leaving Dot

to lock back up, her heart racing at this sudden shift. It had been some time since anyone had asked her out on a date, and she'd nearly forgotten what it felt like. Frankly, she wasn't sure she knew how to do it. Her palms were sweating, along with most of her body, which was a surprise considering the cold air was still sitting in the space. A tiny thrill passed over her at the idea of a date, but it was very short-lived as the situation shifted in her mind and the nerves kicked in.

What did she wear, or bring, or say? Any of it, really. All of the uncertainties that came with the knowledge that she was about to go on a date with a man who she saw nearly every day she was in the shop. What if it was awful? How would she ever look at him again? She couldn't. *Oh God no!*

The panic in her body was causing her heart to race, like it was going to beat right out of her chest. She felt nauseous and completely forgot that she was not alone until Noah coughed behind her, bringing her back to reality.

"So… sodium bicarbonate?" Noah said, holding up his hand, completely unaware of the chaos storming in Dot's body as she laughed nervously.

18

Charlotte

"Yeah, they're not bad," was all Charlotte heard from the kitchen as she struggled to listen in to her son's private conversation with a young girl.

"Not bad? They're incredible," Noah exclaimed. "I don't know what kind of rock you live under when you can't tell an incredible cookie from a *not-bad* cookie."

Charlotte forced herself to stifle a laugh.

She knew it was wrong to listen, but she couldn't help herself. She was too infatuated with the idea that Noah was interested in something other than causing mayhem or distrusting everyone and everything around him. Not that he appeared to trust Cally that much. He actually seemed hell-bent on proving to her, and everyone else, that he didn't care what she thought, despite how obvious it was that he did. It was all rather cute in a way. She tried not to think of all the ways this was going to swing around to be her fault when things went south. It was the reality of being an only parent now. She was blamed for nearly everything.

"I don't live under a rock, Noah, but I do have taste buds,

and I have had Dot's cookies for my entire life. I hate to break it to you, but you are no Dot."

"I know I'm not. But they can still be good."

"Fine, they're good. Happy?"

"I don't want your pity good, thank you," Noah said, and Charlotte heard him stomp into the kitchen.

"That girl is bananas. I mean honestly, I don't see why Nana keeps her around," Noah said putting the small plate of cookies on the counter.

Charlotte eyed them for a second.

"May I?" she asked, curious for herself to see what they tasted like.

"Go ahead. Apparently, they are not bad," Noah said, his voice dripped with sarcasm.

"It's only your second time, Noah. Not bad is impressive. My second batch of cookies looked nothing like these."

"I think I used too much nutmeg," Noah said not really listening to Charlotte despite looking at her as if this was some sort of conversation. So, Charlotte ate a cookie instead. *Damn.*

"These are really good," Charlotte said, tasting the spiced ginger cookie still warm from the oven that had a nice combination of crunch and chewiness to it. "I think Nana will be impressed." *I know I am.*

She kept that last thought to herself since from the expression on his face, Noah didn't seem all that concerned about what she or anyone other than Cally thought about them.

"You have to say that. And Nana is the one who gave me the recipe, which I didn't follow exactly… but I had a vision," Noah said, speaking as though he wasn't referring to a simple ginger cookie.

"A vision?" Charlotte said, unable to stop herself from chuckling, which only caused Noah to scoff and shake his head at her.

"I should have guessed you wouldn't understand," he said, turning to leave but Charlotte reached for his shoulder and turned him around.

"Don't be so dramatic, Noah. I think it is nice that you're putting some thought into this. I just don't think you should put so much pressure on yourself to do it right the first time. Right, Tia?" Charlotte turned to look at the other woman, who was quietly stripping the meat from some roasted chickens for a pot pie. She glared at Charlotte.

"You should keep me out of it," Tia said to Charlotte before letting out a sigh as she picked away at the bird's carcass.

"Why?" Charlotte asked, trying not to focus on the pile of bones surrounding Tia.

"Because satisfaction is death," Tia said, emphasising her point as she ripped off a chicken thigh.

"What?" Noah and Charlotte said, both confused now.

"Food is life," Tia said, pausing to look over at them. "Every time we cook, we are chasing perfection. No two chickens are the same, not two carrots, everything we use is unique. Our job is to take those things and every time, make the best possible meal. We measure things and cut them to size and weigh out our ingredients, trying to create the perfect dish every time. Even once we find the perfect combination, the ones we've tested over and over just to prove it's as good as we think, we still have to tweak it, changing some of the elements, trying to figure out how or if these new factors will affect the dish. And then, let's say we have found 'perfection'. All we need to do now is recreate those same parameters day after day, over and over again. What we do isn't sane. If I were you, I would take the win. Make a cookie that isn't bad and choose satisfaction. Walk away and enjoy that you will make others happy. Because if you continue down this road, too much nutmeg, not enough milk, it will keep you up at night. Trust me," Tia said, shaking her head. "Chasing your own perfection is a type of hell no sane person should be after."

"Thanks, Tia," Charlotte said after a long pause where she'd secretly hoped Tia might have added something a little more encouraging. When it was clear that was unlikely to happen, Charlotte didn't know what to say.

"I told you not to ask me." Tia shrugged.

"No, you're right," Noah said shrugging off Charlotte's hand as he picked up a cookie and walked over to Tia. "What do you think of the cookie?" he said, holding it up and Tia leaned over to eat the cookie right from Noah's hand since her own hands were covered in chicken grease.

Charlotte had a lot of emotions watching the interaction, though the biggest one was hope that when all of this was over, she wasn't left picking up the pieces of a broken son because a young, eccentric chef felt the need to teach him a lesson. Not when Charlotte was so happy that he was finally becoming interested in something other than ignoring her and getting into trouble.

Tia chewed it for a long time before swallowing. Her eyes narrowed a little before she leaned down and took another bite. To Charlotte's surprise, Noah didn't say anything, though she could see and hear his foot tapping uncontrollably against the floor. But to his credit, he just waited.

"That's not bad," Tia finally said.

"I knew it. It's horrible," Noah's arms fell to his sides.

"If it was horrible, I would tell you it was horrible. It is not," Tia said, looking directly into Noah's eyes to make it clear that she was trying to be honest with him. "You ask my opinion and I'll give it to you. If you only ask people to tell you what you want to hear, then you will never get better. If you don't want to get better, then go do something that will make you much more money with far less pain," Tia said, waiting to see what Noah's reaction was going to be.

Charlotte waited too, feeling as though she was witnessing one of those rare life moments in real time, one where her son would be given the opportunity to give up or push through and truthfully, she didn't know which route he was about to take.

"Let's hear it then," Noah said, and with that, Charlotte felt a rush of pride she hadn't known she could feel before. It was not something she had felt for a long time. Not since before Eli's death. She was beginning to wonder if it was a feeling she would ever feel again. She was relieved that wasn't the case.

"Good kid," Tia said, giving Noah a nod. "Truth is, the difference between good and perfect only exists in your own mind. That cookie is good enough to be sold at the Old Mill. That is the truth. People would enjoy it. Some people may even love it."

"Thank you," Noah said, beaming.

"I'm not done," Tia said, and immediately Noah's smile faded. "Don't look so down. I'm not here to shatter your dreams."

Just make my heart do backflips, apparently, Charlotte thought, her heart beating viciously in her chest. She was so worried about how this was going to turn out that she may have forgotten to breathe if her body hadn't already done it automatically.

"But you know you can do better, that's the point. At the end of the day, we're chasing our own perfection. What's perfect for us, we hope, resonates with other people enough to make them happy. But that's the rub. We're cooking for other people. What you think is too much nutmeg might be too little for some."

"So, you think there is too much nutmeg?" Noah asked, sounding surprisingly more confident than Charlotte would have been if she had been the one having this conversation. It was a lot of information, and she thought perhaps there was more to this conversation than simply making cookies.

"Yes," Tia said without question. "But that's not the point, is it."

"It isn't?" Charlotte said under her breath, feeling more confused now than she'd been before.

"No," Tia said, her eyes flicking briefly over toward Charlotte before returning to Noah, who thankfully seemed to not hear Charlotte at all. "The point is that I like my steak medium rare, but I cook steaks rare, or well done, or whatever it is someone else is looking for. Our job isn't just to create perfection for ourselves, it's to try and create perfection for the people who eat our food. Or in this case, your cookie," Tia said, her eyes narrowing in on Noah before flicking back toward the doorway, and it appeared Noah seemed to pick up that she was referring to Cally.

"I'm not making the cookies for me," Noah said thoughtfully, and Tia smiled. "Thanks, Tia," Noah said, running out of the kitchen, and Charlotte managed to hear him ask Cally why she didn't like them before he was too far away for her to listen anymore.

"What just happened?" Charlotte asked, looking over at Tia, who had returned to picking apart chickens.

"Probably depends on what he does next." Tia shrugged. "But with any luck, we just created a young man who has the desire to ask a young woman what she wants so he can give her that rather than a boy who thinks that giving a woman anything deserves her praise."

"You might be a genius." Charlotte chuckled to herself. "And using all that stuff about cooking – incredible."

"Oh no, that was all true." Tia laughed. "Unfortunately, I may have just inadvertently persuaded your son to be a chef, for which I am deeply sorry."

"I think I can live with that." Charlotte said.

"You say that now." Tia stopped her work to think for a moment before shuddering. "Then all of a sudden, he's twenty-eight years old and having to rework his entire life because his dream job has vanished overnight."

"What?" Charlotte said, looking over at Tia, who looked very sad suddenly.

"Oh, I mean, it's nothing. Just thinking about stuff," Tia said. Charlotte thought she look sad and would have liked to ask her what she was thinking about, but a moment later Noah ran into the kitchen with a determined look on his face.

"What's up, Noah?"

"What the heck is a five spice?" he asked, his arms out to the sides, looking puzzled.

Charlotte looked over at Tia and they both started to laugh. "What?"

"Nothing. Come on, I'll show you," Charlotte said.

19

Noah

Noah didn't know what in the world he was trying to prove by spending his afternoon making another batch of cookies. As far as he was concerned, the first batch was great. Sure, there may have been a little too much nutmeg. But in his defence, up until a couple weeks ago, he wasn't sure he would have known what nutmeg was or that you had to grind it from an actual nut.

But here he was, staring at yet another batch of cookies, all because he couldn't get Cally's face out of his head. *Why am I so desperate for this girl to like me?*

Honestly, since the moment he had arrived, Cally had been nothing but rude to him, making fun of him for not wanting to work at the Old Mill. Why anyone would want to work was beyond him. Although he did have to admit, he was beginning to enjoy himself a little. He found that he actually liked cooking. It helped that Nana had been able to explain to him the science behind it and when no one was watching him, he'd even snuck off in the house to peek at some book called *On Food and Cooking* or something like that, which had an interesting way of breaking down cooking to a science.

Sometimes, the book felt a little too much like schoolwork. But since he wasn't doing any schoolwork, he decided to let it slide, and the pleasure of this newfound life away from school was that he could skip the parts of the book he didn't love. Between the book, Bear sleeping at his feet and the early mornings, Noah was finding it very difficult to stay awake. How Nana managed to do it, amazed him. As far as he could tell, that woman never slept. She was just always going off, baking and cooking or sitting in her little room looking at spreadsheets. Even the thought of it now made Noah want to take a nap.

Ding.

"Thank you!" Noah said to no one since Tia was busy mixing some kind of filling and Charlotte was rolling pastry for croissants for the next day, leaving Noah to his own devices.

"They smell good, Noah," Tia said, flashing him a smile.

"They better be," Noah murmured to himself. He was only half-sure he understood what Tia was talking about when she'd told him about food, but he figured he got the gist of it. If he wanted to make Cally jealous of his cookies then he would have to make the cookies the way *she* liked them, not him. Then he could totally rub it in her face when she had to tell him how good they were. At least he hoped that would be the outcome.

"More cookies?" Nana said, stepping in to the kitchen. "Smells good. Can I get a green smoothie please, love?"

"On it," Charlotte said, stepping away from her rolling to fetch the ingredients for the smoothie. Noah was impressed at how quickly she had managed to step into her new role.

As far as he could remember, she hadn't been all that keen on cooking. He vaguely recalled a time when he was younger but after his father got sick, that, and most everything, just stopped.

"I wanted to try and make them a little spicier," Noah said, touching one of the cookies to make sure it was cooled enough. He thought it was, so he picked it up and broke it in half. "Wanna try?"

"Sure," Nana said, taking half of a cookie out of Noah's hand. "You know who really likes spicy ginger cookies? Cally."

Noah didn't think he could feel more embarrassed, but he was wrong as Tia shouted from across the kitchen, "Oh, he knows." She laughed and gave him a playful wink. He didn't know if he should be angry or embarrassed, although she had been right.

"Umm. Wow. That is spicy—"

"Too spicy?!" he asked nervously, taking a bite out of the half he was still holding.

"No." Nana laughed. "It's a good amount. With five spice and everything," Nana said, and Noah only half-caught the glance she gave Charlotte as he was too preoccupied thinking about the cookie. It was different. Not in a bad way but just in a way that made him wonder how different flavours offer different feelings about food. That gave him an idea.

"I think it needs sugar on top," Noah said, more to himself than to anyone else, but Nana gave him a smile.

"Good thought," she said, walking over to a container marked *sugar*. She opened it up, reached inside and sprinkled some on her remaining cookie and then on Noah's. He took a bite.

"Oh yeah!" he said, eyes closed, pumping his fist and

gyrating his hips in a little dance before reopening them and realizing that Nana, Charlotte and Tia were all looking at him, smiling.

"You got to get me one of those cookies," Tia said.

"Don't forget about me," Charlotte said, and Noah was happy to share his creation, as he was feeling quite proud of himself. Although he knew these women were not his target. It was Cally who he needed to impress.

He grabbed more of the sugar and sprinkled it over the remaining cookies before grabbing a couple and taking them to Charlotte and Tia.

"Noah? Would you mind if I sold some of these?" Nana asked as she finished another cookie.

"Really?" Noah said, feeling a rush of excitement at the idea of his nana feeling like his cookies were good enough to be sold at the Old Mill. He'd been a regular customer of the cookies on offer and although he thought his cookies were good, he was surprised Nana thought they were good enough to sell.

"Of course. We are, after all, a store and I think these are a rather impressive batch of cookies. I would be honoured to sell them," Nana said, making Noah giddy with excitement. Even if Cally didn't like them, he would have his cookies sold at the Old Mill. Cally would be so jealous.

"Awesome," Noah said, but he had to remember why he did it in the first place. "Do you mind if I give one to Cally?" Noah asked, picking one up and putting it on a napkin.

"Sure. And you might want to give one to Riley as well. So she isn't jealous. Those girls love a ginger cookie." Nana smiled.

"Will do," Noah said, grabbing a second cookie and running

back out into the front room.

"That's delicious," he heard Charlotte say as he ran out, unable to hide the smile on his face, even if he wanted to.

Cally was running someone through the cash while Riley was busy on the coffee machine making something with steamed milk. He would have liked to break up whatever Cally was doing to tell her he'd made cookies so good, Nana was going to sell them, but he also knew that she was doing her job, and she took her job so seriously that if he interrupted her now, it wouldn't matter if he'd made the best cookie in the world, all she would do is ignore him and then be mad at him for being impatient. So instead, he approached Riley.

"I made a ginger cookie. Nana thought you might like one. She even said we might sell them," he said loud enough for Cally to hear but hopefully not so loud that it was obvious he wanted her to hear it. He laid the cookie beside Riley.

"Looks delicious!" Riley said, spotting the cookie. "I can't wait to eat it. Thank you, Noah."

"Did you say ginger cookies?" the woman Cally had been ringing in asked, her credit card still in her hand.

"Yeah," Noah said.

"I love ginger cookies," she said with a grin.

"Here, Mrs Johnson, have this one," Cally said, turning to take the one from Noah's hand.

"But that one's yours," Noah said, trying not to sound petty, though it was hard to hide his disappointment.

"It's fine, Noah, I'll get another one," Cally said and she looked like her eyes may bulge out of her head as she glared at him.

"That's kind of you dear, but why don't we split it?" she said, breaking the cookie in half, handing half to Cally and taking a bite out of her own. "Mmm," she said, her eyes closing as she chewed the cookie.

Noah had to admit, having a stranger enjoy something he made was almost as good as watching the expression on Cally's face switch from annoyed to what might have been considered pleasant joy.

"That's really good, Noah," Cally finally said.

"I agree. You think I could get six more to go?" Mrs Johnson asked. "We have a book club meeting tonight and I think the girls would love these."

"Umm…" Noah was stunned. Not only had he managed a *really good* from Cally, he'd even managed to make a sale.

"Of course, Mrs Johnson," Cally said. Before Noah could say anything, she added, "Noah will go and bag those up. Won't you, Noah?" Cally turned to look at Noah, her brows raised as she tilted her head. Noah took the hint and ran off.

"That's a nice cookie, Noah," Tia said. The only thing left of her cookie was the crumbs.

"Thanks. Cally just sold six of them," Noah said with a shrug, trying to act like it was no big deal when his heart was hopscotching around his chest as the thrill of a sale slowly rocked his world.

"Six!" Charlotte said, sounding very impressed.

"Yeah. Book club meeting, I guess," Noah said as he used a spatula to shovel the cookies off the tray and into a bag.

"Great work, Noah," Nana said, placing a hand on his back. "We might make a chef out of you yet." She smiled and Noah couldn't help but smile back as he finished the cookies and ran toward the door.

"Wait. How much do we sell them for?" Noah asked.

"Cally will know, love," Nana said. "Best get those cookies

to her," she added and Noah turned and ran out.

"Corner," he added, rounding the side because it was something he'd heard Nana and Charlotte say before when they carried food out. "Here are your cookies, ma'am," Noah said, holding out the bag and handing them to her. "I made sure I got you the best ones," he thought that sounded like the right thing to say, which she appeared to appreciate.

"Thank you, dear."

"Here, let me help," Noah said as he began helping her pack her tote bags with the various goods she'd purchased from the shop.

"You're a good man," she said, giving him a smile.

Once her bags were packed, Noah helped open the door for her and waved as she left before running back to talk to Cally.

"Not bad, Noah," Cally said, her arms folded across her chest. "Feels good when you care, doesn't it?" and Noah had to wonder if that was the reason he was feeling the rush. He didn't know for sure but he had to admit, whatever it was felt great.

"Yeah," he said, not wanting to ruin whatever was happening right now to get praise instead of criticism from Cally.

"It was a really good cookie. I told you the five spice was the way to go," she said with a smile.

Noah had every intention of rubbing it in her face. She might have been the one who suggested the spice, but he had made the cookies, and he was the one who got to sell them. But now that he was talking to her, he didn't think it was the best idea. After all, it had been her idea to use the five spice and she'd been the one to offer Mrs Johnson the cookie. Maybe he could afford to give her a little credit. Though not too much since he did make them.

"Yeah. I guess we make a pretty good team." Noah said the second thing that came to his mind and was surprised when Cally's arms dropped to her sides and smiled at him.

"I guess we do," she said, and the pair looked at each other for a long moment before Cally hooked a thumb back toward the cash register. "I should probably get back to work."

"Yeah. No, of course," Noah said, his pulse beating in his ears, probably from the thrill of selling the cookies and not because Cally was smiling at him.

Cally turned away to go back to the cash but stopped and looked back at Noah.

"Yes," he said before she had a chance to say anything, and he thought he might die from embarrassment had she not replied with a small and very cute laugh.

"I was just going to ask… you know, if you're not busy. If maybe you'd want to go with me to walk around the lights tonight?" Cally asked.

Noah had no idea what the lights were or even if Charlotte would let him go but none of that mattered in that moment as he looked at Cally and said the only answer that he was ever going to give.

"Yes."

20

Charlotte

"Sounds like a date," Charlotte said, giving Dot a wink as she moved around the kitchen. Dot hadn't so much as sat down since she got home from the Old Mill and Charlotte was beginning to think that perhaps she was a little nervous about the dinner, despite being adamant she wasn't.

"Bear, I'm going to need you to go lay down someplace else. Please," Dot said, nudging the old dog with her foot as he stretched his legs as best he could, and without so much as a look in Dot's direction, moved over to nestle up by the fire.

"It's okay, Bear," Charlotte said, giving the old boy a pat on the side, "she's just a little nervous about her date."

"I'm not—it's not a date. It's a thank-you dinner," Dot said, "that's all."

"Sure," Charlotte said, enjoying watching her mother-in-law sweat a little as she pulled a cloth off a handle beside the sink and began wiping down the island countertop. "You already wiped that."

Dot threw her hands up in the air and bunched the cloth up on the table, making an irritated sound in the process.

"What are you so worried about?" Charlotte asked, reaching out to grab Dot's hand.

"I'm not worried… at least I wasn't. Not until you," she waved her free hand in Charlotte's face, "started doing whatever this is."

"I'm just poking fun, Dot. I think it's great you're going out."

"We're not going out. In fact, we are eating in," she said, as if this validated whatever notion she had of what a date should be.

"Fine. Are you taking wine?" Charlotte asked.

"No. Why would I? Wouldn't that be presumptuous? What if he doesn't like wine?"

"Then you'll have more wine for yourself, and maybe then you can calm down enough to have fun."

"It's not a dat—" Dot began as her hands shot to her mouth. "Oh my, is it a date? Is this a date?" She looked genuinely surprised by the concept.

"It's a dinner date. I think you're old enough to know that if you want it to be a date, it's a date," Charlotte said. "Do you want it to be a date?"

"I'm not sure? I haven't been on a date in over a decade, and I can tell you right now, those did not go well," Dot said, shaking her head as if recalling whatever it was that had happened to her. Charlotte didn't know, but she did know that Dot owed it to herself to get out and meet people.

"Stop worrying!" Charlotte laughed. "Worst case, it goes badly, and he stops coming into the store to see you all the time."

"He doesn't come to—"

"Don't be silly, Dot. The man is a tree farmer and he comes in to eat every day we're open and waits to say hi to you."

"Because he's nice."

"He is nice. And he may even like you too."

"Oh, shut up." Dot waved in her direction. "Why would he like me?"

"Because you're a sexy older woman who is fiercely independent, enjoys cooking and is frankly, a catch," Charlotte said. She watched Dot's face blush a remarkable shade of fuchsia as she stumbled around, trying to find a group of words that didn't arrive, landing instead on—

"Stop."

"I will not," Charlotte said. "Dot, you are an incredible woman. You run a business, you support the town… Hell, you opened your home to Noah and me this winter without so much as batting an eye." Charlotte reached over to squeeze Dot's hand, rubbing a thumb over the back of it. "You are remarkable. And I am not surprised that someone has noticed."

"Thank you, love," Dot said giving Charlotte a thin smile.

"And I know what you're thinking," Charlotte said, standing up to pour herself a cup of tea, "but the Old Mill doesn't need you as much as it did. You have a great team and now you can finally spend more time on yourself." She shrugged as she poured a cup of black tea and topped it up with milk and sugar, which Dot had left on the table for her.

Dot looked surprised, though Charlotte couldn't understand why. It's not like this should've been one for her.

"Thank you, love, but you should probably know… it just…" Dot fumbled around, wringing her hands together nervously as she stared at the ground.

"Know what?" Charlotte asked when the tension was building up too much. But before Dot could answer, Noah walked in, running a hand down the front of his shirt as if that was what it needed to get the wrinkles out.

"How do I look?" Noah asked.

"For your date?" Dot grinned, and though she glanced over at Charlotte, the moment and whatever she was planning on telling her had passed. Charlotte couldn't pretend that she didn't want to know what it was, but not enough to press the matter further.

"It's not a date," Noah said, wrinkling his nose at Dot.

"You're right! This *is* fun." Dot giggled at Charlotte as she poured herself a cup of tea while Noah rolled his eyes.

"It's not a big deal," Noah said.

"So you wouldn't mind if I told you you couldn't go?" Charlotte asked, trying to hide her smile behind blowing her tea.

"You wouldn't!" Noah shot back. "Why would you do that? I mean, you keep telling me I need to get out of the house."

"But at night with a young girl—I mean, technically, you're still grounded from getting kicked out of school," Charlotte said, raising her brows.

"Firstly, I wasn't kicked out. They just kindly asked me to not come back until after Christmas break. Secondly, how am I supposed to go out during the day when you have me working at the store? Lastly, she is not some girl, she's Cally and might I add, ew, she practically hates me."

"Hates you so much, she invited you out for a romantic walk through the town's display of lights?" Charlotte said, amused by how visibly awkward Noah was getting.

"It's a walk and yes, there will be lights. But she said the whole town basically walks through it. All one hundred of them, I assume. I'd hardly call that romantic," Noah said but

Charlotte could see his brain working now as he looked at her, wide-eyed, "It isn't, right?"

Charlotte shrugged.

"Why did you have to ruin this for me?" Noah yelled at her, but it was too cute for Charlotte to really feel the weight behind it.

"She's only messing with you, Noah. Trust me."

"Because of your date with Henry tonight?" Noah asked, unable to see the irony in the casual way he threw out the notion.

"Judas," Dot said, shaking her head.

"Who?" Noah asked and Dot shot Charlotte a disapproving look.

"Oh please, it's 2025. I take it as a compliment."

"It's Christmas!" Dot protested.

"I think we're losing focus of what's important here," Charlotte said, diverting away from a conversation she was not equipped to have with anyone at the moment.

"And what is that?" Dot asked.

"That Noah asked if his shirt looked okay," Charlotte said.

"And does it?" he asked again.

"Better question is, why is she going to see your shirt if you're outside?" Charlotte said, pursing her lips.

"What if we get cold and want to get a hot chocolate? Or sit inside cause our feet are cold? You want me to take off my jacket and look like a slob just because I wasn't expecting anyone to see my shirt? Is that what you want, Charlotte?"

"You seem to be putting a lot of pressure on the way you look for a guy not going on a date," Charlotte said and Noah opened his mouth as if to argue and closed it, his eyes narrowing on Charlotte

"I won't take the bait," he said, turning to head back into his room. "I'm going to finish getting ready for my completely casual evening with a colleague who has offered to show me around the town because she is being nice. That's all." Noah turned on his heels and walked back toward his room but stopped before he left the kitchen, turning his head to look at Charlotte. "Unless of course you feel like you want to deny me this small chance to be a kid again and finally hang out with someone my own age."

Charlotte studied him, trying to figure out if what she was seeing was defiance or nerves but she decided either way, it was nice that Noah was finally getting out and meeting people and since she knew Cally, she felt confident he wasn't about to go out and blow anything up.

"Colleagues, huh?" she finally said, giving him a grin.

"You're the worst." Noah walked away.

"Love you too," Charlotte said, turning to look at Dot, rolling her eyes slightly.

"Doesn't it bother you that he calls you Charlotte?" Dot asked.

This was not the direction Charlotte thought that the conversation would be taking once Noah left the room, but she supposed since they had been living at Dot's now for over two weeks that it was probably time for the question to arise.

Charlotte had an answer for her teed up, one she thought was practical and to the point. One that would hopefully put an end to her feeling the need to ask again but now, on the spot, she'd completely forgotten what it was.

"Sometimes. Sorta. Not really. I guess."

"Just one of those feelings then?" Dot smiled.

"Look, it's not ideal, but I think it is some way of creating distance with me since Eli died. At least that's what my therapist told me." Charlotte smiled weakly. "I suppose I would love for him to call me Mom every once in a while, but if it's the difference between him talking to me at all and not, I will take Charlotte for now and pray this is all just a phase."

"Pretty annoying phase."

"Hey, at least you still get Nana. Cherish it, because you never know when that is going to be taken away."

"I'll be long gone by then," Dot said, holding up her tea and toasting the moment.

"Please, not any time soon. I couldn't take it," Charlotte joked but inside, she was feeling the weight of the idea close in around her and she hated it. She wasn't sure what she would have done if it hadn't been for Dot to help her this winter and she still had no way of knowing what on earth she was going to do when she was finally forced to grapple with the reality that she was unemployed and living in one of the most expensive cities in North America on her own with an adolescent child.

She had done an okay job the past couple of weeks ignoring the problem. But she would eventually have to deal with it, though right now, she still could hold onto the lie she'd been selling herself for a little while longer. Bury everything else beneath the mountain of things she'd chosen to ignore in her life at the moment.

"So, you have the house to yourself tonight. What are you going to do?" Dot asked, looking pleased that the conversation was swaying away from her and onto Charlotte, who had half a mind to turn the tables again, but she thought she would give the woman a break.

"Actually, Tia and Riley invited me out for a cocktail at some bar." Charlotte shrugged.

"Riley is letting Cally out on her own? Big step," Dot mused.

"I think it's why she needed a drink," Charlotte said. "I understand." Charlotte's eyes drifted toward Noah's room as she thought about the reality that her little boy was growing up and no longer needed or wanted to be anywhere near her. She understood this was a natural progression of life but after everything they'd gone through, she held on to a small desire that it might all bring them closer together. That hadn't been the case. Her therapist had had plenty to say about that as well.

"Well, I think that's great. You all need a break," Dot said, and Charlotte clocked the shift in Dot's demeanour. It was subtle, so she chalked it up to nerves about her date or not-date.

"Looks like we're all in for a treat tonight." Charlotte grinned, trying to ignore her strong desire, after the week she'd had of trying to get her legs back in the kitchen, to curl up by the fire with a glass of wine and a book and be on her own. But it had been so long since anyone had invited her to hang out and she didn't have Noah so she felt as though she couldn't say no. So, she'd resisted the urge to back out and hoped she wouldn't regret it.

21

Dot

"It's good," Dot said, shaking her head at the absurdity of the comment. It was a tourtière that she'd made and given to him. First of all, of course it was good. If it wasn't, she wouldn't have sold them in the store. But she felt foolish complimenting her own dish.

"I agree," Henry said with a smirk, "but then again, so are most of the things you make," he added with a wink.

"I'm sorry," Dot said, picking up her glass of wine and taking a big swig. "It's been a while."

"Since you've eaten tourtière? Me too. Almost a year now, I suppose," Henry joked.

"No." Dot giggled, feeling a bit like a young girl again. "I mean this. A dinner. With a man."

"Well, I wouldn't have guessed," Henry said as a look of shock moved across his face. "Not that I think you go on many dates. Or that you couldn't if you wanted to… I just mean… umm…"

As much as Dot was enjoying not being the only person in the conversation making a fool of themselves, she decided to put the man out of his misery.

"I know what you meant, Henry." She chuckled.

"Thank you. I swear I'm not always this…" he waved a hand around his head, "together." He laughed.

"Oh good. I was beginning to worry," Dot mused. "At our age, one needs to start being aware of the mind, I suppose."

"Oh Christ, this old thing is gonzo, kaput, one foot out the door, so to speak," Henry said, tapping the side of his head. "I wouldn't blame you for wanting to make a run for it." He laughed awkwardly.

"And miss all the excitement?" Dot said, sipping her wine. "I wouldn't dare."

"I'm afraid it's not all that exciting. You've seen it, mostly. I plant trees, I grow trees, and I cut trees. Nothing nearly as brilliant as what you do."

"You think what I do is exciting?" Dot asked, thinking of the laundry list of words she might use to describe the Old Mill. Perhaps exciting might have been on the list, at least in the early days, but other words had begun to pile up above it. Words like *worry, fear, inadequacy, pressure, future, life,* just to name a few.

"Making incredible food and sharing it with people? Sounds pretty good to me," Henry said as he finished up his slice of tourtière. He looked up at Dot with another pained looked on his face. "I mean, don't get me wrong, I'm sure it's hard work and time-consuming and I know how much effort you put into the store and the food and I'm sure it's not all great, but—"

"You're right. I do like making food," Dot said, letting him off the hook again. For all the years she'd known Henry, she hadn't ever seen him so nervous. He was always chatty and kind and helpful. But this was a side of him she hadn't seen. He was so much shyer than she'd ever expected, though under it all, he was still kind and at least he meant well.

"Sorry. I'm just a little nervous," he said.

"Why?"

"To be honest, I didn't think you would say yes when I asked you to dinner. And then when you actually showed up…"

"You don't give yourself enough credit, Henry."

"I am really happy you were able to make it," Henry said, his eyes glancing nervously up at Dot as if preparing himself for her response.

"I'm really happy you decided to ask me," Dot said as she felt a warm sensation in her chest and she realized she meant it.

22

Noah

The windswept snow from off the river and into the little park that the town used for its light display smacked Noah in the face and he suddenly wished, for the first time in his life, that he had worn a scarf.

"It's cold," Noah said as they walked through the small park. The lights displayed around them depicted various scenes and characters, some of which were obviously Christmas-related while others were decorated with hats, stars and trees to give them a *Christmas theme.*

They'd already walked along the river, spotting dinosaurs with hats on, their lights flickering on and off, giving it the illusion they were walking along the river beside you before vanishing and starting their trek all over again. What dinosaurs had to do with Christmas, Noah didn't know, but he had to admit, it was impressive to see, and from the look of things, it was only the beginning of what appeared to be a long walk around.

"It's winter, Noah. It's cold," Cally said, shaking her head, though Noah could see that she was also trying to pull her own scarf up around her face to protect her nose.

"Doesn't mean I have to accept it," Noah said as they passed a large-scale depiction of the Nativity scene with a three-foot baby Jesus lying in a manger complete with parents, wise men and an assortment of animals.

"You just want to pretend winter doesn't exist?" Cally asked.

"That's exactly what I want to do." Noah laughed. "Don't you?"

"No. I prefer to think of it as something that reminds us of how great summer is."

"That's just something we tell ourselves to deal with this," Noah said, waving his hand to the frigid air around them.

"I happen to like winter," Cally said.

"Come on. You're lying."

"Am not."

"Fine. Then what do you love so much about it?" Noah asked. He tried not to sound skeptical but he had a very hard time covering that up.

"Well, I like hot drinks, a nice fire, snowshoeing—"

"Snowshoeing?" Noah chuckled.

"Yeah. It's great."

"So what? You just walk around in the cold?"

"No, you walk around *on* the snow. Warm because you're walking, dumb dumb. And the sun is out and there is fresh powder. Those are some of the best days of the year," Cally said and Noah had to admit, he almost believed that she believed what she was saying. But he just couldn't get behind it.

"Come on," was all he could think to say.

"I'm being serious. Have you been?" she asked.

"No, but—"

"So, you're willing to judge something that you have never done and write it off as something you don't enjoy just because… what? You think winter's cold? Summer's hot. Do you hate it?"

"You can go swimming in the summer."

"Umm…" Cally walked, her hand running along a life-sized version of Franklin the Turtle.

"What?" Noah asked, rolling his eyes, "What's 'umm'?" he asked again when Cally didn't answer.

"Nothing. You're just…" she said, turning to face him, her head tilted as she examined him. "I don't know?"

"What's so weird about not liking winter? It's basically all people complain about," Noah said.

"So you want to complain about it because everyone else does?" Cally asked.

"No. That's not what I said," Noah protested.

"Seems a little bit like what you said." Cally laughed.

"No, you're… you're putting words in my mouth," Noah said, feeling more than a little frustrated by the fact that he was out with this girl who had done nothing but poke fun at him since he'd got there.

"It's cold, okay. And it sucks. It's just a sucky time of year. We're all supposed to just be happy because it's Christmas and like snow because it's Canada and that is the deal. When really, all of us are just sitting here, silently a little happy that global warming is making it a little hotter," Noah said, kicking a small mound of snow, watching as it flew, hitting a giant Barney the Purple dinosaur light display.

After a moment of silence, Noah finally built up the courage to look over at Cally, who had her hands shoved in her pockets, looking at him with a neutral expression.

"Well, that's the stupidest thing I have ever heard," Cally's eyes somehow managing to bulge and roll at the same time. "Firstly, global warming is no joke and it's not making things warmer, dumb-dumb. It's just causing more extreme weather patterns."

If Noah's hands hadn't been freezing, he may have pulled them out and smacked himself in the forehead for his idiocy. It wasn't like he was happy about global warming. He was trying to make a point.

"I know all of that, okay. I'm not dumb. I'm a pessimistic optimist," he said, hoping his smirk was enough to end the conversation. It was not.

"What?"

"A pessimistic optimist. Short-term pessimist, long-term optimist."

"What does that mean?" Cally asked.

"It means short term pain, long term gains. Or at the very least survival."

"Your big solution is to survive? The boy who can barely survive winter."

"Argh! Why are you so annoying?" Noah wanted to shout, but there were families and people walking around and he didn't want to draw any more attention to himself.

"Yeah, I'm the annoying one." Cally laughed.

"You are!" Noah countered and Cally laughed harder.

"I want hot chocolate," she said, turning round and looking at the small truck off to the corner of the park. She started to walk toward it. After a couple steps, she turned to face him. "Coming?"

"Do you want me to come?" Noah said, sounding a bit petty even to himself.

"I invited you, didn't I?" Cally said.

"Why? All you do is make fun of me."

"All you do is whine."

"I don't whine," Noah was starting to feel a bit mad now at having to stand up for himself.

"Come on, all you've done is whine. I hate these boxes, I hate this town, I hate winter," Cally said, her voice taking on a high-pitched, almost squealing sound, "this dog won't leave me alone, stop telling me what to do, Charlotte. Also, you call your mom Charlotte? That's weird."

"It's her name," Noah countered. "People do it in the city all the time."

"Oh, sorry I don't know what people do in the big city. Here in the sticks, we just say Mom."

"You can call your mom whatever you want," Noah snapped back.

"No, actually, I can't."

"Why, no first name?" Noah said, chuckling at his own joke.

"No. She's dead. My dad too," Cally said, turning and walking off toward the truck, leaving Noah standing in the snow, feeling like he'd punched himself in the gut.

"Shit," Noah said, feeling bad that he'd sworn out loud. But even Charlotte would have agreed that the word fit the moment. He let out a deep breath, watching the hot air billow out from his mouth before closing his eyes. If he left now, he may as well face the reality that he would never be able to look at her again. He would also be finished at the Old Mill because he could never go back there again. And that wasn't really an option.

"Wait up!" he shouted, chasing Cally down.

23

Charlotte

"Interesting spot," Charlotte said, looking around Tom's, a small, dimly lit bar that Riley and Tia had assured her was a nice spot to meet. It wasn't too fancy, but it also wasn't the kind of place where people would be showing up for a cheap pint and unwanted conversation.

The trio sat in the back corner of the bar, at a round table tucked away in a small alcove with four leather chairs. This meant they were more or less alone except for a booth beside them, currently unoccupied. That was convenient, since the background music, if you could even call it that, was so difficult to talk over. It put them somewhere between a conversation and a shouting match. But, for fear of aging herself further, she kept her comments about the music to herself.

It had been a long time since Charlotte had been invited to hang out with anyone who didn't have kids and even longer since she'd had a cocktail, let alone a fifteen-dollar one. But seeing as it had been so long, she decided she wouldn't overthink the cost and instead focus on the potential of just hanging around with women… roughly her own age. *What's a decade when you're over twenty-five?*

"Not a ton of options in town," Tia said, "and even fewer if you're trying to avoid being approached by men who think it is cool to go out for drinks on a Sunday night."

"Aren't we women who think it's cool to go out for drinks on a Sunday night?" Charlotte asked, not wanting to judge them by any means but also trying to understand where the line in the sand was when it came to things like this.

"We are in the service industry. This is our Friday, Charlotte," Tia said, sipping on something that looked spicy, with a candied jalapeño in it.

"Welcome," Riley said, holding up her own martini-style drink. "Though I have to get up with Cally for school in the morning, so I'll have to take it easy," she added quickly, sneaking a glance at Tia.

"What?" Tia's arms rose in defence. "Don't blame me because you can't handle your liquor."

"I'm not blaming you, obviously," Riley said, shaking her head, "but it is usually your idea to do tequila shots," she added, hiding behind her drink as Tia laughed.

"First of all, I drink mezcal." Tia raised a finger. "Don't lump me in with just any fifteen-year-old who found a bottle in the basement. Secondly, Riley, you're an adult. I do not force them on you."

"Yet somehow, I always feel pressure."

"Don't put that on me," Tia said, waving her hands in the air to stop the conversation there. "Look, you're scaring our new friend."

Charlotte wouldn't have said she was scared. In her mind, scared was a feeling reserved for attempting to watch scary movies without success, or Halloween in general. What she was feeling right now was something closer to apprehension, though perhaps fear was linked in there too.

"I'd hardly call either of you scary," Charlotte offered, though admittedly, she had always found men to be far less intimidating than women. Perhaps it was because she'd spent a good chunk of her teens at an all-girls school, trapped in an emotional tinderbox with overly hormonal and judgemental young women. It had not been a wonderful experience, although it did allow her the freedom to do pretty much anything she wanted to at school without the fear of impressing boys. She was grateful for that, despite damaging at least part of her relationship with women.

But for the past couple of weeks, Charlotte had worked with these two women nearly every day and still she knew nothing about either of them, except from what she picked up in passing. She was hoping that tonight, she might be able to help close that gap.

"You say that now, but the night's still young." Tia winked.

Charlotte really enjoyed spending time with Tia in the kitchens. She was easy to talk to, hardly ever appeared to be overwhelmed and was always happy to help her out when she needed it. This was a good thing because Charlotte needed the help.

"How are you holding up, Charlotte?" Riley asked. "You know, being back in the kitchens and all of that."

This had been a question Charlotte had been thinking a lot about. The first week at the Old Mill for her had been a lesson in patience for everyone else in the store. She wished she could have shown up and immediately returned to her former skills but the reality was, between the nerves and the efficiency in which everyone else around her worked, she felt as though she was doing more harm than good.

By the second week, she had thankfully gotten over the nerves, but she was still slow. It was a shame because she really wanted to be a help to Dot over the holidays and she had no idea if she was helping Dot or if Dot was helping her. But maybe that was a good thing.

"Good," Charlotte said with a thin smile as her head rocked awkwardly from side to side. "Maybe ask me after a few more of these." She waved her drink in the air.

"Come on," Tia said, waving a hand in her direction, "you've been killing it."

"Thank you." Charlotte smiled, feeling good about herself, even if she didn't believe it entirely.

"I'm serious," Tia said, leaning in to lock eyes with Charlotte across the small table, her face lit up by the flickering fake candle between them.

"You have been crushing it. You know how long it took for Dot to let me handle the quiches on my own?" Tia shook her head. "I'll give you a hint. It wasn't a week." She laughed.

"Agreed. I wasn't allowed to make coffee for two weeks after I started to work there for anyone outside of the staff," Riley mused. "I mean, I was fifteen. She's only just started to let Cally do it and she's been there for a year. Granted, she doesn't even drink coffee yet. But still."

"Well, I appreciate the support. Honestly, I forgot how much fun it can be," Charlotte said.

"Fun is an interesting word for something that requires you to get up at four in the morning." Tia laughed.

"Honestly, I'd take that over my last job."

"What was that?" Riley asked.

"I was… am a sales rep for a tech company that helps digitize operations manuals for companies, and other slightly more boring things," Charlotte said. "Trust me, waking up at four in the morning to make food is a dream. You guys have it made."

"Not for long," Tia said, sipping her drink, and Charlotte caught her share a look with Riley but she couldn't tell what it was.

"What do you mean?" Charlotte asked.

"We shut down for a couple months in January," Riley said with a shrug after a long beat. "Gives us a little time to think about what we want to do with our lives."

"Right. Yeah. I always forget about that," Charlotte said, though from the look on both of their faces, there was something that wasn't being said. Charlotte wasn't about to start the night off with trying to dig into a conversation that, it was clear, neither of them wanted to have.

"Well, we are happy to have you with us now," Tia said, finishing her drink and waving the empty glass toward the bartender. "Another round?"

24

Dot

Henry refilled Dot's wine glass and the pair laughed, though at this point, Dot wasn't so sure she knew exactly what she was laughing about. All she knew was she was feeling pretty good and enjoying herself, which was pleasant-enough.

To her surprise and perhaps she shouldn't have been so surprised to learn that Henry was very funny, and there were many things she didn't know about him.

"Thank you." Dot smiled as she mentally counted her drinks, figuring she should start to wind down if she planned on driving herself home at the end of the night. Henry refilled his own glass, finishing off the remainder of the bottle and setting it down between them.

"I don't usually like wine," Henry said, holding up his glass and looking at it with a curious eye, "but this is very good."

"I feel fortunate enough to have picked up a few things over the years, and good wines have been one of them," Dot said having a sip of the cabernet sauvignon she'd picked up from the LCBO.

"I suppose food and wine must go together."

"Don't be silly, Henry. Food goes with everything!" Dot laughed.

"How did you get into cooking? Have you always done it?"

"No." Dot thought about it for a moment. "Well, sure, I suppose. I have always liked food and I trained when I was younger for a little bit, but life got in the way. Family, money, you know how it goes, and well… it just sort of fell to the wayside," Dot said, feeling a little unnerved about opening up with someone she didn't know overly well.

"Life has a funny way of telling us what to do," Henry said. "Best-laid plans and all of that."

"Sounds like you have your own story."

"We all have a story, Dot." Henry smiled. "Just like we all still think we are twenty-five with our whole life in front of us, only to wake up with a sore back and aching knees."

"Isn't that the truth," Dot said. "I only wish I'd had the courage to take control of my life sooner rather than waiting for as long as I did." Dot realized she had not said those words out loud to another human being ever in her life. She'd always felt that was the case but until now, she'd not actually admitted it and for a moment, she felt guilty.

"At least you did it. Too many people don't ever take the leap," Henry said, "and what you've created is incredible."

"I'd hardly call the Old Mill incredible. All we do is serve food," Dot said, swirling her wine.

"Oh, don't undervalue what you do for this community, Dot. You've provided us with a place to have great local food. That's rare these days. Not only that, but you support other producers in the area. You're the epitome of buying local. Without you starting the Old Mill, all we would have in town are chain stores."

"I think you give us too much credit." Dot chuckled awkwardly.

"I don't think you give yourself enough credit," Henry said, shaking his head. "I remember the days when we'd have the butcher and the baker, and we supported various shops in the community. All that money that was spent here stayed here. Maybe you didn't get rich, but you made yourself a living. Now we get box stores and fast-food chains and sure, they might be 'locally owned and operated' or what have you, but they lack… something. All that money just sent away to people somewhere else who have no interest in the livelihood of the people in this town. You created a place where local artists and food producers can survive and make a living. It's important," Henry said, nodding affectionately.

Dot hadn't thought about the Old Mill like that. In her mind, all she ever wanted was to make food that people liked. She supposed the fact that she did everything in her power to buy what she could from the area was a good thing. But she didn't do that because it was helpful. She did it because the food was fresh. Why wouldn't she want that?

"Thank you, Henry," she said with a subdued smile. "Is that why you created the Christmas tree farm?"

Henry laughed. "Oh no, this is a hobby farm. I rent out most of my land for cash crop and then I keep some acreage for the trees because Christmas is the best time of year, and I believe everyone should have a Christmas tree in their home. Nothing says Christmas like the smell of a tree," Henry said with a smile. "My late wife used to plant them on the property, and it was her idea to invite people to come chop them down. We started with ten trees, then twenty, and then, well… perhaps I got a little carried away. But I enjoy it. And I suppose in some ways, it reminds me of her." He ran a finger around the rim of his glass.

"She sounds like a lovely woman. What was her name?" Dot asked.

"Margrette. And she was quite lovely," Henry said. "She passed away about eleven years ago now."

"I'm sorry," Dot said, seeing the pain in the man's eyes which were usually so filled with warmth that she felt terrible about bringing it all up for him.

"Don't be. She lived a full life and in the end, she was ready to go. Well, as ready as anyone can be, I suppose. She was fearless." He chuckled, reminiscing about something. "Sorry, I didn't mean to bring down the mood."

"Being proud of the woman you love is nothing to apologise for. When Eli passed away, it shattered me. He was the only thing I truly loved about my life, before moving here, and I'm not sure I would have ever had the courage to do any of this without him," Dot said as an empty feeling settled in her gut. She always tried her best not to think about Eli, and particularly what he meant to her since it never really stopped hurting and she hated feeling that pain. But she imagined Henry's own pain was similar and if he was willing to share, then so was she. And since she was already in the spirit of bravery, she figured she might as well keep going. "Can I tell you a secret?"

"Sure," Henry said, giving her a curious look.

"When we close the store at the end of the month, I won't be reopening it in the New Year."

"Wait? You mean you're closing the Old Mill?" Henry said and his face looked a little stunned. "But why?"

"Lots of reasons, I suppose. The main one being that I think

I am ready for the next stage of my life," Dot said, taking a sip of her wine.

She wasn't sure why she was telling Henry any of this, not after he'd given her such praise for the store in the first place, but somewhere inside, she felt guilty, like she was letting him down in some way, which was a ridiculous thing to think since it was her life and she should be allowed to do what she wanted with it. It was too late to think about what his reaction was going to be now that it was out there. She would just have to wait. But she didn't have to wait long.

"I understand that," Henry said, and Dot felt a tiny weight lift. "I mean, I won't lie, I'll be disappointed for sure. It will come as no surprise that I enjoy your food and your company. And I understand how hard it is to let go of something you love, even if it might be the best thing for you. I think that takes courage."

"Thank you," Dot said, a little taken aback by the reaction. Henry was someone who she had been a little nervous to break the news to, not that she realized that until this moment, but to have him understand was gratifying. "There are things I think I need to do with my life, while I can." Dot felt like it was important for her to discover who she was and travel more, without the Old Mill. People relied on her at the moment, and she couldn't let them down by vanishing for months at a time. It wasn't fair to anyone, including herself. But she still loved the store, which meant she would never be one hundred percent okay with closing its doors.

"It's easy to feel comfortable. And the older we get, the harder it becomes to allow ourselves to be uncomfortable," Henry said, and Dot found herself nodding, pleased that someone else understood. "I'm sure it wasn't an easy decision to make."

"It wasn't. Isn't," Dot corrected. "But only Riley, Tia and some of the suppliers have been told. I had planned to wait until after Christmas because… well, I'm not really all that keen on having those conversations for a month. It's Christmas and it shouldn't be sad." Dot smiled weakly. "But I've decided I'll do it at the Tree decorating party now."

"Seems as good a time as any."

"So, you're not mad at me for closing my doors?" Dot asked the question she knew she desperately didn't want to know the answer to. But just because she might not like the answer wasn't a great reason not to ask.

"How can I be mad at you?" Henry said, getting up from his chair and moving to sit in the chair next to Dot. She was surprised but didn't pull her hand away when Henry reached out and grabbed it. "You created something so wonderful for this town. You built it from the ground up, kept it going through some incredibly difficult times, and you always did it with a smile. How could I ever be mad at someone who inspires me so much?" Henry said with a full smile. "You, Dot Williams, are one of the bravest people I have ever met." He gave her hand a light squeeze, and Dot wasn't sure if it was the fact that he smelt like pine trees and wood shavings or the two (and a bit) glasses of wine, but as she looked into his eyes, for the first time in a long time, Dot leaned in and kissed a man.

And she was happy when he kissed her back.

25

Noah

"I didn't know," Noah tried again but Cally remained silent as she waited in line for a hot chocolate. She hadn't said a word to him since he'd made his stupid comment which he regretted now more than anything else he'd ever done in his life. "I wasn't trying… I'm not…" He still didn't have a great way of explaining any of this and he felt as though he was trying to climb out of a hole, which was gradually getting deeper with each merciless attempt.

"Stop," Cally said, turning to face him as she placed a gloved hand in front of him. "This is starting to become embarrassing," she added calmly.

"I'm just—"

"You feel bad and now you're desperately trying to make it better. But there is nothing to say because it's so awful and there is no way to actually make it better. Right?" she said, looking at him, and he wasn't sure if this was rhetorical or not and the last thing he wanted to do was ruin the fact that she was at least speaking to him again, so he nodded slightly. "I've been dealing with that for nearly half my life." She turned to look away again but she continued to talk. "You ever think that maybe I liked the fact that someone in this town wasn't aware of what happened to me and Riley? That I enjoyed not being treated differently because everyone just sees me as the girl who lost her parents?" Her voice was low as she looked around. She moved up to stand by the open window out the side of a large truck.

"And what can I get you on this fine evening?" said a quirky-looking teen with rounded glasses and a stack of books sitting on the counter behind him. Despite the warmth from the little truck, he wore a long, brown jacket with a colourful scarf wrapped around him.

"Two hot chocolates, please," Cally said.

Noah hoped one was for him, though he still didn't have the courage to say anything out loud. His mind was going a million miles a minute. He had some idea what she was going through—after all, his father passed away—although he supposed that living in a small town might have been a little different than the city, where you were just one of thousands of kids all dealing with problems, which made it a little easier to fly under the radar.

"I would prefer it if you didn't treat me any differently." Cally finally turned to look at him.

"I'm not going to treat you differently," Noah said, feeling exasperated. "Hell, I'm not even sure I know if you like me or not."

"Of course I like you. Why else would I invite you out?" Cally rolled her eyes. "Boys are so stupid."

"But you're mean to me."

"Because you're stupid. I literally just told you. I am trying to help you be less stupid," she said.

"Here you are," said the young man. "That will be five dollars." He looked at Cally and then over at Noah, who was looking at Cally and the hot chocolate, and for a moment, everyone looked confused.

"Go on, pay the man," Cally said, turning to walk over to a section of the park where some heat lamps and picnic tables had been set up for people to watch the lights from. Before Noah could object, Cally was gone.

"Relationship problems?" the young man asked.

"What? No… I mean, we're not… It's just… We're friends," Noah finally managed to say.

The young man looked sympathetically at Noah. "People can be complicated," he said, giving Noah a shrug.

"I'm starting to get that impression," Noah said, fumbling in his pocket for his wallet which, up until a few weeks ago, was just something he carried around to feel older. But now that it held some actual money, he pulled out a five-dollar bill and handed it to the guy. Feeling generous, he decided to add a loonie to a small paper cup that read, *help with books*, which amused Noah.

"Cheers, friend. Stay warm," he added as Noah ran off to meet Cally at the table she'd selected.

"Thanks for the hot chocolate," Cally said, sliding his across the table to him.

"You're welcome," Noah said, still very confused by what on earth had just happened to him as he struggled to understand Cally and his relationship with her. He still didn't know if she hated him or not but the fact that she was still sitting there must mean something.

They each sat in silence for a moment, taking a sip of the hot chocolate, which was okay but nothing like the one Nana made at the shop.

"You think I'm stupid?" Noah asked.

"Sometimes. But don't think much about it. It's not just you—most boys are," Cally said as if this were as true a fact as the sun rising in the east.

"Girls are stupid too," Noah said, feeling the urge to stand up for all the boys in the world in that moment. But Cally only rolled her eyes at him again.

The pair sat in silence again while they sipped, each of them watching people pass around them.

Noah was taken aback by how many people were out just walking around this little park looking at lights. It seemed odd to him but given what he knew about the little town, perhaps it was all anyone could think of doing on a Sunday night.

"I think Nana's hot chocolate is better," Noah finally said when he couldn't handle the silence anymore.

"Of course it is. Everything your Nana does is great."

"You really like my nana."

"Yes. Because she's awesome," Cally said shaking her head and sipping her hot chocolate.

"She is pretty cool. Though I guess I never really noticed."

"That's because you're…" Cally looked at Noah and he suspected he knew what she was going to say but something stopped her as she tilted her head and looked at him, until letting out a deep breath. The hot air formed a cloud around her face for a moment before dissipating into the night air. "I'm sorry," she said, which caught him entirely off guard. He'd been preparing for many things but an apology was not one of them.

"You're sorry?" Noah asked. "Why?"

"I don't mean to pick on you so much. I just find you so frustrating sometimes. I mean, you seem like a good kid. You know, once you get the stick out of your butt," she added and Noah didn't know what to say to that.

"I don't… have a stick up my butt." He felt odd just saying the words.

"You do. A little," Cally said holding up her two gloved hands about a foot apart.

"That's a big stick," Noah said.

"It's getting smaller if it makes you feel any better."

"How could it not?" Noah chuckled. "Look, I am sorry about your parents," Noah said before he had a chance to think about the words. He felt terrible and he also didn't want to ruin the only friendship he had with anyone in this town because he was too stubborn to acknowledge that he'd hurt them.

"Yeah, it sucks," Cally said looking down at her hot chocolate. "I'm sorry about your dad," she offered in return and Noah felt a pang of guilt lurch in his stomach at the thought of him. He hadn't enjoyed thinking about him all that much since he died. It had been a little over a year now and every time he tried to think about it, the pain welled up inside and he hated it so much that he would press it back down and lock it into whatever little place in his body held on to the pain.

"Yeah," he said, locking down the emotions that threatened to come up while he sat there, "it sucks," he admitted after he was sure it was locked away.

"I remember how hard it all was on Dot. It was one of the reasons Riley suggested I start working more at the Old Mill. Give Dot a little extra time for herself. Not that I needed any persuading to work there. I spent most of my time there anyways. Just made it official," Cally said.

"Why do you love it so much?" Noah asked. "The Old Mill, I mean."

"You know, after our parents died, it was just Riley and me. I was a bit of a mistake, although my parents never really said it out loud. It wasn't like having two kids eleven years apart was the plan for most people." Cally smiled. "But after that, Riley and I were on our own. It was Dot who helped us out. Gave Riley a flexible job so she could finish school and I had a place to come that wasn't the house. Dot is like a second mother to me—well, third, I guess, if you count Riley, and Tia too."

"Odd family," Noah said with a grin, and to his joy, it made Cally laugh, which was a nice sound.

"I suppose it is."

"Can I ask you a question?" Noah asked, his eyes looking everywhere but at Cally.

"Sure," she said as he finally risked glancing up at her.

"How did you, you know… umm…" He was fumbling with the right words. He hoped maybe Cally might instinctively understand what he was trying to ask but she didn't budge. Her face looked at him without showing any signs that she would jump in and save him. It meant that if Noah wanted an answer to his question, he would need to ask it. "Never mind," he said, tapping the side of his cup.

"Okay," Cally said with a shrug.

"Well, it's just… how do you get over it?"

"Get over what?" Cally asked and from the way she looked at him, he understood she knew what he was talking about.

"You're going to make me say it?"

"If you can't ask the question, how can you expect to understand the answer?" Cally said.

"What are you, some sort of Buddha?" Noah chuckled.

"More like a child with years of therapy." Cally shrugged. "You pick up a thing or two."

"Fair," Noah said, taking a sip of his drink and looking around, wishing he didn't need to have to build up the courage to say any of this, but he did, and he hated every second of it. Finally, he just blurted it out.

"How do you get over the death of your parents? How do I get over my dad?" he said, letting the words run out of him. To his relief, he didn't feel as terrible asking as he supposed he would. But the answer wasn't the one he was expecting.

"Truthfully? You don't," Cally said.

"Oh," Noah said, shaking his head as he tried to grasp the reality of the words she was saying. He'd spent the better part of the year trying to lock this part of his life away, distracting himself in any way he could just so he didn't have to think about it, at all. Now, he was hearing he would have to do this for the rest of his life.

"What was your dad like?" Cally asked. Noah looked up at her and his confusion must have shown because she asked him again. "Your Dad. What was he like?"

"I don't know. A dad. He had a job, and he liked movies, I guess," Noah said, though he wasn't entirely sure if that last one was accurate. He remembered him watching movies, but he also remembered the criticism he gave them afterwards. "Well, he liked to pretend he enjoyed movies. Really, he just liked to watch them so he and my mom could complain about all the plot holes they could find," Noah said, and the thought made him laugh. "They had a funny way of appreciating them. Until one of them would pick at some tiny thread in the story and they'd start pulling it all apart until they agreed it wasn't that great. It would last for days afterwards sometimes. It was annoying. But I loved how much fun the two of them had doing it. I miss that." Noah felt a tear fall to his mitt and suddenly, he felt so embarrassed about crying. He tried wiping his face unnoticed, but it was too late. Cally was watching him and had already seen it.

"I get it. My parents used to bicker so much about going out to dinner until they would inevitably cook something with Riley and me at home and then complain about how hard it was to get a decent meal. It was so annoying," Cally said, looking at Noah. "And I miss that every day." She shrugged.

"So why would you ask me?" Noah said as the feeling of embarrassment was beginning to wear off and, in its stead, he felt angry. Not just at having to relive that memory but also at Cally for making him.

"Because it's hard," Cally said evenly. "But we don't get to change what happened to us. And we don't get to pretend like it didn't happen either. All we get to do is decide how we want what happened to us to affect how we move forward. We don't get to forget that they died. But we do get to decide how they are remembered. At least to us." Cally shrugged.

Noah wanted to continue to be angry, but he knew that he wasn't the only one here who was dealing with pain and if Cally wasn't going to get upset and walk away then he wouldn't either. No matter how much he resented having to think about it all.

"What if I don't want to think about it… ever?" Noah asked. Admitting this only made him feel guilty. But he couldn't understand why he should have to do anything that made him feel awful.

"I suppose you could lock it all up and ignore it." Cally offered. "It's certainly one way of doing things. You could just build up walls, giving it the power to dictate how you live your life until one day, it all shatters apart and you're left there picking up the pieces of your existence all because you thought it was too hard."

Noah looked at her, waiting to see if she was kidding or not and when it was clear that she was being entirely serious about this prediction of his life, he looked at her with a very different point of view.

"You are a very scary girl, you know that?"

"Please, Noah," Cally said as she started to smile, "I'm thirteen. I'm a very scary woman." She reached across the table and grabbed his hand. "But enough about our trauma. I want to take you on the ice slide." She waved her hand toward a hill in the distance that looked to have a series of winding slides made of ice.

"Trauma? I'm not sure—"

"You're going to love it," Cally said, standing up and pulling Noah to his feet and off toward the ice slide.

Noah finished the last of his drink and tossed it in a bin as they passed, nearly missing the bin altogether. He was about to asked her to slow down when Cally stopped and turned to face him.

"What?" Noah asked, trying to read her face but so far, he had yet to read anything about this confusing girl… woman, correctly.

"It does get easier if you talk about it. I promise," she said softly. "And I'm sorry that it happened to you." She looked at him and before he had the chance to say he was sorry for her loss or any of the numerous things that rattled around in his brain, he watched in awe as she leaned in and gave him a kiss on the cheek. And everything in his mind, for that brief moment, went blank.

26

Charlotte

"Coffee!" Charlotte moaned she as dragged herself out of her bedroom and into the kitchen where both Noah and Dot were sitting around the island, a plate loaded with pancakes at its centre.

"Not as young as we used to be, are we?" Dot said, giving Noah a nudge in the arm and Charlotte a wink, although Charlotte didn't have the energy to acknowledge it.

"Rough night, Mom?" Noah asked, and Charlotte had to take a double take to make sure that it was actually her son that was sitting at the table and not a stranger.

"Oh no. The night was fun, at least from what I remember," Charlotte said, pinching the bridge of her nose as Dot placed a hot cup of coffee in front of her. "You know Tia is a bad influence!" Charlotte said as the memories flooded into her mind of what had started out as some cocktails at a tiny bar and had led into a dance party at some place they'd just called "the tavern".

"She certainly knows how to let loose." Dot smiled. "I probably should have warned you before you left but then what fun would that have been?" She chuckled.

"Oh, she is fun alright." Charlotte shook her head and immediately regretted it. "And to answer your question my dear little one, it isn't the night that is rough, it's the morning. Remember that when someone invites you out for a 'fun night'. There is always a cost." Charlotte waved a finger at Noah as she took a deep breath.

"Weird time to be teaching me a lesson when you look like you want to vomit." Noah shrugged.

"We don't get to stop parenting just because we don't feel well."

"Is that another thing I should remember?" Noah asked, tapping his head.

"Don't be cheeky," Charlotte said, pulling out a stool and sitting in it. "Oh God, I said I would take Bear out for his walk this morning!" Charlotte's head rolled slightly and she felt a little dizzy just getting up to move at all.

"Don't worry, I took him out," Noah said as he pulled another pancake off the top of the larger plate.

"You did?" Charlotte asked.

"Yeah. Figured you could use a sleep-in. What with stumbling into the house past two in the morning."

"Was I that late? And that loud?" Charlotte felt embarrassment wash over her, though the alcohol was leaving little room to feel much more than terrible, so the feeling faded quickly. Although she knew she would be dealing with that one later.

"Not so loud," Dot said, trying her best to sound reassuring, though Charlotte could tell from the grin on her face that she was only doing it to be nice.

"No!!" Charlotte said her arms folded on the table as her

head dropped down to rest on them.

"It's okay, Mom. From what I hear, we should all just be happy you peed in the toilet," Noah said, patting Charlotte's arm.

Charlotte's eyes widened as she looked up toward Dot, who was doing a poor job at pretending not to look at her.

"I did that one time!" Charlotte said. "And you and Eli could never let it go. Now you have to bring our son into it? *J'accuse, madame! J'accuse!*" Charlotte said, pointing her finger at Dot, who held her hands up.

"In my defence, I thought it would be funny."

"You thought telling Noah I peed in the bathtub would be funny?" Charlotte said, shaking her head.

"She didn't tell me where you peed." Noah laughed. "Why would you do that?"

Charlotte's cheeks reddened as she scrambled to figure out what she was going to say. She wasn't able to think of much. Her brain was too muddled and all she wanted to do was sit and drink her coffee, not have to explain to her son the horrors of alcohol.

"I didn't want… It wasn't like I was trying…" Each attempt was getting worse than the one before and finally, she just looked at him.

In her mind, she had this formulated idea that she would tell Noah that drinking can be fun if it is controlled and that you shouldn't let it or your friends control how you live your life. Because once you do, it is a slippery slope, and you end up feeling lousy and terrible the next day.

But she said none of that. Instead, all she could manage in her current state was, "Do yourself a favour and never drink. It's poison and it sucks… it sucks." She hoped the finger pointing would help emphasize her conviction but truthfully, like the statement itself, it felt weak.

"Thank you for that," Noah said, as he covered his pancakes in maple syrup.

"Thank you for taking Bear out. And for letting me sleep in," Charlotte said, praying she was able to move away from any more talk about her, her emotions, or her embarrassing history.

"You're welcome," Noah said as he cut off a piece of his pancake and "accidentally" nudged it onto the floor, where a happy Bear was waiting to gobble it up. "Whoops."

"Careful, he will never leave you alone," Dot said, before sipping her own coffee.

"I think I could live with that," Noah said, leaning over to pat the old dog's head.

Who is this kid and what has he done with Noah? Charlotte thought as she looked in wonder at the boy in front of her. He was calling her Mom, he liked Bear all of a sudden, and so far, he hadn't complained once about the fact that he had to go out in the snow to walk him. Charlotte began to wonder if perhaps she'd drunk herself into an alternate reality. She knew there was only one way to deal with a situation that was too good to be true. Ignore it.

"So," Charlotte said, sliding a plate in front of her as she grabbed a fork and pulled off the top pancake. She contemplated taking a second but decided she would wait to see what her stomach did with the first one before risking it. "I think that's enough about me. How were your nights?"

Charlotte sipped her coffee and watched as Noah and Dot shared a look with one another, then they both shrugged as if she hadn't caught any of whatever little unspoken dialogue had just occurred. Her head throbbed and she would have loved to just go back to sleep but if she couldn't then she would have to put her mind toward something other than the pain it and her stomach were in. It seemed that the coffee and pancake she'd taken in were starting to help the stomach affliction. But still, she wouldn't mind a little distraction.

"What was that?" she asked, her eyes narrowing on the pair.

"What was what?" Dot asked, her cool composure weakening slightly.

"That look?" Charlotte asked.

"What, we're not allowed to look at each other?" Noah asked. "You disappoint me, Mother," he added, and Charlotte cringed at the word. *I think I preferred Charlotte.*

"I just thought we were all sharing our nights out and now I find out that this little gathering was just to embarrass me? I don't see how that's fair." Charlotte had no doubt that Noah and Dot had been waiting in the kitchen for this very reason, not that she was able to hide what she had done, and she would have to live with that. But only if that meant they were also going to share.

"You thought wrong," Dot said with a soft smile. Charlotte began to feel like she wasn't going to win this game, but she still had one card to play.

"Come on, please! I just want to know how your evenings went. Can you blame me for being curious? You were on a date Dot and Noah… how were the lights?" She wasn't quite ready to push that button with her son, and certainly not when he appeared to be in a good mood.

"If you must know…" Dot sighed.

"I must. Honestly," Charlotte said, taking another nibble of her pancake.

From the look on Dot's face, Charlotte would need to be patient, hold out and wait for her to engage. Unfortunately for her, the alcohol from the night before hadn't completely left her system, which left her the perfect amount of courage to say the first thing that popped in her head. She felt a slight numbness that often triggered her inability to silence herself. So she quickly shoved another piece of pancake in her mouth and mimed zipping it closed.

"It was a nice evening. Henry is a good man," Dot said, thinking for a moment and then sipping her coffee.

"That's it?" Charlotte asked. "You didn't want to tell me that? I already know Henry is a nice guy," she said, gesturing toward the tree. "Did you enjoy yourself? Would you do it again?"

"Yes." Dot grinned and Charlotte knew now that she was enjoying this little game that Charlotte had started, and she was discreetly winning.

"You're no fun, you know that?" Charlotte reached over to grab the maple syrup and poured a little extra on her plate. "And you? I assume it was fun," she said sarcastically.

"It was, actually," Noah said with a smile. "She's a cool girl. Took me on the ice slides."

"What are ice slides?" Charlotte asked.

"Feels like the name gives it away." Noah said. "They are trails made of ice that people slide down."

"And it was fun?" Charlotte asked as she began to feel like her attempts to learn anything about their nights were going nowhere.

"Yeah. Totally," Noah said, giving her a big smile. *I suppose I should be grateful he had a good time.*

"That's great. What's everyone up to today?" she asked,

taking a different approach.

"You don't want to go for a walk?" Noah asked, which caught Charlotte off guard. She had been making Noah go out for walks on the days where they hadn't been working—and some of the days they were—in order to teach him a lesson for getting kicked out of school. She'd meant the entire thing to be a punishment but now he was getting up and walking Bear on his own and asking if they were doing it. Her instincts at this point were to pinch herself to find out if she was dreaming still, but then again, that would end what was turning out to be a very interesting morning.

"Right. Yeah, we can head into town. Maybe we can get things for the tree-decorating party?" Charlotte asked.

"I was thinking about that," Noah said, his eyes drifting down to his pancakes, "and I thought, maybe, that... well, it would be cool if we had like a craft table set up. Maybe we could get kids to make their own decorations to hang on the tree?"

"That's a great idea, Noah," Charlotte said. A feeling of warmth and pure joy rushed through her as she looked at the smile Noah gave her. She couldn't remember the last time he'd smiled at her like that. With it came an old memory, one she hadn't thought about in a while. "You know, your dad and I used to do that with you and your friends."

"I know. I remember," Noah said with a little laugh. "Why do you think I thought of it?"

Charlotte fought back the tears from her overly emotional body as she sipped her coffee and nodded for what felt like an embarrassingly long time. She wasn't prepared for any of this today. If it hadn't been for her phone going off in her bedroom, she likely would have broken down.

"I should get that," she said, sneaking off before she had a chance to lose herself in the moment.

She took a breath to compose herself before she picked up the phone, not bothering to look at who it was. If she had, she might have let it go to voicemail.

"Charlotte? Hi, it's Andrew," he said from the other end of the line. "I told you I would give you a call before Christmas. So, we could work out—"

"I remember," Charlotte's fist clenched so tightly she could see the whites of her knuckles, hating this man for ruining her morning, along with everything else in her life.

"I hope this is a good time to chat, but we really do need to know if you're willing to accept the terms of your release."

"You mean you firing me?" Charlotte hissed. Since she hadn't told anyone that yet, she didn't want to start shouting it.

"You know this is difficult for all of us."

"No, you'll be fine. You have a job, Andrew," Charlotte shot back. She knew it wasn't Andrew himself who'd fired her. But still it felt good to take her frustration out on someone. "I'm visiting my family. Do we really have to do this now?"

"Charlotte, we need you to sign those documents. They outline the terms of your release."

"For fuck's sake, Andrew, stop calling it a release."

"It's company procedure, Charlotte, I'm sorry."

"I know," Charlotte said, letting some of the anger she was feeling drift away before she engaged him again. "Can't I sign it when I get home?"

"We need them signed before the New Year. We've already given you more time than usual. We understand with the year you've had that this is difficult."

"You mean because my husband died?" Charlotte wanted to scream into the phone, calling him a long list of names she'd thought of after they'd told her she was fired. At the time, she'd been so shocked by it all that she'd not even raised her voice. She'd just grabbed her things and left. It wasn't until later when it finally hit her that she was prepared to yell. Now that she was away and starting to enjoy herself, the last thing she wanted to do was give them the satisfaction of ruining her day. Again.

"Yes. It's been a hard year. And we have tried to be accommodating but you missed nearly all of your targets this year, Charlotte. You can hardly blame us for—"

"Don't you dare tell me what I can and can't do." Charlotte's words pinched out of her mouth in a bad attempt to keep her voice down. "I will email you the details of where you can send the documents."

"Thank you, Charlotte, and for what it's worth, I'm—"

Charlotte hung up the phone before he could finish the thought. She wasn't about to let this man ease his own conscience while she was out in the real world, trying to figure out how the hell she was going to tell her son that not only had she managed to lose her job but there was a good chance that come the New Year, they would no longer be able to afford their apartment in the city. That would mean him likely changing schools. All of this was because she couldn't keep it together. She had inadvertently destroyed their lives, again.

27

Dot

The little shop was crammed with people. It was the first official day of holidays for the kids not currently expelled from classes. It appeared the entire town was picking up the odds and ends they needed to prep for Christmas the next week.

Dot hadn't "taken a day off" in some time and she promised Noah and Charlotte that she would not go into the shop at all. This was of course a lie, since she would need to look at a few things for the week, but still, it was the closest thing to a day off that she could remember.

Charlotte, who had had a very long shower that morning, still didn't look herself when she came out into the living room, but she was determined to stick to her promise of going into town with Noah.

She appeared to turn a corner after her fourth coffee, but even still, Dot couldn't shake the idea she appeared a little flat and distant. Something she wasn't convinced was just about her night out.

"I didn't realize there were this many people in town,"

Charlotte said as she forced a smile and shimmied past a couple looking at various rolls of wrapping paper. She leaned in to grab one and Dot held up her hand.

"Not those. I have enough wrapping paper to last me till the end of time." Dot recalled the moment she decided that three rolls of Costco wrapping paper was a great deal. That had been five years ago now and she still hadn't managed to use it all.

"Noted," Charlotte said, glancing down to look at Noah. "So, what do we have on the list?"

Noah studied it carefully. "Markers, ribbons, wooden tree ornaments, glue, glitter, and three takeaway lasagna trays?" Obvious confusion arose from this last one, so Dot raised her hand.

"Those are for me. I like to make a few lasagnas for the house for when I am too lazy to make dinner."

"You work at a store that prepares meals," Charlotte said, looking a little confused.

"And I like to bring those home too. But sometimes, I like to switch up my recipes to try something new. Keep this old thing thinking," Dot tapped her head thoughtfully.

"Fair enough," Charlotte said, giving her a shrug. "Seems like an easy enough—Glue!" She practically shouted the words, causing more than a few heads to turn their way. Charlotte didn't seem to notice, but Noah did.

"Maybe take it down a notch, it's not a *Where's Waldo.*"

"Sorry, my brain only has two speeds right now. All in or asleep. And since I'm not asleep, I suggest you get onboard with all in," Charlotte said, sipping her coffee.

"Oh good, can't wait for whatever this is," Noah said, waving a hand in front of Charlotte, "to wear off."

"Easy," Charlotte said, pushing her sunglasses up even though they were inside now.

"How many people are you expecting to show up on Friday?" Dot asked knowing that at the very least, she could have a good time with the five of them. Six if you included Henry, who had made it abundantly clear that he wouldn't miss it for anything.

"Not sure," Charlotte said, bringing Dot out from her thoughts and back into the chaos that was Adi's Art and Supply Store, which had been around for even longer than the Mill, and was considered a staple for anyone looking for their next creative endeavour. Since Dot wasn't in need of more creative endeavours, she'd only ever been in the store once.

It was filled to the rafters with everything someone might need to get any art project finished. Bristol boards, markers, paints (acrylic and oil), walls of yarns in various sizes and colours, sewing machines, needles—crocheting, sewing and knitting. A section of custom high-end toys like wooden crib boards, handstitched teddy bears, porcelain dolls which always tended to frighten Dot, though she had no idea why. It was likely their faces.

It was nice to see the shop so busy. From her experience, getting a small community out to support a local shop wasn't always as easy as it sounded. It was often more expensive and that was hard for people to wrap their heads around. Especially as the cost of living was getting so high. Since she'd been considering selling the Old Mill, she knew that if she hadn't purchased the property when she had, there was no way her store would have had the success it had had. It was no wonder that new stores in town were having so much trouble. The thought made her sad.

"Henry said he's been sharing the news at the farm to people coming, and we have set up posters around town so hopefully, we can get a few people," Charlotte said.

"Cally has been telling all the kids at school about it. She thinks there should be a few that come," Noah offered up and Dot couldn't help but smile at Noah mentioning Cally.

She was so pleased the pair were able to get along. She'd had her doubts from the beginning, seeing as the pair had had a rocky start, but Noah had confided in her, and only when she'd promised not to make a big deal of it or to tell Charlotte about any of it, that Cally had kissed him on the cheek. It wasn't a real kiss, he'd said, but Dot remembered the preciousness of a kiss on the cheek. Like many things, it was something appreciated more as you got older.

"Well, that is all good to hear," Dot said, hoping she sounded more optimistic than she felt, and she must have succeeded because neither Noah nor Charlotte said anything about it. "I feel like you two have things covered here. I might sneak off to go speak with my friend Betty over at the Reading Nook. It's just around the corner. I'll take Bear with me too, so he doesn't need to sit in the cold," Dot said and when there were no serious objections, she took her leave, finding a well-behaved Bear curled up on the snowy sidewalk.

Dot might have felt bad for the old boy, but she'd had him long enough to know that Bear was the type of dog happy to be anywhere and with all the passersby on the street giving him attention, he was a happy camper.

"Cooling the old bones?" Dot asked Bear, who struggled up to his feet and gave her a big stretch and a yawn. "What do you say we go visit Betty? I'm sure she's got a treat or two for you," Dot said, watching Bear's tail wag playfully at the mention of treats.

Dot unhooked the leash from the bench and started walking with Bear down the road. St Martins wasn't a big town by any means, mostly just the one main road with a few lights, which meant that she only had a block to cover before she entered the tiny bookstore.

"Welco—Dot!" Betty said with enthusiasm as she came out from behind her little desk to give her friend a welcoming hug. Dot hugged back, enjoying the tall woman's long arms wrap around her as she felt Bear nudge his way between them. "I haven't forgotten about you, little one," Betty said, kneeling down and giving Bear a couple of scratches behind the ears. She reached into her pocket, pulled out a treat and fed it to an eagerly awaiting Bear.

Betty had been retired for some time. But like most retired boomers. she'd been unable to sit down and do nothing for long, and although Dot had offered many times for her friend to come help out at the Old Mill, Betty had taken up a small residency at the Reading Nook, which suited the old teacher well.

"Busy day?" Dot asked, looking at the half-dozen or so people walking through the little bookstore. It had been a relatively recent addition to the small community and apparently, from its continued success, an important one. In the short time that it had been around, they'd managed to attract a waiting list for their reading groups and had pushed to work with other local business to create events to help promote both the store and the books. The owner had even approached Dot about doing a dinner night where they would bring in cookbook authors and do a special meal at the Old Mill. Dot thought the idea was brilliant and they had managed to do their first one in the fall, which was a huge success, selling out in a matter of days. But since then, Dot had been reluctant to do another knowing she would be closing her doors soon.

"It's the last day to order books if you want them in by Christmas. So people have been coming in all day and putting in requests," Betty said with a smile.

"Good to see people haven't completely forgotten how to wait for things," Dot said, feeling the crunch every business owner felt at having to deal with anything you want delivered the next day. It was hard to compete with. But in her mind, all that did was send money out to somewhere that had no interest in the community you lived in. Convenience always came at a cost, and in this instance, it was the local economy.

"Truer words have never been spoken," Betty said, still squatted down, giving Bear some much-needed attention. "Speaking of, your order has arrived." Betty stood as she clapped her hands. "It's all brand spanking new and everything." Hurrying off behind the counter, Betty knelt down, pulled out a large book and placed it on the table in front of her. "It's certainly a heavy one."

"It looks gorgeous," Dot said, running her hand down the front of the book, which had a glossy, almost simplistic, white cover. Although the *Food Lab*, Dot knew, was anything but simple, and she was sure that it was the perfect gift for a young chef. And it never hurt to help to teach a young man how to cook good food. The thought caused Dot to turn around quickly to make sure Charlotte and Noah weren't right behind her.

"This a gift?" Betty asked, pulling it from the counter and tucking it back under the desk.

"Yes. For Noah," Dot said. "I think he will enjoy the science behind all of it. He has quite the mind."

"Nothing better than indulging the curiosity of youth," Betty said with so much reverence, Dot thought she might have taken up residence as the church pastor.

"Well, so long as he's not blowing up chemistry labs, I think it's a win," Dot mused, and the comment caught Betty by surprise. "It's a long story and one for another time." Dot smiled. "But would you mind holding it for me and I'll pick it up another time? Noah and Charlotte are meeting me here at any moment." Dot dropped her voice conspiratorially, as if Charlotte or Noah would be able to hear her from some other building.

"Of course," Betty said with a wink, her own tone dipping to match Dot's. "Speaking of stories," Betty said, looking around the shop to make sure no one was listening in. Although there were a handful of customers in the store, they were happily running fingers along the spines of books, paying no mind to the two women. "How was your date with Henry?" Betty's brows rose so high, Dot lost them behind her bangs.

"I would hardly call it a date," Dot said, feeling flushed by the conversation swinging around to her.

"You're right. It was just two grown adults having dinner together in one home," Betty said.

"Exactly." Dot smiled.

"That is a date, you ninny." Betty playfully smacked Dot in the arm. "And the more you try and fight me on it, the more I know it was one."

Dot opened her mouth to protest and suddenly felt trapped. "Okay, fine, it may have been a date."

"And how did it go?" Betty asked eagerly.

"Good, I suppose," Dot said, purposefully holding back now just to frustrate her friend.

"Don't you dare. You know this might be the most exciting thing to happen to us in a long time."

"Us?" Dot asked, amused. "When did our lives become about us?"

"The moment you got asked out on a date by one of the nicest men in town. Now spill, you little—"

"Easy now," Dot said, looking around the room but still, no one was paying much attention to them. "Well, we had dinner and wine and things went really well."

"You're so dull. That's it?" Betty asked.

"Well, there was the kiss," Dot said, her cheeks blushing like a schoolgirl at the mention of it. Still, after all these years, and with the energy she was picking up from Betty, she felt like it was her first kiss all over again. And perhaps it was, in a way. It was certainly her first with Henry.

"You kissed!" Betty said, trying to quell her excitement by hissing the words out but still, this reaction caused a couple of glances their way.

"We did. And if it's all the same to you, I would like to keep it so the whole town doesn't hear about it in the bookstore." Dot said, though she too felt giddy at the memory.

"And...? Was it...?"

"It was good," Dot said, a giggle coming out before she could allow herself to stop it. She was beginning to feel foolish, chatting on like this in the bookstore, but still, it felt nice to share the news with someone and truthfully, there was no one she wanted to share it with more. Betty, like her, understood what things like these meant as you got older. Young people always assumed that just because you were older, you were supposed to act a particular way, but that couldn't be further from the truth. Yes, the older you got, the more responsible you were supposed to become, but deep down, there was nothing better in the world then letting yourself get swept up in something as mysterious as romance. When it came to matters of the heart, everyone was a child.

"My God, you little minx. What's next? Another date? Another kiss?" Betty said. This last suggestion came with so much gusto that the two women started laughing even harder. The attention was most definitely on them now. Even Bear's head perked up from his resting place on the floor, which was impressive for the old boy.

"He is coming to help on Friday. We will see what happens then. I've also decided that I will tell the community my plans to close the shop."

"And you're sure about that?" Betty asked. She was supportive, but Dot knew her friend had her reservations about her closing it down for good. Dot needed to do what was best for her now, and it wasn't the time to be thinking about what everyone else wanted.

"I am," Dot said with as much conviction as she could muster. "Charlotte invited the paper, and it will be easier to tell them there and they can share it."

"If that is what you want," Betty said, reaching over to give her hand a squeeze.

"I think it is," Dot said, adding the "think" for Betty's sake and not her own. All she'd been doing for the past few months was thinking about it and she'd not found any good reason to keep the store going, not when it meant occupying so much of her time. Sooner or later, something was going to have to give, and she wasn't prepared for it to be her. Who knew how much time she had left, and she wanted to make sure she made the most of it.

"Charlotte, Noah!" Betty said, releasing Dot's hand and waving to the pair coming in.

"They don't know," Dot said quickly under her breath and her friend gave a tight nod. Her expression faltered once before she moved in to give Charlotte a hug, and noticed the pair were holding a couple of bags loaded with party supplies.

"Oh good, you found everything," Dot smiled, thinking about the mess that was sure to come after all of this.

"Nearly," Noah said proudly, and she knew that her best course of action as this point was to get on the train.

"Well then, what else do we need?" Dot asked.

"Coffee." Charlotte smiled weakly.

"And lunch," Noah said, patting his belly.

"I think we can manage that," Dot said, giving Betty a hug. "Thank you." Dot hoped her friend understood just how much she was thankful for in that moment.

"Of course," she said, wrapping her arms around Dot and nearly suffocating her in a hug, loving every second of it.

28

Noah

"So, you're done with school now?" Noah asked as he placed a warm quiche into one of the boxes Cally had laid out for him.

"Until the New Year," Cally said as she stamped the side of one of the takeaway coffee cups with an Old Mill logo. "Just in time too. I need a break. You know, like the one you're having."

"You think this is a break?" Noah huffed as he closed the box and stacked it neatly on the other two quiches he'd already boxed. "Waking up at five in the morning, making cookies, cleaning, stamping, boxing, repeating. I'm the one who needs the break."

"Don't be a baby. You're getting paid. I'm here, aren't I?"

"Yeah, but you're a weirdo," Noah teased. "Who else enjoys work?"

"Oh come on, like you don't like working here. Free cookies, hot chocolate, scones!" Cally finished the stack of cups and moved to place them under the coffee maker.

"Maybe you two can stop flirting long enough to help me out here?" Riley said as she placed a croissant into a takeaway bag.

"We're not—" Cally said but didn't finish. She just looked over at Noah and rolled her eyes. "She's just jealous cause we're not talking to her."

"Don't be jealous, Riley," Noah said with a grin. "We would be happy to talk to you if you're feeling left out."

"I'm not feeling—" Riley said, putting the croissant in front of a young couple, who looked amused by the banter. "You too are just—" She appeared flustered now as she looked up at the younger couple. "I'm not jealous."

"It's okay, Riley. We won't leave you out," Cally said, giving her sister a pat on the back as she turned to give Noah a little wink. "One croissant, a pecan square and two Americanos, black. Anything else?" Cally said, stepping up to the cash and running the pair through.

Noah was impressed she could remember any of that considering he hadn't even been paying attention. But that was the thing about Cally. She always seemed to be paying much more attention to everything, even if it was just happening in the background.

Neither of them had said anything about the kiss she'd given him the night they went out to see the lights and he wasn't going to be the one to bring it up. Not when he had worked so hard to create this kind of rapport with her. He wasn't about to blow it all up because he wanted to talk about it. That would be silly. No, it was much better to accept that things were going well and that he finally had a friend to talk with in town.

Not just any friend. Cally had been a little rough around the edges when they had first met but Noah understood now that she was just being protective of Dot and the Old Mill and knowing what he knew now, he could understand why. This was practically her second home.

Plus, she was right. Despite being tired all the time and having odd hours, he did have to admit he was actually enjoying himself at work. Riley was kind, Nana was always encouraging him to help her with some of her dishes, and Tia let him try all the delicious things she was cooking—plus chunks of cookie dough. She'd made him promise not to tell his mom about that.

Not that he was about to risk a good thing by telling her, since for the first time in a long time, he felt as though they were getting along. More importantly, she seemed happy.

"Noah, you have hands free up there?" Charlotte called back from the kitchen.

"Sure," he said as he boxed up the quiche, stickered it closed and walked around the corner and into the kitchen. Charlotte was standing at one of the long, stainless-steel tables in the centre of the kitchen, Tia was covering pies while Dot was mixing up something that apparently required a mountain of cheese. "What's up?" Noah asked.

"I'm just about to roll some of these croissants, and thought you might want to try it out," Charlotte said as she used a chef's knife to cut triangles into the long sheet of pastry.

"You want me to help you?" Noah asked, feeling a little taken aback by her request.

"Only if you want to. Wouldn't want to pull you away from anything important out front," Charlotte said, clearly baiting him into acknowledging that he would prefer to be working with Cally. But he wasn't about to give her the satisfaction. Still, he couldn't help but share a glance with Nana, who shook her head.

Noah had no choice but to trust that Nana hadn't told Charlotte about what had happened with him and Cally the other night. She'd promised him that it was his news to share and that she wouldn't tell a soul. But like his relationship with Cally, Noah wasn't about to ruin the good thing he had going with his mom and start sharing the more intimate details of his life with her. Not at this moment in time, anyway.

This meant she was fishing. Trying to get something out of him without asking him directly.

"Nope, I would love to learn," Noah said, rolling up his sleeves and moving over to the sink to wash his hands even before his mom had to remind him. He hadn't been doing much in the kitchens but the first thing Nana made him do before cooking anything was to wash his hands.

"Good boy," he heard Nana say behind him.

"So how does this work?" Noah asked, looking down at the table of triangles.

"Okay, well I'm going to continue to cut them out while you, roll them up and place them on the tray."

"Sounds easy enough. What's the catch?" he asked, feeling like there had to be more to it than that.

"No catch. You just need to roll them tight enough that they don't fall apart, and not so tight that you squish them. Here, watch," she said, reaching for one of the triangles and working from the wider base she rolled up the dough in one smooth motion. Then she picked it up and placed it on a tray lined with parchment paper. "Easy-peasy. We need four rows of three, staggering them slightly if you can."

"Of course I can." Noah smirked as he moved to the first triangle and went to roll it. To his dismay, it was not as easy as his mother had made it look, and it came out a little wonky.

"Shoot."

"You'll get the hang of it," Charlotte said. "Once you have the tray filled, put them in that plastic bag and leave them there to proof for a little while and start a new tray. Got it?" Charlotte asked, gesturing to a tall tray standing by the ovens.

Noah nodded as he reached for the next triangle and attempted another roll. This one was better, but it still wasn't as good as the one his mom had done.

"Just wait, you'll be a master by the end of this," Charlotte said with a grin.

"I'm aiming for not terrible," Noah said, reaching for the next croissant.

There was something different about his mom and he wasn't quite sure what it was. She was still off at times, sneaking away and when she thought no one was looking, she always looked a little sad. Even still, being in the kitchen and watching her work and get better, Noah had never seen this side of her before. She was usually so preoccupied with one thing or another that she rarely allowed herself to have fun. Maybe it was the kitchen or being around new people, but it seemed to bring out the best of her.

Noah wished it had been him who had noticed it but if he was being honest, it was Cally who brought it up. He wondered if maybe it was because for the past year, it had just been the two of them tiptoeing around one another, waiting for their next blow-up, that he couldn't actually see the change this place had had on her. Or on him, he supposed. But something about the way Cally had talked about her had made him think.

*

"You're lucky, you know," Cally said, her feet dangling off

the edge of playground. Noah was beside her and the pair sat nearly ten feet off the ground, looking over the field of lights. He knew soon enough he would have to be home but for the time being, he felt so grateful to be sitting there.

"Why's that?" he asked, feeling like she wasn't going to say the reason he was thinking of, which was that he was sitting there with her. And he wasn't about to allude to that because he didn't know if she also felt lucky to be sitting there with him. He doubted it. But still, it was better to hope for it in his mind, where it could be a possibility.

"You get to spend all that time at the Old Mill. With Dot, Riley, Tia… your mom." She said this last name looking at him.

"Yeah. Maybe. I guess. Charlotte is just trying to teach me a lesson, I think."

"Maybe." Cally said. "It's a fun lesson, though. I'm jealous."

"We could switch places if you want," Noah joked, but Cally didn't laugh.

"I would in a heartbeat." Her voice seemed heavy and Noah didn't think it was because of the cold air. "Can I ask you something?"

"Anything." Noah hoped he sounded casual and cool, even though he felt anything but. His body was freezing, and he was pretty sure his butt was going numb from the snow and ice on the landing at the top of a small rock wall, but he would happily let it get frostbitten if it meant getting to spend more time with Cally.

"Why do you call your mom Charlotte?"

"It's her name," Noah said instinctually.

"Yeah, but she's your mom."

"I know," Noah said, not sure what to say. Of course she

was his mom, but sometimes, it just didn't feel that way.

"I just don't understand it," Cally said, glancing over at Noah, who pretended not to notice, which was so hard, it almost hurt.

Noah opened his mouth to speak and he immediately regretted saying that she could ask him anything. He wished it had been something that was embarrassing or silly, not this. How could he possibly explain something so complicated to anyone? To be honest, he wasn't even sure how he had managed to get to this point himself. All he knew was that over the past year, their relationship had morphed into something that he could only describe as roommates, not a mother and her son.

"You couldn't understand," Noah said, feeling the tension in his voice thicken. He hated that he was beginning to build up his walls like he had with all the other kids at his school. He thought for sure Cally was different, and what made it worse was he couldn't even be mad at her. After all, he said it was fine, that she could ask him anything. *Stupid!*

"Oh, I think I could," Cally said, chuckling, which only served to make Noah even more upset with her. How could she possibly think that she could understand something so complicated that he didn't even understand it himself? Not only did she think she understood but she found the idea amusing.

"It's not funny. You don't understand."

"Why? Because you're the first kid in the world to struggle with a parent?" Cally said.

"You don't get it, Cally. You don't have your parents. It's different," Noah said, and even as the words came out of his mouth, he regretted saying them. It wasn't as if he was trying to be malicious or anything, he was simply stating a fact, but still, it was a stupid thing to say, and he knew it immediately. "I'm sorry. I didn't mean—"

"You're right. I don't," Cally said but she didn't move or turn to hit him. She just stared off, looking at the lights, unmoving.

Noah was shocked, mostly because he expected that he'd just crossed over a boundary that no one should ever step. He knew that because he would and had pushed back on comments like that. But she just sat there, staring.

"I didn't mean—"

"Yes, you did. You wanted to hurt me," Cally said, turning to face him now.

"I didn't—"

"Yes. You did. But you don't get to hurt me, Noah. You don't get to take your frustrations out on me because you don't like the conversation," Cally said. "We don't have to talk about this if you don't want to, you can say that, and I will respect that. But don't get mad at me because you're uncomfortable."

Noah opened his mouth to say something but Cally beat him to it.

"Don't pretend like it wasn't what you were doing. You said it to hurt me. But you failed."

Noah sat in shock for a moment, feeling so much guilt at what he'd said, it felt as though his insides were rotting out. *I never wanted to hurt her... Did I?*

The thought stung almost as much as knowing what he'd said. He understood the gravity of his words even before he'd said them. He knew because people had been saying things like that to him for the past year. They weren't always trying, but it still hurt. And here he was, turning that same thing around on Cally because he was upset she'd asked him a question. He was mostly surprised that he wasn't on his back with a black eye or a bloody lip since it would have been what he deserved.

"I don't think Charlotte… Mom, ever really wanted me," Noah said so softly, he wasn't sure if the words had actually come out. But Cally must have heard because she turned to face him but didn't say anything. He waited, unsure if he should continue or not but when she didn't say anything, he just kept speaking. "I mean, she must have, maybe, at some point. She agreed to it, I guess. But she was never… I don't know, it seems so stupid saying it all out loud."

"It's not stupid to have feelings, Noah," Cally said.

"I know. But… well… after Dad died, she shut down, like a part of her had just stopped existing. She stopped joking around and everything became so serious, as if we weren't allowed to have fun anymore. She kept telling me to grow up and get my act together. Like I was the problem."

"Were you?" Cally asked.

"I mean, sure, maybe, sometimes. But she stopped too. She just wanted me to be something I wasn't. So I tried to give her what she wanted. I grew up."

"No, you didn't," Cally said, chuckling to herself, and if it wasn't Cally, Noah might have been angry at her for making his thoughts feel silly. "Calling your mom by her first name doesn't mean you've grown up, Noah. It just changed your relationship with her, no longer seeing her as a mom."

"Only because she didn't want me as a son," Noah protested, feeling his defences pop up again.

"Calm down, of course she wants you as a son." Cally shook her head. "Has it ever occurred to you that maybe your mom is also just scared? She lost someone too. Someone she thought would be around for a long time. Riley was only eighteen when our parents died, and I was horrible to her."

"Somehow, I doubt that. You have to be the most rational thirteen-year-old I've ever met." Noah laughed.

"Maybe now. With some help." Cally laughed. "But after it happened, I was awful. I felt like my whole world had been taken away from me. I hated everyone and everything. Even Riley."

"So, what happened?"

"Riley had to fight to keep me, even though I'm sure there were times she would have rather let someone else take me. But then Dot offered her a job at the Old Mill, allowed me to be there as much as I wanted. She was the one who encouraged me to go and talk to someone, which I did."

"Did it help?" Noah asked, knowing that his mom had been trying to get him to talk to someone for a long time but he kept refusing since he didn't see a point in bringing up something he hated talking about in the first place. At least, he usually hated to talk about it.

"Eventually. Slowly, I started to realize that my whole world hadn't been taken away from me, just a massive part of it. She also helped me realize that it wasn't just me who lost people. Riley had too, and like me, she was trying to deal with it," Cally said. "It's easy to get so caught up in our own world that we forget there are other people in it, also struggling."

"Are you trying to tell me my mom is struggling?" Noah asked.

"Of course she is, dumb dumb. She lost her husband. Dot lost a son. Death affects people in so many ways. It's like a ripple effect."

"So what? I should just get over it?" Noah asked, and to his shock, Cally laughed.

"No, you idiot. Boys," Cally scoffed, "you just think you can push it in a box and forget about it. That's not how this works."

"So, what then?" Noah said.

"I don't know." Cally said and Noah's annoyed feelings returned.

"You don't know? That was the point of this whole thing?" Noah said, wishing now that she would have just punched him and moved on.

"There was no point, Noah. I don't know what to do because I'm not you. Only you can decide what you do next. It's your life. But you're right, I don't have my parents. They died. But I would give anything to have one of them back," she said, looking at Noah as her mouth twitched to one side.

*

"That one is perfect!" Charlotte said, nodding at Noah as he looked down at the croissant he'd been working on. It was by far the best one that he had made yet and he placed it on the tray with the others. "I told you you'd be a master in no time," she mused.

Noah gave her a thin smile, feeling almost embarrassed about the approval after looking down at the four others he'd been not nearly as precise with. But he did have to admit, he was getting better.

He wasn't sure why but looking up at Charlotte laughing and smiling, sent a warmth through him, as if all the ovens in the kitchen had opened at the same time.

Ignoring the part of his brain telling him otherwise, Noah ran over and wrapped his arms around her waist, catching Charlotte off guard as she raised her arms in the air partially, it appeared, to get the knife she'd been holding out away from him.

"Thanks, Mom," Noah said softly, and a moment later, he heard the knife drop down on the table and he felt her arms wrap around him as a fresh source of warmth filled him.

29

Charlotte

It had been such a long time since Charlotte could remember being as happy as she was that day. She'd shared a special moment with her son, and for the past year, those moments had been few and far between, and she was working in a place that gave her joy. Still, she sat in the bathroom, wrapped in a towel, crying on the toilet while the shower splashed in the tub, covering up the sounds of her weeping.

"What the fuck," she mumbled to herself as she wiped the tears away from her eyes. Somehow, despite the overwhelming joy, she felt as though she were seeing a rainbow in the eye of a hurricane. Sure, it was beautiful, but she was still in the middle of a hurricane.

"You okay in there?" Dot said as she tapped on the door.

She wasn't, but she wasn't about to admit that to anyone. Truthfully, she was falling apart at the seams. Whatever little wonderland she was living in was going to end, and soon, she would be back to reality. A reality that consisted of a life she could no longer afford because she'd managed to let that all implode.

"Out in a minute," Charlotte said.

"Well, Noah and I are making dinner," Dot said, which stabbed at Charlotte's heart as she realized that she should be the one making dinner with Noah, not moping around in a shower, crying.

"Can't wait!" Charlotte said, choking back the sobs that threatened to tear out of her. She paused a moment, waiting until she was sure Dot had left from her spot behind the door before she removed her towel, hung it carefully on the hook and eased herself into the shower, careful not to make too much noise in case someone was listening. It was an insane thought, considering most normal people weren't in the habit of hanging around bathrooms to make sure people weren't lying about being in the shower. Still, she crept her way into the shower, hoping the change in the sound of water from hitting the base of the tub to now her body wasn't enough to give her away.

"I'm losing my mind," she said, looking up to the bathroom ceiling. The water sprayed down on her chest as steam billowed up.

Sometimes, she imagined herself looking up in the sky and talking to Eli, which was also an illogical thing to do. Charlotte had never been the religious type, despite the pressures of her parents. She'd never got into the whole church thing. That wasn't to say that over the years, she hadn't come to develop her own understanding of what she thought about people, and death, and honestly, none of it was likely to make any sense to anyone else but her. But since she was the one in the shower speaking to the ceiling, it didn't matter.

"It only took one year for me to fuck it all up, Eli. One.

That's it. You'd laughed at me when I said two but look who's laughing now. It's not me. And it certainly isn't you, unless you can laugh while you're dead," Charlotte said as she pressed her face into the water. She was shocked by how nice the water pressure was. She lived in one of the most expensive cities in the world and yet her building must have the worst shower pressure of all time. Compared to this, it was a sprinkle.

"My God, that's nice," she said, breathing in deeply letting the steam and warmth fill her nostrils. "You remember when we used to come up here on the weekends? How you always thought this was an insane idea for your mom to do on her own. Leaving all of her friends and life in the city to renovate a beaten-down mill. I know we didn't get a chance to come up here much the last few years but if you are seeing this now, I think you would be surprised. I mean, she really did it."

Charlotte didn't make a habit of talking to Eli. Not for some time at least. Her therapist had suggested it might help to think about him. Charlotte had thought the whole thing was stupid. But desperate times call for desperate measures.

"I don't know what to do," she said, running her hands down her face. "I feel that is something I should know how to do. I feel like you would know what to do. You'd probably be great at this. Processing things in a positive manner. Talking to Noah, making him feel good. While all I seem to do is push him away." Charlotte grabbed the bar of lavender soap and began washing herself down, making quick work of it since she'd already been occupying the shower, or rather the bathroom, for some time. She was starting to think if she didn't get out of there soon, they might decide to send a search and rescue team.

"He hugged me today," Charlotte said, rubbing the suds off her body. "That was a welcome surprise. I had kind of forgotten what it felt like. Christ, who am I kidding? That's sad, isn't it? Yeah, it is. You would probably tell me if I wanted more hugs, to hug him or something as stupidly simple as that. Like it was the most obvious thing in the world. But I'm not you and I'm not good at taking the things I need, or asking for them, or whatever the hell it is rational humans do. It's hard for me, Eli."

Charlotte heard a creak from the door. She looked out of the curtain towards it and glanced at the floor to see if there was a shadow from someone listening in the hall. But there was nothing.

"Oh good. I am officially losing my mind," Charlotte said, leaning over to turn off the shower before reaching out and grabbing her towel. She began drying herself off, tilting her head up to the ceiling, unsure if she was still crying or not. "I could go for you telling me everything is going to work out. That it will all be fine. But you said that before and well, now you're not here and honestly, it's not fine. So, I'm not sure how much I can trust you at the moment." Charlotte closed her eyes and dropped her face into her towel, fighting the urge to scream into it, since explaining such an action would be too hard at dinner. Instead, just forced herself to dry off.

*

"Smells delicious," Charlotte said, stepping into the kitchen as she ran her fingers through her hair to detangle it a little.

"Spinach and ricotta ravioli," Noah said as he pressed a mason jar into a piece of folded pasta dough.

"You don't say," Charlotte said, looking at the trays of pasta. "Are you planning some sort of party I don't know about?"

"I figured we could freeze some." Dot offered. "Put in all this effort so might as well make it last a couple of meals."

"Fair enough," Charlotte said, rubbing her hands together. "What can I do to help?"

"I think we are nearly done with the pasta, and the marinara is on the stove," Dot said, looking around.

"What kind of sauce is it?" Charlotte said, moving over to the stove and picking up the wooden spoon to give it a stir.

"Roasted tomato, basil and garlic. Nothing special," Dot said. Although from the smell of the sauce, Charlotte would hardly say nothing special. Everything Dot made was special. She had some sort of sixth sense when it came to making food that made your mouth water.

"It smells incredible."

"Wait till you taste it!" Noah said as he pressed his palms into the mason jar, which was a little amusing because he had to use most of his body weight to press the jar all the way through the pasta.

"I can't wait," Charlotte said, resisting the urge to taste it right then and there. "So, pasta done, sauce done, umm... Can I grate some parmigiana?" she asked, trying to be of some help.

"Sure, the grater is just in there," Dot said, gesturing to a shelf beside the sink. "And you know what else I could use?"

"A glass of wine?" Charlotte asked, her brows lifting as she tilted her head at Dot.

"Well, if you insist." Dot grinned coolly.

"That I know where to look," Charlotte said, going into the pantry where she knew Dot kept more than a few bottles of nice wine. There had been many pleasant things to go along with staying at Dot's house for the holiday season, but one of the best was the steady flow of good wine hanging around. She was always hunting for new wines that she wouldn't mind offering in the store. Some of them were nice local wines from various regions around Canada. Charlotte hadn't known Nova Scotia had so many vineyards and she was pleasantly surprised at how good they were.

She found a bottle of red Montepulciano that looked good, and she thought would be a great addition to the pasta they had made for dinner.

"How's this?" Charlotte asked.

Dot took one glance at the bottle and nodded her approval. Dot wasn't overly snobbish about wine, and since Charlotte was picking a bottle out of her own pantry, in theory she would probably enjoy it. But she did have a few rules that she stuck to and many of those were about how the wine would pair with the food.

"Great." Charlotte opened the bottle and poured two glasses.

"What about my glass?" Noah asked when he saw just the two glasses being filled.

"You're thirteen." Charlotte laughed.

"Nearly fourteen," Noah countered.

Charlotte pretended to think about it. "So, you're still four years from being able to drink in Quebec."

"Come on, Nana. Why can't I try it?"

"If it were up to me, you could," Dot said with a devilish grin to Charlotte.

"Come on! You let Eli drink when he was his age?" Charlotte asked.

"Drink? Of course not." Dot waved a hand in Charlotte direction. "But try some wine? Of course."

"Really?" Charlotte asked, almost mystified. If parenting books were to be believed, then her allowing Noah to have any type of alcohol was grounds for becoming the worst parent in the world.

"Of course. I appreciate food. Wine in many countries is as much a part of the meal as anything else."

"Really?" Charlotte said, still trying to figure out if Dot was messing with her or not.

"Come on, Mom. Be cool. Be a cool mom."

"Drinking doesn't make you cool, Noah," Charlotte said.

"I know that," Noah said. "But still, Italian food and Italian wine. Wouldn't this be like an educational experience?"

"You know you can be quite cheeky when you want to be," Charlotte said, but she was thinking about it now. In her house, alcohol was just something no one ever talked about but people always had. She herself had certainly had some experiences with alcohol she would have preferred never would have happened. But maybe this would be a chance to change that for Noah, to show him that alcohol wasn't just something that is designed to get you drunk, but to maybe enhance an experience if it was enjoyed wisely. She also couldn't tell if this was all a load of crap and she was being peer pressured by a thirteen-year-old and tested by her mother-in-law. *But what is the test?*

"Fine," Charlotte said after giving it lots of thought. "You can try it, but I can't promise you're going to like it."

"It's just grape juice, isn't it?" Noah asked.

"Sort of," Charlotte mused as she pulled another wine glass from the shelf. "My guess is that you won't even like it, and for the record, this is not a regular occurrence. But I don't see a harm in giving you the chance to appreciate wine on a special occasion."

"What's the occasion?" Noah asked.

"It's the first time you've made ravioli." Charlotte smiled as she poured a small glass of wine and slid it across the table to Noah. "Here you are, sir," she said, nodding to the glass.

Dot held up her own glass. "Cheers," she said looking to Charlotte and then to Noah, watching as their glasses clinked. Both Charlotte and Dot were homed in as Noah tilted the glass to his lips.

"Kind of smells like plums," he said, giving it another sniff.

"You're a natural already." Dot laughed.

Noah sipped the wine. His face lit up and for a moment, Charlotte thought he was going to spit it all up over the table. But he grimaced and swallowed it.

"It burns a little," he said, coughing, "And it tastes nothing like grape juice."

This made Dot laugh even more.

"I told you, you might not like it," Charlotte mused.

"Here," Dot said, grabbing the glass and going over to the fridge. She pulled out a small container of water and filled it up so that it was about half and half. "This will allow you to appreciate it with the food, and you can still smell it, but you won't have the same burning sensation." Dot handed the cup back to Noah. "It's what I did for Eli after he tried it the first time." Dot smiled.

"So no one likes it the first time?" Noah asked.

"Some people never do," Dot said. "Though I think it is a shame not to be able to appreciate something that someone has taken so much time and care into developing, sometimes for hundreds of years. Wine and beer have been as much a part of human civilization as spices, and although we tend to take these things for granted now, it is important to remember that quality things take time." Dot took a sip from her own wine.

"Is that why you love cooking, Nana?" Noah asked, trying a tentative sip of his new wine. He still grimaced but not nearly as much as he had before.

"Maybe. I'm not sure. I suppose in a way, it is. I think too much of our world prioritizes an abundance of fast and cheap things. But what's the point in knowing how to do so many amazing things if all we do with them is rob them of what makes them special?" Dot said. "The Old Mill is my own little oasis. I may not make a ton of money doing it, but I'm proud of what we do and I think people appreciate that we care about it." Dot smiled thinly and Charlotte got the impression that there was more on her mind than just the quality of her food.

"To the Old Mill," Charlotte said after a few moments.

Noah and Dot held up their glasses and when Noah put the wine up to his lips, he waited a second.

"I think I'll wait for the food," he said, setting the glass town on the table.

"Smart boy." Dot smiled and like that, she was out of whatever thought had pulled her down and she was there, present in the kitchen. "I think it's about time we get these things boiling. What do you say, Noah?"

"You got it, chef," Noah said, eagerly picking up one of the trays and going to the water as Charlotte watched from the island, trying not to think about how all of this was going to end and sooner or later, they would need to go home and face the realities of their lives. But for now, she had cheese to grate.

30

Dot

"So, are you ready?" Henry asked as Dot loaded a tray of butter tarts onto the wooden cutting board in the display area.

"Define ready?" Dot's brows rose slightly. "Something to have with your coffee?" she asked as Henry gave her curious look.

"You know I'm not in this for the butter tarts, don't you?" Henry said.

"I know. But I don't see why they can't be an added bonus," Dot said, sliding the plate over to him.

"Well, it isn't the worst perk, I suppose," Henry said, playfully grabbing the plate. Dot felt giddy looking at Henry, a feeling she was sure she would have gone the rest of her life not feeling again. It was like someone had replaced her with a sixteen-year-old girl who was trying her best to be cool and flirt at the same time with a boy she liked.

She hadn't had too much opportunity to speak with Henry since their dinner, though he still came into the shop every morning. But given that it was the week before Christmas, it was all hands on deck as orders were constantly being called in and picked up, leaving Dot with very little time to think about what it was she was doing with this man.

"You know it's going to be great, right?" Henry said, sipping his coffee.

"Nana, why don't you take a break," Noah said, coming to grab the tray from out of Dot's hand. "You haven't sat down all morning."

"Thank you," she said, reaching over to give Noah's shoulder an affectionate squeeze. "And that's because we're busy."

"Not right now we're not," Cally said, gesturing to the room. There was a smattering of people perusing the shelves, looking at various cookware and knick-knacks Dot had put out for the holiday season.

"What about orders?" Dot asked.

"I'll get those," Riley said, gesturing to the open table. "The kids are right. Go sit down, enjoy a coffee. We can handle it."

"Who you calling kids?" Cally asked.

"Yeah. I believe you mean responsible young employees?" Noah offered.

"I think for now, I'll stick to kids. Save the responsible for a later date." Riley laughed.

"Rude," Noah and Cally said at the same time, and Dot noticed when Noah's cheeks flushed a little at the shared moment.

"Well, if you think you'll be fine," Dot said, and though she wasn't about to say any of this out loud, she was very happy to have the chance to get off her feet. There was a time when she could go an entire day without ever needing to rest, but those days were gone and replaced with an increased desire to sit.

"I'll save us a table," Henry picked up the plate and his

coffee as he moved toward the table before stopping. "That is assuming I am allowed to sit with you. I would hate to—"

"Grab the table, Henry." Dot waved a dismissive hand in his direction. She may have felt like a youthful child but that didn't mean she was one.

"Dot," Charlotte said, poking her head out from the kitchen. "Question for you." She wiped her hands down on a towel tied up at her waist.

"What is it, love?" Dot said, grabbing an empty mug to pour herself a coffee as Noah took the now empty tray which had held the butter tarts around Charlotte and into the kitchen. The pair shared a cute smile as he passed.

Dot didn't know exactly what had changed between them, but she was very happy to see that they were no longer bickering as much and although she was afraid to say it out loud since she didn't want to jinx it, they were actually getting along.

"You don't by any chance have a fax machine or a printer or something that I could use in the office, do you?" Charlotte asked.

"A printer. No fax machine, though."

"What the heck is a fax machine?" Cally asked.

"Stop eavesdropping, Cally," Riley said. "And don't be so young."

"I'm not eavesdropping, they're standing right there," Cally said, waving a hand at Dot and Charlotte, "and I can't stop being young because that's not how life works, Riley." She rolled her eyes as she reached under the table to grab a cloth and a spray bottle, eyeing up one of the tables that an older couple had just left.

"Why? What are you expecting?" Dot asked, though it was

none of her business.

"I just need to sign some documents for work and send them back. They were asking what I had available," Charlotte said, a thin smile on her lips.

"Everything alright?" Dot asked, getting a sense that there was something Charlotte wasn't saying but she couldn't tell what.

"All good," Charlotte said. "Just thinking about what else I need to grab for tomorrow night. Brain's a little all over the place, you know."

"Better than you think." Dot smiled. "But yes, the printer is in the back room. Help yourself," Dot said, not wanting to get herself involved in anything to do with the Friday night tree-decorating ceremony. She'd been dreading it all week, since she still had no idea how many people were going to be there and therefore no idea how much food she should have on hand. Not to mention all of the orders she needed to fill over the weekend for the final pick-up on Christmas Eve that following Tuesday.

The only benefit to this whole tree-decorating thing was that Charlotte had suggested it was on the Friday night. That meant she would still have the weekend and all day Monday to prepare. Tuesday was the last day the store would be open before they shut down for Christmas. By then, everyone should know the store would be closing for good in the New Year which left Dot with only a handful of days left of working at the Old Mill.

She might have felt sad about the whole thing, and perhaps when she allowed herself time to think, she would. But lately, she'd been so busy with Noah and Charlotte and the holiday shopping that she hadn't had much time to reflect on the reality of it all. She supposed that was for the best, though, considering if she allowed too much time to think about it, she would likely find a way to talk herself out of it, and that wasn't what she needed right now. She needed to be strong and brave or else the fear of it all would cripple her.

"Fair enough." Charlotte laughed. "I don't think I realized just how busy you got here over the holidays."

"I did try to warn you," Dot said. "It's not too late to—"

"Don't even try!" Charlotte said, holding up a finger. "We have nearly everything in place for this thing and I'll be damned if I'm going to let myself get carried away and not make it happen."

"So, you'll make it happen out of spite?" Dot joked, pouring herself a cup of coffee.

"Call it whatever you want. But I need a win right now," Charlotte said, "and this is going to be my win," she added more to herself than to Dot.

"I'm sure it will be great," Dot said, turning to grab herself a pecan tart from a tray and put it on a plate. "I have no doubt in my mind that if anyone can pull it off, it's you, love."

"Thank you," Charlotte said and clearly the words resonated with her, which was good because Dot herself wasn't sure any of this was going to work. For all she knew, it would be eight people, if Henry and Betty decided to show up as well. But she wasn't about to share her hesitations with anyone, certainly not Charlotte. Clearly there was more going on in her life if this seemingly innocuous event mattered so much to her.

"You're welcome. Now if you need me for anything, I'll just be over there talking to Henry."

"Yeah you are," Charlotte said, giving Dot a wink.

"It's not like that."

"Whatever you say, Dot," Charlotte said as she slowly backed away, her brows rising and falling as she disappeared back behind the kitchen doors.

"It's not—" Dot began but she knew a losing battle when she saw one. Charlotte was going to believe whatever she wanted, whether Dot said otherwise or not. Sure, Henry had kissed her at dinner the other night and sure, he had expressed a desire to hang out more. But Dot didn't know what any of that meant since he had no idea that for her, selling the store meant she planned on travelling more. Would he still be so keen on hanging out when he learned she wouldn't be in town as much? Would he want to travel with her? Would she want him to?

All of these questions swam around her mind as she walked over to meet him. Sure, he was an incredible man and she would be lucky to have the chance to spend time with him. But she had put her life on hold once for a man and when that had fallen apart, she'd done it for the Old Mill, and right now, she wasn't all too sure she wanted to be a part of anything that stopped her from living this new chapter of her life.

None of this she'd had the courage to tell Henry since they had only gone on one date and frankly, she didn't have the time to discuss it with anyone else because she didn't need anyone to tell her it was a bad idea. Perhaps it was, but if it was then it was her bad idea to make and no one else's. If he had a problem with her plans, then she would deal with that then. For the time being, she was happy to enjoy the company of a nice man. Future her would deal with the consequences.

31

Noah

"I think it would be better over there," Noah said, pointing to the long wooden table that usually held pies, flowers and various goods that the store sold but was now set up as a makeshift craft table and covered with brown paper for protection, as per Nana's instructions.

Noah hadn't really understood why Nana cared about an old table that looked as though it was going to fall apart at any minute, but he wasn't about to risk getting yelled at either when someone wrote on it with marker. So, he and Cally had covered it. It was also why he felt the only logical place to put the cookies was on the table as well, since that was where the kids would most likely congregate.

"And your thoughts would be wrong," Cally said, placing the cookies on the counter near the till.

"Explain to me why I am wrong?" Noah said, his arms folded defensively against his chest.

"I shouldn't need to. It's obvious."

"If it were obvious then don't you think I would get it?"

"No. I don't," Cally said with a smug grin.

Noah should have realized he was walking into that one but still, he wasn't ready to admit defeat, especially when he still couldn't understand why putting them in the area with all the kids wasn't a good idea.

"If we put the cookies there, we eliminate how much people need to walk around," Noah said, shaking his head. "Unless you think it is a good idea to have little kids running around with markers? Is that what you want? To clean up more messes later? Cause you know it's going to happen."

"Ye of little faith, Noah," Cally said, as if that were a response that even remotely qualified as answering the question.

"What!?" Noah threw his arms up in confusion.

"If you put the cookies over there, they are going to be gone in two minutes. You can't put cookies around kids and think they won't be cramming them in their mouths. We'll be out of cookies before anyone arrives." Cally sounded exasperated. "Besides, if the cookies are over here, people will have to pass the counter where there are things that they can purchase. Which means we have a better chance of selling more things while everyone is here. Things like the hot cocoa." Cally grinned, gesturing to the small sign she'd made displaying the deals for the evening, which had various kid-friendly options, along with some wine and cocktails for the adults. "Or did you forget that this is a business as well?"

"Cally's right on this one, Noah," Charlotte said, coming out of the kitchen with a tray of cookies. "It would be nice if people came and actually bought things."

"See?" Cally said, holding her hand up toward Charlotte and nodding approvingly.

Noah didn't like when Cally was right about things. Not that he had a problem with being wrong or anything, but he just didn't like when she was right.

"Fine," Noah said, shoving his hands in his pockets.

"Don't be a baby, Noah," Cally said, going to check on the tree.

"I'm not being a baby," Noah said unconvincingly.

"There is no right way or wrong way," Nana said, coming out from the kitchen with a tray of warm pies. "This is the first time we have ever tried this. All we can do is hope we break even and a few people from town show up."

Noah wasn't too sure, but he was confident Nana wasn't all that convinced this was going to work. It might have been the fact that she continuously insisted on not making it a big deal, or that she kept telling Mom how fun it was going to be in the most unconvincing ways possible.

That afternoon, he'd seen her on her phone bragging about how her friend Betty was going to come by, "so that would make at least two", and Noah knew the second person was Henry, who had been in and out that afternoon with Christmas decorations, like a wreath for the front door and some garlands to hang in the windows.

Noah liked Henry, not just because he thought the old man was funny or how he'd helped Noah cut down his first and second trees, but he was fun to talk to. Since Noah wasn't in school, the only boy he'd managed to meet was Henry. Sure, Cally was fun to hang out with but there was something nice about being around a boy. Or man, he supposed, in Henry's case. It was funny. Despite Charlotte's insistence, Noah had never been all that eager to grow up. From what he'd managed to make out so far, all growing up ever got anyone was stress. But hanging out with Henry was a little like hanging out with a kid, only he had money to spend on things.

"She's only saying that to be nice," Cally whispered in Noah's ear and he turned and smacked her on the arm. "Ouch!" she cried out but was unable to hide her smile.

"The room looks great, you two," Nana said, appearing to ignore their bickering as she laid her pies out on one of the side tables. Noah noticed Bear trailing behind her, his nose lifted in the air, sniffing intently at the pleasant aroma of pumpkin pies. "Don't you even think about it." She turned, pointing a finger at the old dog, who parked himself on the floor, looking indifferent to the threat.

"The rest of the lights should be ready for tonight," Henry said, stepping down from the small step ladder he'd been using to hang lights around the windows. He was the tallest of the lot of them, and therefore the only one able to reach the top of the frames.

"I'm sure they will be great. Thank you for doing that, Henry," Nana said, giving the big man an affectionate pat on the back.

"You don't want to test them? Make sure they all work?" Riley asked from behind the counter.

"I think Henry has done enough for us," Nana said, shaking her head.

"Riley's right. Best to make sure they work before I head home."

"Oh, you're leaving?" Nana asked, sounding disappointed.

"Just to change. Hardly want to show up looking like I just climbed out of the woods now, do I?" Henry grinned, gesturing down at the dirty, green coveralls he wore for work. "I'll be back when the doors open."

"Oh. Good." Nana smiled and the pair looked at each other for a moment before Henry dusted his hands together and gestured at the lights. "Why don't you fire them up? See how they look"

Nana's hands immediately shot up. "No, no, it shouldn't be me."

"Of course it should," Charlotte said, coming out from the kitchen. "None of this would be possible without you."

"Ok, if that's what you want." Nana said as she walked behind the tree and Henry bent down and handed her a little switch. "Just press this?" She asked Henry gesturing to the little button. Henry nodded. "Here it goes." A moment later all of the lights in the store lit up.

"Wow," Noah and Cally said at the same time.

"That looks incredible, Henry," Riley said.

Noah looked over at his mom and she remained quiet, just looking at the overly tall and well-lit tree.

"Did I miss i—" Tia said, coming out from the kitchen. "Damn!" She grinned as she gave the tree a satisfactory nod. "Why does it seem bigger?"

"It's the angel," Noah said, nodding to the little decorative tree topper Henry had helped him place. He glanced at Tia, who shot him a thumbs up. It was still without a doubt the biggest tree Noah had ever seen inside before. It was certainly the best one he'd ever cut down.

"It's, umm…" Nana said, stepping away from the tree to get a better look at the entire thing. "Impressive," she said with a smile. "Thank you again, Henry."

"My pleasure," he said, admiring his workmanship.

Nana moved herself to face the room. "Well, I think now would be a great opportunity to say thank you to all of you for setting this up. I'll admit, I had my doubts about doing this—"

"You did?" Charlotte asked, getting a round of laughter from the rest of them, though from the look on her face, she was being serious.

"I did. It's not in my nature to want to create more work than is necessary," she said, holding up a finger to stop Charlotte from saying anything else, "but I'm glad that you suggested this. No matter the outcome tonight, I'm proud of you for making it happen and… well… I'm grateful that all of you were here to help this month. It's been special. Truly," Nana pressed her hands against her heart.

"Agreed," Riley said and though Noah thought all of this should be making people happy, he couldn't help but feel sadness fill the room.

But he didn't have time to think too much on it, as the buzzer for the oven went off.

"That's me," Tia said, wiping her eyes as she left the front room.

"I should get home to change," Henry said, walking over to give Dot's hand a squeeze before heading out the back entrance.

"I suppose we should finish up in here," Riley said, patting Cally on the back, which just left Nana, Charlotte, and Noah standing still looking at the tree.

Charlotte, who looked as though she was only seconds away from breaking down, walked over to Nana, not saying anything as she wrapped the older woman in a hug. A second later, she waved a hand at Noah and he took the opportunity to run in and embrace them both.

"Easy now. It's just a decoration party," Nana said, stepping away and giving the tree another look over. Noah still had his mom's arm draped around him.

"You know this isn't about the party," Charlotte said.

"I know," Nana said.

"I don't." Noah felt confused now.

"Don't worry about it, love. I think you have other things to think about," Nana gave him an amused look.

"I do?" Noah asked.

"Yes. Like taking that little guy out for a walk before people start to arrive," Nana said, gesturing to Bear on the floor by the cash table.

"Come on. Why do I have to?" Noah protested.

"Because he likes you."

"Bear likes everyone."

"But he particularly likes you. Besides, we have some things in the kitchen that we—"

"I can help in the kitchen," Noah said eagerly. He liked the kitchen, and it had started to snow and truthfully, the idea of dressing up and going back out in the cold wasn't all that appealing to him, and from the look of it, not to Bear either.

"When you get back maybe," Nana said.

"Fine. But I would like to point out that I am doing this under protest."

"Noted," Nana said with a smile.

"Come on, Bear," Noah said, realizing the only way he was going to get this over with was to do it. Bear looked as though he would be perfectly content lying on the floor all night but he reluctantly stood up. His hind legs shot out as he let out an impressive-looking stretch for such an old dog. "Good one, Bear."

"Noah!" Cally said, rounding the corner, and his heart skipped a beat.

"Yeah?" he said eagerly, his mind racing with all the things

Cally could ask him. Though his fancies were short-lived as she offered him a slight smile.

"I meant to print off the new sign for the drink specials. When you're in the back, do you mind doing that for me before you go?"

"Yeah, of course." Hoping his deflation wasn't as obvious as he felt it had been.

"Thank you," she said before running off.

Noah muttered to himself, feeling a little bit like an errand boy rather than a real help. Considering he'd been the one who helped cut down the tree and come up with the idea, he thought he would at least get some credit. But everyone just seemed too wrapped up in their own worlds to realize what a great job he had done.

Not that he was about to complain about any of this to any of them. Cally would likely laugh in his face and list all the numerous things everyone else had done to make it happen, which would only make him feel worse. So instead, he chose to just let himself feel a little pity while he was out walking Bear in the snow, and then when he got back and the night was a success, he would just take a small amount of joy in knowing he'd helped. And then maybe if he was feeling up for it, brag about it to Cally.

Noah walked into the back room, hearing the click clack of Bear's nails on the floor as he followed him. He spotted his jacket resting on the couch with everyone else's. He reached in to grab it and began dressing for winter.

Before he headed out, he opened the computer, found the document that Cally had made for the drinks and pressed print. An error popped up on the screen and he realized the printer wasn't connected to the computer.

"Old people," Noah said, chuckling to himself. He wasn't sure if it was his mom or Nana but either way, they needed to learn how to use electronics. Noah managed to track down the cord for the printer and plug it into the side of the computer. Once he'd finally set it up, he printed the document.

"Noah! You have the sign?" Cally shouted from the other room.

"I'm printing it now!"

"Stop yelling!" Riley called out. "You're ruining the music."

Noah knew she was joking because Riley hated Christmas music. Well, she said she didn't hate it, just hated that it played non-stop for all of December.

The printer started to go, and he had to wait a few seconds for the document to print. But when he went to grab it, he realized it wasn't the drinks list at all. He was about to ignore it until he saw that it was for his mom. He knew it wasn't his to read but still, it was there in his hands. He couldn't help himself. He scanned the top of the page and immediately regretted touching it at all.

The pages kept coming but he didn't need to read it all to understand the importance of them.

"Noah? Do you have it?" Cally asked, poking her head around the door.

Noah was silently looking at the document.

"Noah?"

"You know if you were going to go through all the trouble of coming back here, you could have just done it yourself," Noah finally said, grabbing Bear's leash off the wall and hooked it on to the old dog.

"Noah, I was just playing—"

"Here," he said, shoving the paper into Cally's hands. He knew it was rude, but he was mad. And she was there.

"Noah I wasn't—"

"I need to take Bear for a walk," he said, feeling guilt rush through him at the pained look on Cally's face. She had no idea what was going on but he didn't care. All he knew was that Charlotte had been lying to him this whole time.

"I can come with you if you want," Cally offered but Noah was already out the door, dragging Bear along with him.

32

Charlotte

"Have you seen Noah?" Charlotte asked Cally. She'd been looking around the store trying to find him, thinking he should have been back by now. It had been at least thirty minutes since he'd said he was taking Bear out for a walk.

"Not since he stormed out," Cally said, "I swear that kid is all over the map tonight."

"What do you mean, stormed out?" Charlotte asked.

"I don't know. He was just in the office printing out those signs and then he freaked out and ran off. Didn't say anything to me." Cally rolled her eyes. "You know he is not very good at communicating."

"It's been a rough year," Charlotte said, though her mind was somewhere else. Something about him being in the office wasn't sitting right with her, but the realization hit her like a punch to the stomach. "Shit," she whispered but not so quietly, Cally didn't hear.

"What?" she asked, clearly not at all thrown off by curse words, though she must have seen something on Charlotte's face before placing a hand on her arm. "Hey, tonight's going to be great. Look how many people are already here." She gestured to the room.

She wasn't wrong. It had surprised everyone, including Charlotte, to find a small line forming outside of the Old Mill along the sidewalk at seven when they'd opened the doors. There were only a dozen or so, but since then it had almost doubled in size. Many of the kids had already started making their own decorations to hang on the tree while parents mingled in the corner. Some of them were drinking wine, others hot chocolate.

"I know… I just need to check on something," Charlotte said, forcing a smile, though she doubted it was all that convincing.

Cally didn't say anything because she didn't have time as another person came over to purchase a special strawberry and rhubarb pie that Tia had decided to make for the night.

Charlotte tried to cut through the kitchen but was stopped before she could by Dot, who was having a glass of wine with Betty and Henry.

"I should never have doubted you, Charlotte. Tonight looks like it is going really well," Dot said with a grin. "Everything okay? You look pale."

"Fine," Charlotte lied. She thought her stomach was about to empty on the floor if what she suspected to be true, was true.

"Well maybe grab some water, or a wine. Relax a little. This is all because of you and Noah." She looked around the room. "Speaking of, where is he? I wouldn't have thought Bear needed that long of a walk."

"I'm not sure. I'm sure he'll pop up soon." Charlotte forced a laugh. "If you'll excuse me," she said.

The formality of the comment stirred something in Dot but

she didn't stop Charlotte.

"You look great, Henry, and thank you for coming, Betty," Charlotte added quickly, her mind already in the office.

She didn't have to search hard to find what she was looking for, although a massive part of her wished she'd been wrong about it all. But there it was, crumpled up on the floor beside the desk.

"Shit."

She bent to pick it up but before she could unfold it and make sure it was what she knew it would be, a shiver of cold air filled the room.

"Oh. Hi," Noah said as he unhooked Bear, putting the leash on a small knob before he dusted himself off and removed his jacket. "People actually showed up, I guess." Noah tossed his jacket on the couch and turned to leave.

"Noah, I think we should talk," Charlotte said.

"About what?" Noah turned, giving her a shrug.

"This," she said, holding up the documents that outlined the terms of her termination.

"You want to talk about this now?" Noah's head shook before he turned to leave.

"Noah, get back here." Charlotte reached out and grabbed his shoulder, turning him around to look at her.

"Don't," Noah said, pulling his shoulder aside and swatting her hand away. "There is nothing to talk about, okay?"

"What are you talking about? Yes, there is," Charlotte said.

"You mean this thing that you have been keeping from me for… who knows how long? The thing I found because you made a mistake? The thing that if I hadn't found, you wouldn't have told me about? That thing?"

"That's not true. I was going to talk to you about it,"

Charlotte said, wishing she didn't sound so defensive.

"Right. Just like you talk to me about everything else." Noah scoffed and turned to leave again, but Charlotte stopped him.

"Hey, I'm sorry. But I didn't know how to tell you about any of this."

"So, you thought not telling me was your best option. Great parenting, Charlotte." Noah shook his head.

"Don't speak to me like that," Charlotte said, her voice low, realizing there were more than a few people in the other room who she certainly didn't want to hear about her troubled life.

"Fine," Noah said, shrugging as he attempted to turn. But Charlotte grabbed his arm again.

"Ouch," Noah said, louder than she would have liked, and she immediately let go.

"I'm sorry, it's just, we need to talk about this."

"Stop it!" Noah shouted. "You don't want to talk about any of this. You're just upset that you got caught. Now you feel like you have to answer for it. But you don't, I get it. I'm just a kid and wouldn't understand the pressures you're under or whatever excuse you want to use to make yourself feel better."

"Noah—"

"No. I'm done. You brought us up here to this sad little town making me feel like it was all my fault because I got kicked out of school. That I'm some kind of troubled kid who needed to be taught a lesson, and the entire time you've been keeping the fact that you," he jabbed his finger in Charlotte's direction, "lost your job. What was your plan, Charlotte? Move away from our home, my friends, and come up here and pretend like everything isn't screwed up?" Noah's eyes never left hers as his chest heaved.

Charlotte could feel her mouth hanging open and she

wished she could say something that would fix the problem, but this was all her fault and he was right. She'd done all of this to both of them. She was even fairly certain that if she boiled everything right down to it, Noah's incident was somehow her fault too. After all, she was the adult here and all she'd managed to do was isolate her son even more. There were countless things she could have said to help the situation, but she wouldn't get the chance as a shadow passed in the corner of her eye and she turned to see Cally standing just outside, her arms folded against her chest, her eyes tearing through Noah.

"Stupid little town, huh?" she said, shaking her head.

"Cally?" Noah said, turning to face her, his mind catching up to his words as he tried to double back but she was having none of it. "I didn't—"

"Whatever," she said, rolling her eyes before focusing in on Charlotte. "Dot just wanted me to get you. She's going to make an announcement or something." She didn't wait for a reply. She just turned, leaving the two of them alone again.

"Cally, wait," Noah tried but she was gone.

"We're not done here," Charlotte said.

"Look what you did!" Noah shouted. "You ruin everything." His voice dropped, making each word more hurtful then the last. Charlotte would have preferred anything else over the cold disappointment spilling out of her son's mouth. She didn't think it could get any worse, but he shook his head as tears welled up in his eyes. "I hate you."

It was as if he'd reached into her chest and torn out her insides. Charlotte had never felt more vulnerable than she did in that moment. Her breath caught and even though she wanted to say anything in that moment to keep him there, she just watched as he walked away. She didn't even have the strength to try and stop him.

What happened after that was like a tormented dream that she wasn't able to wake from. She was watching herself from another world, drifting in and out of some weird hellscape.

Eventually, she found her way into the main area, poured herself a large glass of wine, and attempted small talk with various people in the room. She was pretty sure people around her were complimenting her on the success of the night but all of it just washed over her.

Vaguely, she remembered talking to Riley asking about Cally, who was actively avoiding Noah at every turn. Charlotte's world was spinning. She was filled with a strong desire to vomit but thankfully, she didn't. From the concerned looks people were giving her, she suspected the chill she felt in the air was a by-product of all the blood draining from her face.

"You should say a few words."

Charlotte stared at her now empty glass, wondering when she'd finished her wine and if it had only been the one glass, before finally looking up at Dot.

"Charlotte?"

"I, umm… What?"

"Are you alright? You look a little faint."

"No… I mean, yes. Just… yeah."

"I was going to make an announcement," Dot said, glancing down at her own glass nervously.

"Okay," Charlotte said, hoping that the expression she was holding on her face was a smile. She had relinquished all control of her body and hated every second of it.

"I just thought, well, I should tell you first, before I tell everyone else."

"What's that?" Charlotte asked, half as a question, half-unsure of what it was they were discussing. From the serious look Dot had on her face, she knew it was important, and she wasn't entirely sure she was prepared for anything else at the moment. She was, however, beginning to realize how little control she had on how her life was playing out.

"Are you sure you're okay?"

"What is it, Dot?" Charlotte said, annoyed, which she immediately regretted. "Sorry, I didn't mean to… It's just I have some things I need to tell you too." She let out a heavy sigh, which threatened to break down the last of her defences.

"Maybe I should wait?" Dot said, looking around the room now hesitantly.

"No. Please. Just tell me now," she said, feeling like there wasn't any way she was going to feel any worse. But then she'd been wrong about everything else so far.

"Okay. It's just, well… You know I've enjoyed having you and Noah here this month. It's been great. But, well, before I got the call from you, I had decided to, well, in the New Year, I am going to shut down the Old Mill. For good."

The words barely registered, nor did the nods that she felt her head doing without the confirmation from her brain. It was as if her whole system was slowly shutting down and her body was struggling to keep up. She had no words, just a nauseating feeling of her world collapsing around her, as one by one, she felt the dominos of her life topple over.

"Sure," was the only thing she could manage to muster before she drained the bottom of her glass, or she would have had it not already been empty. Not only did her son hate her but the one thing left in her life that served as a reminder of all the amazing times she'd shared with Eli was closing, stripping her of the last tether she held on to.

"Are you sure you're alright?" Dot's voice sounded distant, even though she felt as though she was practically on top of her.

"Sure." She was starting to skip like a broken record, and she certainly felt more broken than ever. She could feel her life slipping through her fingers. In a month, she'd somehow managed to build back what small bond was left between her and her son, and find a purpose again at the Old Mill, doing something that made her happy for the first time in a long time. Then she managed to ruin it all again in one night.

Perhaps she shouldn't have been surprised, knowing that at the end of the day she wasn't destined for a good life. She just continuously destroyed things. It was the reason she never wanted to have any kids in the first place. She was so afraid that she would mess up their lives, but Eli convinced her that she had something to offer a child. She knew now, she only had something to offer a child if it was with him, because he always knew how to bring the best out in her.

Without Eli, she was a shell of who she could be. They had been the perfect team and now with only her around to manage their lives, she had barely managed to keep her head above water and now she was fully submerged, and sinking.

Charlotte watched from the side of the room, her stomach in knots as she tried to keep what she thought was a smile plastered on her face, listening to Dot say what she was sure was an emotional farewell to the town she'd been a part of for the past fifteen years. She heard words like, "life-changing" and "gratitude". It was undoubtably a well-delivered speech that summed up the feeling of pride from a thankful woman, ready to experience the next chapter of her life. But Charlotte missed all of it. Her mind was so loud she barely heard Noah shouting.

"Bear? Bear!"

Charlotte managed to pull herself out of her misery long enough to see Henry running over to Noah, who was kneeling over Bear, looking as though he was sleeping under the table with a pool of vomit on the floor. The room fell silent as everyone watched Henry pick Bear up in his arms before rushing out of the store with Noah and Dot behind him.

33

Dot

"Any news?" Charlotte asked when she stepped into the kitchen, looking around presumably to see if Noah was in there as well.

He was not. Dot hadn't seen him all morning, not since they'd got home from the emergency vet clinic late the night before. She hoped he was trying to get a little sleep, something she herself should have been doing but was unable to. She'd woken that morning at 4 a.m., well before her alarm clock was set to go off.

"Nothing yet. But the vet said he would need to watch him for the night, then take some more tests today," Dot said solemnly. She'd been holding onto the tiny piece of optimism that told her if she wasn't hearing from the vet, it was likely a good thing. She would be keeping her phone tight to her today.

"That is good news, I suppose," Charlotte said, sitting at the island while Dot poured her a cup of coffee. "Thanks."

"I appreciate you staying to close up last night. Sorry we just ran off," Dot said, though truthfully, she had more things on her mind than the store. Still, having someone able to stick around and make sure everything was in order was a small blessing she was happy about.

"Of course. I'm just sorry I couldn't be there for you," Charlotte said, but something in the way she was carrying herself that morning made Dot feel as though she was happy to have had the distraction.

"I'm also sorry to hit you with the news about the Old Mill. That wasn't fair. I should have told you ear—"

"It's fine. I probably could have handled a lot of things better last night and I am sure that I will have a lot to clean up over the next couple days, assuming I can," Charlotte said as she pinched the bridge of her nose.

"I'm sure you will sort it all out, love," Dot said, giving her as much of a smile as she could muster that morning. She hoped it conveyed the sympathy she was reaching for, though she could tell Charlotte wasn't paying too much attention to her.

"Poor Bear," Charlotte said, shaking her head. "How was… umm, did…?" She couldn't get the words out, but Dot picked up her meaning as she tilted her head toward Noah's room.

"He was sad. But Henry managed to talk to him a little while I was in with the vet. It seemed to help."

"Good," Charlotte said, letting out a weighted breath that carried more than any words could have.

"What happened? With—?" Dot nodded to Noah's room.

"He didn't tell you?" Charlotte asked, and Dot shook her head. "I really made a mess of things, I guess."

"I hope it wasn't the tree event. You know, before things took a turn, I thought it was going really well," Dot offered, but it did little to cheer Charlotte up. Noah hadn't told Dot anything about what had happened with Charlotte. Dot would have liked to know more but even now, her mind drifted back to Bear and how much she needed him to be alright.

Next to the Old Mill, Bear had been the only other thing to have helped Dot alleviate the loneliness she'd felt when she'd first moved to town. She could still hear Eli telling her how terrible of an idea it was for her to buy a puppy. But Eli didn't understand what it was like to be alone, and although she knew it was going to come with its own set of challenges, which it had, Bear had been such a pivotal connection in Dot's growth over the years, it would be impossible to explain to someone else what he'd meant to her.

It didn't mean that it was always easy, and the early days of trying to start a small business and look after a new dog had left her with some very sleepless nights. She'd been exhausted and it had challenged her in a way she didn't think she was capable of handling anymore.

But eventually, Bear got older, the store became easier to run, and life fell into a smooth rhythm that reaffirmed Dot was not incapable of change. Change was an inevitability, and she supposed that was why she was ready for one now. Despite being fifteen years older than she'd been when she got divorced and uprooted her life to St Martins, Dot knew she was still young enough to change again. This time into, hopefully, something with a little more rest and relaxation.

She never suspected that change could be without Bear. She knew he was old and she felt this particularly over the last couple of years. But that didn't mean she was ready for it to happen.

All dog owners knew eventually their dogs would break

their hearts. It was their blessing and their curse. To love another living being knowing it will be for such a short time is not for the faint of heart.

Deep down, Dot had hoped that Bear would be there to help her start her next journey, to help her through that first and hardest part of any transition. But the reality that he might not was only just starting to sink in and if she was being honest with herself, she was terrified.

"It wasn't the event. Honestly, I was surprised myself at how well it was going." Charlotte laughed as Dot was happily pulled back to the present. "It was, well, umm…"

Dot remained silent, giving Charlotte the space to say whatever it was that had set her off the night before, assuming she was ready to talk about it.

"I lost my job," she finally said, shaking her head as it dropped to study her feet tucked in under the high stool at the island.

"I'm sorry, love," Dot said, knowing for herself that at times like these, there was usually not much anyone could say to fix the problem, and what she needed was just a little support. If she needed anything more than that then she would have to trust Charlotte to ask her for it.

"Thanks," Charlotte said. "I feel like the truth is, I think I saw it coming for some time but never really wanted to admit to myself that it was happening. I just didn't think I could handle another thing falling apart."

"Things are not falling apart, Charlotte. They are changing. You won't know if things are changing for the better or the worse until all the pieces are played."

"You can't honestly believe that?" Charlotte said, sounding more incredulous than Dot would have imagined.

"Yes. I do," Dot said, not having to give it thought at all. She knew from her own experience that even the worst things happening to you could offer you a perspective you never knew was possible.

"But what about—"

"Eli?" Dot offered, and Charlotte gave her a nod. "I'll admit that was not an easy thing to deal with, and I wouldn't wish that situation on anyone. I miss him and still think about him every day. But Eli wasn't the kind of person who let life pass him by. He made the most of everything he did."

"He did, didn't he." Charlotte smiled.

"Yes. Which is why I doubt that he would want any of us using him as an excuse not to live our own lives."

"I just don't know how to do all of this without him," Charlotte said, her arms gesturing symbolically around the room.

"The same way you did it with him. One day at a time, relying on the people you have in your life to support you when they can. Just because he isn't here doesn't mean you're alone, Charlotte."

"Feels like I am. Sometimes, at least," she said, tilting her head, a hint of a smile creasing her lips.

"I'm sure it does."

"He was just so… good at this."

"No, he wasn't." Dot laughed and the sudden outburst startled Charlotte. "Sorry. It's just… He really wasn't. He used to call me all the time, telling me he wished he was more like you, how you kept everything together and he just felt like he was messing it all up."

"What!?" Charlotte shouted, shaking her head adamantly. "No, he didn't."

"Oh yes, he did! He would be so down on himself, trying to figure out how he could do more, help out, or organize things. He was a mess."

"You're just trying to make me feel better."

"No. I'm not." Dot said, careful to keep her tone even. If nothing else, she needed Charlotte to understand that whatever she believed was just her perception, it was not the actual truth. Dot recalled endless calls from Eli, wondering how on earth he was supposed to step up even half as much as Charlotte had. She was the organized one who made sure their life was in order, while he felt like the fool trying his best not to let her realize just how useless he was.

"He admired you. How you made sure you were all taken care of. He only wished he had half as much determination as you did. He always said the only thing stopping you from taking over the world was the confidence to pull it off. That if you had his blind confidence, there was nothing you couldn't do."

"He did have an abundance of confidence," Charlotte mused. "Remember when he wanted to sand the floors at the Old Mill?"

"Absolutely." Dot laughed. "I still have the rivets in the wood as a reminder."

"He'd never touched a tool in his life, let alone an industrial sander."

"But he did it. More or less," she added after some thought.

"Yeah, more or less," Charlotte said softly, and without warning, memories of Eli flashed in Dot's mind. Things she hadn't thought about in ages. The first time she'd taken him out skating or when she'd tried to teach him to bake, but he lacked any ability to follow instructions. Or when he'd told her she was going to be a grandmother.

"I miss him so much," Charlotte said, her eyes red and puffy as she fought back tears that desperately wanted to come out. But as always, Charlotte remained strong, even in her weakest moments. A trait Dot admired in her daughter-in-law, but also knew it wasn't necessary, at least not around her.

Before Charlotte had a chance to put up her walls again, Dot walked around the table and embraced her.

"Me too," she said softly.

The two women hugged for a long time and Dot had never felt more grateful for the chance to share in her grief with someone else. It wasn't that she and Charlotte didn't get along, but in the past, Dot had always felt like Charlotte was a little guarded, especially around her. A feeling that had only grown stronger since Eli passed away. She'd always assumed it was because of something she'd done or not done in the past.

Eli had promised her this wasn't true, that it was just Charlotte's way of protecting herself. She rarely let people past her walls because she hated feeling vulnerable. Dot had assumed this was all something he just told her to make her feel better. But having Charlotte here this month and seeing her slowly open her world to Dot, she was beginning to understand exactly what Eli was talking about.

"You," Dot said, feeling her fingers grip Charlotte's shoulders firmly, "are going to be alright. Because you're a smart and strong woman who cares so much about that boy."

"You mean that boy who hates me?"

"He doesn't hate you," Dot said.

"No. He does. He told me in no uncertain words last night."

"He's a kid, Charlotte," Dot chuckled to herself. "He's going to hate you a lot. Then love you. And need you. Then hate you again. You just need to be there for him."

"I just feel like he doesn't want me there."

"Maybe. But he will. I promise." Dot leaned over to give Charlotte a kiss on the forehead. "Just like you'll always have me."

"I don't know. I show up for less than a month and you decide to close your doors," Charlotte joked.

"Oh please. I decided that long before you and Noah got here."

"Why are you closing, Dot? I thought you loved it?" Charlotte asked.

"I do," Dot said evenly, "I'm just not sure I love it as much as I used to and if I am going to go out, I want to go out on a high."

"I can understand that," Charlotte said, nodding, but her face said a world of other things. "It's just…"

"What?" Dot asked, forcing Charlotte to look up at her. "Tell me."

"It's stupid." Charlotte laughed. "I just kinda always thought it would be around, you know?"

"Maybe we're all just in need of a little change?" Dot offered hoping that it was a touch of the comfort Charlotte needed.

"Well shit," Charlotte said. "At least you're getting to decide you need the change."

"Maybe some of us need a bit of a push," Dot said, her words causing Charlotte to snort unexpectedly, sending a ripple of laughter between them.

Not for the first time, Dot considered the relationship between sadness and joy and how the two weren't all that distant from one another.

34

Noah

"Do you need any help?" Noah asked, knowing the answer even before Cally brushed him off and walked away with a stack of quiches ready for the display table. He knew this was going to be her response because consistent avoidance had been the only thing he managed to get out of her that entire morning.

He didn't want to be anywhere near the Old Mill, not after everything that had happened the night before. Somehow in one night, all of the happy feelings that had surrounded the building had vanished and what was left was utterly uncomfortable.

He'd gone so far as to pretend that he was sick, but Nana had seen right through it. He'd tried to use Bear as his excuse, which wasn't all too far off reality since he hated the fact that they'd still not received word on how he was doing. But since Bear had been Nana's dog and she was going into work, he could hardly claim it was too much for him.

Everything about that morning had been off. He wasn't sure what he was expecting. It certainly hadn't been Charlotte and

Nana hugging in the kitchen when he'd finally managed to climb out of bed. The whole thing seemed to be a very special moment, so it only seemed right to interrupt it. After all, as far as Noah was concerned, Charlotte deserved to feel bad. Not only did she lie about everything, but she tried to pretend like it was all Noah's fault.

He supposed that was what really stung the most about all of this—that she expected him to grow up and be responsible, but when it came time for her to treat him like an adult, she didn't trust him. How was any of that fair?

"Well, I guess I'll just go fold boxes," Noah said, calling after Cally.

"Might as well do something useful," she called back, which might have been a positive sign had it not been for the coldness with which she said it.

"Why don't you help me with these cookies?" Nana said, startling Noah, who thought no one was around him.

"I think I'll stick to the boxes, Nana," Noah said after composing himself a little.

"We have enough boxes." Nana said as she placed a guiding hand on his back. "Come with me. We are going to make some macadamia nut cookies."

Noah hadn't ever made macadamia nut cookies, but he did enjoy eating them. Still, the idea of being in the kitchen with Charlotte and Tia and knowing Cally would be out here stamping cups or folding boxes, or whatever it was Cally did when he wasn't around, only made his desire to crawl into the dark basement and fold or count, or do anything other than be around people, stronger.

"I really don't—"

"In case you forgot, I'm your boss. And your nana. So

basically, you have to do what I say," she said and though there was a clear playfulness in her tone, it left little room for negotiation. She would be expecting him to come and help regardless of what he wanted.

"Fine," he said, slumping his shoulders and following beside her as she dragged him into the kitchen. He'd been avoiding the area all morning, having no desire to see or speak to Charlotte at the moment. She'd tried to talk to him, but he had brushed her off and since then, she had stuck to the kitchen while he stayed in the front or the basement. It made things complicated, especially when Riley asked him to grab items from the kitchen. But thankfully, Cally was always there and looking for any excuse to get away from him.

Despite some small understanding that maybe there was a chance that he was to blame for some of his current situation, it certainly wasn't all his fault and he didn't understand why he was suddenly made to feel like he wasn't welcome. What was he supposed to do? Force Cally to forgive him? Tell Charlotte why he was so mad? None of these things were easy and why should he be the one to have to reach out? He was as much a victim in all of this as anyone.

"You grab the butter and sugar. I'll get the nuts and flour," Nana said, giving him a warm smile and he made a lame attempt to reciprocate it.

"If you want," Noah said with a shrug. From the looks of things, Charlotte wasn't in the kitchen, which was a pleasant surprise.

"I had your mom run out to grab some ingredients we need for some orders this week. Only a few more days left before Christmas," Nana said, and Noah was surprised she caught him looking around the kitchen for her. He was happy

Charlotte wasn't there, but he didn't want Nana to think that was why he didn't want to come back here. Even if it was.

"What are you making, Tia?" Noah asked, grabbing the bins of sugar and heading over to the table. Tia was off in the back of the kitchen, cutting designs in the tops of some recently covered pies.

"Chicken curry pot pies," she said, biting down on her tongue, which was sticking out of the side of her mouth, in deep concentration as she carved intricate designs in the top of the pie.

"You know it's not a Picasso," Nana said with a laugh.

"Not all of us find this as easy as you do, Dot," Tia said, tilting her head to examine her work. She must have been satisfied as she continued on to the next pie.

"Practise, practise, practise," Nana said.

"You said that three years ago. And I won't lie, I think I'm getting worse."

"You're becoming more critical of your work, Tia. Because I can tell you right now, you are not worse," Nana said as she rummaged through a shelf before pulling out a large bottle of vanilla paste. Noah caught the smile Tia give Nana, though she didn't say anything else.

"Did you know Nana was getting rid of the Old Mill?" Noah asked, regretting the question the moment he asked it, especially when Tia looked at him and then at Nana, before ducking her head back into her work.

"I did. She let Riley and me know so we could start looking for other jobs," Tia said and Noah was surprised she didn't seem angrier about the whole thing. After all, she'd supposedly been a part of the Old Mill for years. Surely, she would be devastated by the news. But from the way she appeared now, Noah wondered if she even cared.

"You don't seem too bothered by it," Noah said.

"Noah!" Dot said and Noah figured he'd crossed a line but that didn't mean he didn't want to know. Surely, this place had to mean something to people? Before everything had fallen apart the night before, Noah had witnessed it for himself what it meant to the community and was even beginning to enjoy it here himself. If it hadn't been for Bear's collapse and Charlotte's betrayal, Noah was confident everything would have been great.

"What?" Noah said, trying to sound like it wasn't a big deal. Because apparently, it wasn't to anyone else. "Wait, did Cally not know?" Noah asked, suddenly realizing she wasn't listed in the people that knew. He wondered if she was as blindsided by all of this as he was, in which case, maybe it wasn't just him she was upset about.

"We thought it was best to wait to tell Cally. Although I suspect Riley let her know at some point before I announced it. Same as your mom," Nana said.

"So, you told Mom last night?" Noah asked.

"I did. Though I don't think she handled the news all that well," Nana said with a grim smile.

Noah knew that even if she had found out about the Old Mill last night, he doubted that was the only thing that had been bothering her. Their own conversation replayed in his mind like a bad record, but each time, he found it difficult to change how he felt.

"So why keep everyone in the dark?" Noah asked, feeling a sudden urge to take his frustrations out on someone else, even if they didn't really deserve it.

"Noah!" Tia stopped her work to look up at him, waving a

knife in his direction. "I hardly think that's fair."

"No, he's right," Nana said with a sigh. "I made a choice not to tell people."

"Yeah. See," Noah said, giving Tia a smug look.

She rolled her eyes and went back to cutting her pies. "Doesn't mean you're not being a weenie," she muttered under her breath.

"Hey!" Noah shouted as he grabbed a scale for them to start measuring out their ingredients.

"Well, you're both right," Nana said, catching Noah a little by surprise. He wasn't used to her not always being on his side and he wasn't sure he enjoyed it very much.

"But you said—" Noah began but was stopped by Nana's raised hand.

"I know what I said," she said quickly. "I made a choice, but it was my choice to make. I understood that maybe it wasn't the best way to announce shutting down the Old Mill. But you have to understand how difficult that decision was for me, Noah. This place has been like a baby to me for the past fifteen years, and now I am going to shut its doors for good. That is really hard for me and the last thing I needed was more people telling me how hard that was going to be on them. I came to this decision on my own because I feel like what I need right now is to focus on the next chapter of my life. I can't do that while I am here every day trying to keep this place running."

"But Tia could run it," Noah offered. "Couldn't you, Tia?"

"Ha." She laughed. "Maybe if we had more hands. This little town is great for many things but housing talent capable enough to fill Dot's shoes would be difficult. No. After this, I suppose I'll go into the city, test my skills in one of the restaurants there. Maybe even start my own?" Tia said and Noah got the impression she was trying really hard to feel excited by the prospect, though she wasn't very good at selling it.

"You don't want to do that," Noah said.

"Sometimes, what's best for us isn't always doing what we want to do," Tia said with a shrug. "It's one of the ways we grow."

"But—"

"Noah," Nana said. Her voice was more assertive than usual but still held a tone that suggested she was talking to a child, and maybe if Noah wasn't so caught up in trying to understand why all of this was happening, he might have heard it himself. But he was confused and still angry from the night before and if he was being honest, all he wanted to do was let out his frustration—which unfortunately, at the moment, was directed towards Nana and Tia.

"Fine. Just give up on this place. Who cares," Noah said, slamming the stick of butter he was holding on the table.

"Hold on," Dot placed a firm her hand on Noah's shoulder and turned him to face her, "You just stop that talk right now, Noah. I understand that this has been a rough year for you and your mom. But don't you think for a second that it hasn't been hard for me too. Your dad was my son, and when he died, it broke my heart." Nana's voice caught for a second as she looked away before once again meeting Noah's eye. "When I bought this place, everyone thought I was crazy, but your dad knew that it was my dream. So he supported me. He and your mom would drive up on their weekends and help me rip out walls and sand floors. The only reason I was able to start any of this is because the two of them gave up so much of their time to come and help me. Even after you were born, your mom would be up here on weekends. You would be bundled up in your stroller in the corner, right there," she said, gesturing to the side of the room. "And she would be making filling and pie crust while your dad was trying to fix whatever had fallen apart that week or needed doing—the kitchen sinks, bathroom, setting up signs. Everywhere I look in this store, I see him. You understand what I mean, don't you?"

Noah knew exactly what she was talking about. It was one of the reasons he found living in their apartment to be so hard, but it was still where he remembered him and that made Noah feel like he couldn't leave.

"I do and we're about to lose the one place that holds all of the memories we had with him. It's the only place I've ever lived and now because of Charlotte, we're going to lose the apartment and he's going to be gone for good," Noah said, and he hated that he could feel tears coming down his cheeks. He wiped them away, wishing he could be stronger than he was.

"It's okay to be sad, Noah," Nana gave his shoulders a light squeeze before using the sleeve of her shirt to wipe at his eyes. "Just like it is important to remember that those memories of your father don't go away because you no longer live at your house. You will always remember the important things, no matter where you are in the world."

"But what if I don't want to be anywhere else in the world? What if I'm not ready to leave?" Noah asked, feeling his chest tighten at the thought.

"Change isn't something you should be afraid of, Noah," Nana said with a smile. "Change is an inevitability in life, whether we are ready for it or not. Change offers us new perspective and more importantly, it gives us new goals to work toward. You're not the boy you were a year ago, and you will be someone completely new in a few more years. That isn't a bad thing. So long as you stay true to yourself and give space to the people in your life who you care for and who care for you."

Nana's words floated in the air around him as he questioned himself and his actions over the last couple of days. He'd somehow managed to push all the people in his life away and if he was being honest, he was pretty sure he understood why none of them wanted to talk to him. He'd been mean.

"What if I ruined everything?" he asked.

"Oh, love," Nana said, sniffling slightly as she chuckled to herself, "I'm willing to bet that you didn't ruin anything."

"I did, though."

"Noah," Nana said, holding him firmly in her arms. "The only way you ruin things is when you refuse to accept when you're wrong. There are very few things in this world that can't be resolved by being honest with yourself about what you could have handled better, then offering a good apology."

"What if I don't think I was wrong? What if I think I have every right to be angry?" he asked, knowing full well that there were things he said that he meant, and why should he have to apologise for what other people did wrong?

"You're right. But an apology isn't for the other person. It's for you. It's an opportunity to change the way you feel about a situation. To make yourself proud of the person you are."

"But how's that fair? Why should I apologise and take the blame?" Noah asked, feeling like this line of thought was becoming more confusing to him. Perhaps he could understand wanting to feel better by apologizing but it wasn't all his fault.

"You're not taking the blame, Noah. You're acknowledging where *you* were wrong. After all, it's your life, and only you get to decide how you want to live it. Just like everyone else has to decide how they live theirs."

Noah thought about this, already feeling as though he knew what he had to do. But first, "I'm sorry I got mad about you selling the Old Mill," Noah said softly. "I think… I don't know… I just think this place is really special. You know?" Noah wrapped his arms around Nana and gave her a big hug, "Thank you."

"You're welcome."

"And I'm sorry, Tia," Noah said, turning to look at the young woman still carving the tops of the pies, pausing briefly to wipe at her eyes. "I think you'll make a great chef!" he added.

"Thanks, buddy," Tia said, looking over at him and wiping her eyes again. "Bloody onions."

35

Charlotte

The weekend passed and thankfully, Charlotte had managed to get through it without any breakdowns, although her stomach was still tied up in a million knots which threatened to make her throw up at any moment. Remarkably, she managed to keep that in as well.

She was having a difficult time remembering the last time, or if there had ever been a time, where she had felt so embarrassed by her actions. Even now, she wasn't overly confident about what had happened on that Friday night.

Somewhere between being told she was the worst mother of all time, Dot breaking the news about the Old Mill, and Bear collapsing on the ground, Charlotte fell into default mode.

She'd managed to assist Riley and Cally with getting everyone settled up, the kids decorations all hung up, and everyone out the door as planned. Not that she could recall any of that. All she could remember was the look on Noah's face as he confronted her about why they were really in St Martins.

She wasn't sure her heart could take another confrontation with him and so mercifully, for the past two days, she'd managed to occupy herself well enough so as to avoid him, since it was clear she was the last person on earth her son wanted to see.

After all, he'd made it quite clear that he did, in fact, hate her. That was all the proof she needed to know that deep down, she was single-handedly the worst mother on this planet. Not only did her son have to deal with the death of his father—he had to live with a mother who could never be the person he needed her to be.

As if this realization wasn't bad enough, Charlotte had entered the kitchen that morning, hoping she might be able to make an early escape to the Old Mill, where she could bury her head into work and baking and trying to think of anything other than the absolute shit storm she had created in her family. However, it appeared Dot had her own thoughts on the matter, as outlined in the note she'd left her in the kitchen.

I've gone into the shop to prep for tomorrow. Should be fine with just Tia this morning – feel free to sleep in and come in the afternoon. Expecting news about Bear today so please stay by the phone, and while you're home, maybe you can set up the living room for Christmas. You still have a few boxes left to unpack, and it would be a waste to not set them up now.

Best, Dot

"Well, damn," Charlotte said, tapping the island countertop with her fingers as she tried to figure out how in the world she was going to make this happen. She doubted Noah was going to just turn around suddenly and start helping her put up Christmas decorations. Not after she'd systematically ruined Christmas.

One thing was for certain. None of this was going to be

easier without coffee and since she apparently had nowhere to be, she got to work making some.

By the time her morning French press had finished, she'd decided the only course of action was to get a move on with her life. There was little point in sitting around and feeling sorry for herself, not when she was perfectly capable of feeling sorry for herself while being mildly productive. Of course, that meant doing as Dot suggested and going through the rest of the boxes of Christmas stuff she and Noah had brought from Toronto.

Somewhere deep within her overwhelming languishing, Charlotte did have many emotions surrounding opening the boxes of Christmas stuff. It had been too hard the year before to open anything up, and so she and Noah had decided that it might be worthwhile to take the year off from Christmas. Well, she had decided, and Noah went along for the ride. It just felt like too much to have to go through all their family belongings so soon after Eli's death. Even now, Charlotte didn't love the idea, but at least they weren't going to be in the apartment alone. Despite everything going on between her and Noah, she couldn't deny how wonderful it had been, at least for the briefest of moments, to have other people in their life to surround them.

Toronto had always been a place where anything could happen at any moment, and when she and Eli had first moved there, the opportunities had been endless. Amazing food, art, theatre, along with a nearly endless supply of concerts and shows that you couldn't get anywhere else. It was like a dream for two kids living in the world on their own for the first time. But eventually, as all dreams seem to do, things change. Things get complicated.

"Hi," Noah said, walking into the kitchen, causing Charlotte to nearly jump out of her skin. She supposed she shouldn't have been surprised, but she was.

"You're up early," she said, staring at the hot water in with her coffee grounds, trying to act as normal as possible and not like the pair of them hadn't talked for the past two days.

"Feels like I slept in," Noah said, going to the fridge and grabbing the orange juice from inside.

"I suppose you have been getting up early this month. Sorry," Charlotte said, looking over at the clock showing that it was just past seven.

"Don't be. I kind of like getting up early," Noah said, using a small stool to reach up and grab a glass from one of the cupboards.

That's good, Charlotte thought, feeling the makeshift conversation coming to a natural head and unsure of what to say next. She supposed she could always go with a more sincere apology, take the blame for why they left home and why she made him work in a shop for a month because she couldn't face telling him the truth. Tell him that all she wanted was for them to have a relatively okay Christmas before she once again destroyed her son's world and made him uproot everything just because she wasn't able to handle things on her own.

But none of that came naturally for her and instead, she grabbed the French press and moved silently into the living room where Dot had placed the remaining boxes they'd brought with them on the floor, along with one of her own, it looked like.

"What are you doing?" Noah asked, surprising Charlotte again with any form of conversation.

"Nana said she didn't need my help in the store this morning and suggested getting things set up for Christmas. These were the last of the boxes. The ones we didn't get to the other night."

"I still can't believe you managed to get them all in the trunk." Noah chuckled as he poured himself a glass of orange juice.

"It was tight." Charlotte joked. "It was a lot I suppose."

"A lot is being asked to leave the moment you get up." Noah's words stung but she knew deep down he was right. It was a terrible way to handle things, but at the time, she'd felt as though she was at her wit's end and just needed to go.

"I'm sorry about that. I didn't mean—"

"It doesn't matter." Noah sighed, which was almost worse than him getting mad at her. She remembered when her own indifference started with her parents and how that initiated the end of whatever relationship she'd had with them. She refused to let that happened to her with her only son. But before she had a chance to interject, Noah was walking over toward her. "You want help with the boxes?"

"Yeah… sure," Charlotte said, wondering when she would stop being surprised that morning. She hoped never but knew sooner or later, her luck was bound to run out. "Only if you want to," she added quickly.

"Yeah. I mean, what else am I supposed to do?"

"Anything you want." Charlotte suggested.

"The last time we opened these was with Dad," Noah said, looking down at the boxes, completely ignoring Charlotte's offer to leave.

"I would understand if you didn't want—"

"Not opening them isn't going to make him come back," Noah said.

Charlotte felt the knots in her stomach tighten up. She

busied herself by pressing down the French press, trying to return herself too normal. Or as normal as she was likely to get.

"No, it won't," she said, focusing on her coffee and not her son, since only one of them was likely to make her feel better that morning.

"I just mean… it's Christmas. What are we supposed to do, never celebrate it again? He would have hated that," Noah said.

Charlotte forced herself to look up at him and noticed he was looking back at her.

"He did love Christmas," Charlotte said, allowing herself a little joy at the memory of Eli.

"You both did," Noah said, crossing his legs and sitting down beside the boxes. "I remember how excited you two would get. How the two of you tried to sneak a tree into the building on November first because neither of you wanted to ask if you were allowed to have trees in the building. Better to beg forgiveness…"

"Than ask permission," Charlotte said. "But only about trees. Not with me."

"I hardly think now is your moment to be trying to lecture me on what's fair," Noah said, shaking his head at Charlotte.

"Fair enough," Charlotte said, raising her hands up in defence. "To be honest, I'm just happy you're even talking to me."

"Well, Bear's not here and talking to yourself gets a little weird after a while. So, I'm out of options really," Noah said, taking the top off one of the boxes and laying it beside him before looking up at Charlotte, who must have worn a stunned look on her face because he cracked a smile. "I'm kidding. You're my mom. What am I supposed to do? Not talk to you?"

"I think you have every right not to," Charlotte said, pulling the top off the other box beside her as she began pretending to rummage through it, all the while trying to build up the courage to say everything she wanted—no, needed—to say to Noah.

"I'm sorry."

The words came out and settled in the air between them like a buoy tossed out to a drowning person, that last bit of lifeline waiting for them to grab hold and pull themselves to safety. The only problem was it was tossed by the wrong person. Because it wasn't Charlotte who said it.

"What?" Her face must have confused him as much as his words had confused her, because he barreled through his meaning, not bothering to stop for breath.

"I shouldn't have said I hate you. I don't hate you. I was just angry, and mad, I guess. I don't know, I think for a moment, I did actually hate you, but it was just for the moment, not for all time, like for the rest of my life, and now you don't want to talk to me and I'm sorry, I'm so sorry."

His words fell out of him like a waterfall and each one pounded into Charlotte, washing over her in waves as she grappled to make sense of what was happening. How Noah could feel like any of this was his fault hurt her more than any words ever could. Her mind was failing her and, in that moment, she did the only thing she could think of—she hugged him.

She squeezed his little body so hard, feeling it tense in her arms, feeling his big heart beat against her chest until slowly, his body eased into hers. He was sobbing, or rather, they both were. Her own chest was heaving now as she choked back sobs. Her tears fell freely until her voice managed to crawl its way back, saying the words that took too long to come.

"I'm sorry. You have no reason to apologise to me, Noah. What I did, it was wrong. I lied to you and I made you feel like leaving was your fault and it wasn't. It was mine. I was so ashamed of letting you down, of letting your father down. I promised I would take care of you and all I've done is ruin everything. I couldn't even get through a year without him." She sniffled and her discomfort turned to mild amusement at how pathetic she felt. She held him tightly in her arms for a long moment until she had enough courage to finally look him in the eyes. "You are not the problem here. I am."

"I'm not mad that you blamed me," Noah said, his gaze not leaving her.

"What?" Charlotte said as Noah reached up and wiped her eyes with the sleeve of his shirt, which only caused more tears to run out of them.

"You said I was mad that you blamed me. And I guess maybe I was a little mad, but honestly, I was just upset that you never told me. You always told me we could share anything with each other. But then you didn't," Noah said. "That hurt."

"You're right," Charlotte said, feeling somehow both horrifically disappointed in herself and tremendously proud of her son in the same moment, creating a real juxtaposition of emotions. "I did say that. I wasn't honest with you. I should have trusted you'd be able to handle it. With everything that's happened, I just wanted to protect you from this."

"You think keeping me in the dark while you suffer in the background protects me?" Noah said.

"When you say it like that, no. No, it doesn't." She was

unsure if having a him explain it in such a blunt fashion stunted the blow or made it worse. Once again, waves of pride and embarrassment washed over her.

The pair looked at each other for a long moment before Noah broke off and began looking through his box, picking out different things.

"We brought so much stuff." Noah laughed.

"I didn't know what to bring so I brought everything." Charlotte shrugged.

The pair searched through the boxes, and Charlotte was beginning to feel like a small part of herself was being put back together. A piece she wasn't sure would ever be able to be restored. Maybe it was because Charlotte always believed that her luck had run its course when she and Eli had met.

Charlotte never imagined a world where she could love another human as much as she did Eli. Her life had always been filled with people on the fringe, considering the people that were supposed to love her the most only saw her for the worst of what they saw in one another. But then Eli came along and began picking away at her, revealing all the truly wonderful things about herself that she'd never realized were there. Only then he was taken from her, and she began to think all those things he had unearthed disappeared along with him. But she had Noah. And Dot. And for the first time in a long time, Charlotte felt hopeful.

"What are we going to do?" Noah asked. "When we go home?" he clarified when Charlotte wasn't prepared with an answer.

"I don't know," she said, feeling like honesty was the only course she could take, even if it meant admitting her weakness. "But I promise we will figure it out together," she said, finding it surprisingly easy to match the brave smile Noah was giving her.

"Yeah, we will," he said with a blind confidence that reminded her so much of Eli that it threatened to break her heart all over again, had it not been for the phone going off in the kitchen.

"Yeah, we will," she said, standing to get the phone. "Hold on. See if you can't find anything worth putting up in those." She smiled to him as she walked away, taking a moment to wipe her eyes and compose herself as she picked up the phone. "Hello?" she said. "Oh hi, yeah, I heard you might call. How is he?"

The vet on the other line began describing Bear's condition. She watched Noah's ears, as he held on to an old-looking elf on a ladder, perk up at the mention of the old dog.

"Great news. I'll let her know," Charlotte said with a grin as she hung up the phone.

"Bear?" Noah asked, sounding hopeful.

"Yes. It sounds like he had to have emergency surgery, which Dot did not tell us about, for severe bloating. I guess his intestines were all twisted up. But they fixed the problem and said he is making a good recovery. They will need to keep him for observation for another night but they don't see why he shouldn't be home by tomorrow, albeit heavily medicated," Charlotte said, watching as relief passed over Noah's face. Though he may not admit it, Charlotte knew he had become quite taken with the dog over the past month and if she was being honest with herself, the idea of losing him now would not be something any of them could take.

"Good," Noah said, letting out a sigh of relief.

"I'll call Dot and let her know the good news," Charlotte

said, picking up the phone to dial the shop.

"Mom," Noah said, standing up, "I really want to help you go through this stuff, but do you think maybe it would be okay if I went and did something quick?"

"What do you need to do?"

"If it's alright with you, I would like to handle this one on my own," Noah said, his face turning a slight shade of pink Charlotte hadn't seen on him before.

After feeling as though she'd lost her son and was now in the process of getting him back, a massive part of her wanted time to stand still. Surely whatever it was could wait until later. But that would be selfish and after the courage he showed her this morning, Charlotte knew that if there was something he needed to do, there was nothing she was going to say to prevent him. Her only course of action was to trust that he knew what he was doing.

"You sure you don't need help?" Charlotte asked in a last-ditch effort to hold on to the little boy who needed her for everything. Inside though, she knew that boy was gone and for better or worse, she was the one who had sent him on his way. All she could do now was be a supportive spectator. *At least until he asked.*

"No. I need to do this myself," Noah said, and she appreciated how sure he was of himself.

"Of course. We can do the boxes later," she said.

"Thanks, Mom."

Charlotte watched him gather his things and run out the door, knowing whether she liked it or not, something had changed.

36

Noah

Noah ran down the street, playing this big, elaborate scene out in his head as he did. One where he would run into the school, barge into Cally's class and start apologising. There were a few hurdles with the scenario, the first being that Cally wasn't in school since it was the holidays.

The second was all the embarrassing images that no matter how he played them out in his mind, never seemed to shy away from weird. His only saving grace was it wasn't his school and therefore no one would know who he was other than Cally, who may never talk to him again after embarrassing her like that.

He'd barely made it down the block before realizing that option number one was off the table. That meant option number two, which was to go to her house. But since the pair had only ever met at the Old Mill or the park, Noah had no idea where she lived.

This meant a tiny detour to the Old Mill to see Nana, who he found in the kitchen baking when he ran in and made his request. She tried to ask him questions which he managed to evade since he still didn't know what he was doing. He wasn't about to go laying out his plan before he got there. *No, it will be better to see her and then I'll know exactly what to do.*

His loose plan began to take form when he knocked on the yellow wooden door of a small apartment in a larger house.

"Noah?" Riley asked, looking around as if expecting to see someone with him. But she would not be finding anyone today, since what Noah needed to do, he had to do on his own.

"Hi, Riley. I was wondering if Cally was here?" he asked, his voice creaking a little but finding its place as he worked through the sentence.

"Sorry bud, she's out somewhere. The park, I think? Said something about ice sliding?"

Noah didn't wait for her to finish before he was off again.

"Thanks," he called back.

"Can you tell her to be home by five?" she shouted after him.

"Yep!" he called back as he started to jog again, though it was beginning to look more like a brisk walk since his initial run had already had one too many detours and it was hardly easy to run on the iced-up sidewalks. But at least now he had a location, or he hoped he did.

By the time he reached the park where they'd gone sliding the week before, Noah's run had dwindled to a full-fledged walk as he huffed in the cold air, which was hardly making his breathing any better.

He stood at the side of the park, looking around, focusing on the hills where the tubes were going down. It was a nice day and the park was crowded with kids all trying to make the most of what little time they had off from school, and a sunny day. If Noah hadn't been there for a specific reason, he might have found the whole thing fun. But he didn't have any friends in this town besides Cally and he had hoped he hadn't destroyed that the other night. *Stay positive, Noah!*

He'd been repeating that mantra to himself since the running-around portion of the journey had taken so long, causing him to second-guess and overthink every little thing he was doing.

What if she just thought he was weird and never wanted to talk to him again? What if she wasn't willing to forgive him? Or worse, what if he was running up to her, he slipped on ice and tackled her to the ground, the weight of his body slamming into her legs and breaking them, and she was forced to walk on crutches for Christmas, and she let everyone in town sign her cast except for him?

He had his doubts about the last one, but still, stranger things had happened. He once went to school with a guy who tried to ask a girl to a school dance but ended up tripping on his shoelace and stabbing her in the side of the head with his pencil. He ended up going to the school dance alone and people still hold their hands up around him when he's got a pencil, as if they might be his next victim.

No matter how hard he tried to stop them, terrible images of him messing up around Cally persisted in his mind while he searched around the park. There had to be hundreds of kids of all ages in snowsuits running around, while parents sat talking at park benches drinking coffees or whatever parents drank at eleven in the morning during the holidays.

The only thing Noah could think to look for was Cally's knitted, sparkly green hat with a ball hanging off it. He thought it would be easy to spot until he realized she could have a hood up or not be wearing it or—*There!*

Cally stood with a small group of kids at the base of the hill near a high metal fence that, if it were night-time, would have depicted a very large Nativity scene. He remembered that from the last time he was there. But he was stalling. All this time, he'd been thinking about what he would do when he saw her and now the time had come for him to actually go and say something and his stomach was doing backflips and despite it being well below zero, he could feel his palms sweating. He hoped it was just from all the running.

Noah took a deep breath and looked down at his feet, forcing himself to take that first step in her direction, followed by the second and soon enough, he was standing only a short distance away from her while his mind, which only moments before had been running wild, was now silent. He began to wonder if he could even remember his own name.

"Noah?"

That definitely sounded right.

But he heard the name in his head as he looked up to see Cally staring at him, her eyes narrowing with each passing second. He needed to say something before this whole situation became even more awkward than it already was.

"Hi, Cally." Feeling like he could have done better but knowing this was the best he could do in his current situation.

"What are you doing here?" she asked, her guard still up as her friends created an intimidating half-circle around her, as if they were preparing to maul him if he said the wrong thing.

"I came to see you," Noah said as he tried to dig up all the things he wished he could say. *At least I haven't broken her leg.*

"Just wanted to see what I was doing in this sad little town?" Cally said, turning away, her friends following her lead.

"Yes. Wait, no. I mean… yeah, I did come to see you. Because I wanted to, umm…"

"Noah?" Cally said, her foot tapping the snow-packed ice impatiently.

"Right, yeah. It's just…" He paused for a moment, taking a second to take a deep breath before letting the words fall out of him. "I'm sorry. For everything that I said the other night. There was a lot of stuff happening and I said some horrible things. I don't expect you to forgive me, but I just wanted you to know that my intention was never to hurt you and I am sorry that I did." Noah looked at her for a moment as a weight he hadn't realized was pressing down on him dissipated. He'd said what he came to say. He could be proud of that. No matter what happened next. "That's it," he added, desperately trying to read her face, but it was like trying to read a stone.

A couple of breaths later, he turned to leave as something else popped in his mind. "Wait!" he said, startling the group, whose faces were much simpler to read since it was mostly confusion and what he supposed might be mild embarrassment, but he couldn't tell. Or rather, he chose to ignore. "I heard you also found out about the Old Mill that night and I'm sorry. I know how much that place means to you and for what it's worth, I'm disappointed it's going too. I was just starting to like it." Noah chuckled to himself. "Okay, that's it." He turned to leave again.

"Noah, wait," Cally said, and he turned to see her shoulders drop and her head shake. "Thank you for your apology." She took a tentative step toward him. "We were just about to go get a hot chocolate. You want to come?" She gestured to the truck by the edge of the park.

"Really?" Noah asked.

"Sure. Just try not to be too weird around my friends," she said, waving for him to come join them. "Everyone, this is Noah. He works at the Old Mill with me. Well, I work. He basically tries not to mess everything up." She threw an arm around him and the last little bits of torment stuck to him disappeared with the gesture.

To his surprise, Cally's friends were much nicer than he would have imagined. He'd expected them all to have heard what he'd said to Cally, but if they had, they kept it to themselves.

*

"You guys want to hit the slide?" Jasleen asked, waving a hand at them.

Noah, who still hadn't finished his hot chocolate, shook his head and Cally, who had finished her cup, shook her head no as well.

"We'll catch up with you later," Cally said.

"Suit yourself." Jasleen said, before running over to catch up with the rest of the group.

"Cool friends you've got," Noah said when it was just the two of them sitting on the swings. His arms were tucked at his sides, holding his hot chocolate while Cally kicked her feet, swinging beside him.

"Yeah, they're not bad." Cally smiled. "So," she said after what felt like minutes of silence, though, it might have only been seconds. Her feet shoved into the snow, crushing stones as she brought herself to a stop.

"So," Noah said when he couldn't think of anything better to say, taking a sip of his hot chocolate, which was more like lukewarm chocolate now.

"Are you okay?" Cally asked.

"What makes you think anything is wrong?" Noah asked, feeling more defensive than he would have liked.

"Well, I have to assume there was more going on the other night than just you being mean and calling me and this town stupid." Cally shrugged. "But I suppose I could just go on believing the worst of you… if you want."

"No. I don't want that. And yes, it's just a lot was happening with my mom and me. I was mad. I'm not even sure why I said all those things. I mean, I suppose I wanted to hurt her in some way, you know. Like the way she hurt me," Noah said.

"Been there." Cally chuckled to herself and Noah, who maybe at one time would have been upset that she was finding his struggles amusing, was just happy to hear her laugh "I appreciate your apology, even if you did have to stalk me through town to give it." She gave him a cheeky grin.

"I wouldn't say stalked." Noah held up a finger. "I just had a wide search area since I didn't know where you'd be."

"Calm down. I'm only messing with you," she said, rocking her swing sideways to nudge him lightly. "I knew, by the way."

It was so out of the blue, Noah had to think about what in the world she was talking about.

"About the Old Mill. Riley told me shortly after she found out. Made me promise not to tell anyone." She kicked a loose stone in front of her and it shot across the snow and into the wooden barrier.

"You did?" Noah asked.

"Don't sound so surprised. I am good at keeping myself together when I want to be, Noah."

"I'm sure you are. I'm just impressed you didn't say anything to me or Nana."

"Say what? Don't retire? Work here forever? How could

you do this to me?" Cally laughed. "It all seems a little selfish, doesn't it?"

"Sure, maybe. But Riley and Tia, I don't understand why—"

"Dot offered them the store. Tia wasn't sure she could manage it, or if she would ever want to without Dot. And Riley doesn't have the skills to run it on her own. Not like Dot did."

"You don't think Tia would stay on with Riley?" Noah asked.

"I think she is worried that if she owned the store, she would never leave town."

"Doesn't seem too bad."

"Not as stupid as you thought, huh?" Cally jabbed.

"No, it isn't. I kinda like it here, actually," Noah said, finishing the last of his cold hot chocolate.

"It grows on you. When you let it."

"Like a fungus," Noah said, and he felt an actual jab in the arm from Cally.

"Only I get to insult my town," she mused.

"Point taken," Noah said, rubbing his arm. "I'm going to miss having you around so much." Noah said the words before he had a chance to regret them in his mind. "I just mean—"

"I'm going to miss you too, Noah," Cally said, thankfully not giving him the space to double back.

"Weird question, but do you think we would be friends if I lived here?" Noah asked.

"No," Cally said, shrugging it away as if it didn't matter. She looked at him, her brows raised with mock-confusion. "What? You're needy. I mean, you've been here a month and you're already obsessed with me," she said coolly. Noah was shocked but thankfully, she put him out of his misery quickly. "Come on, Noah, I'm joking. Of course we'd be friends. We *are* friends. I mean, I'm sure you will come back here, right? Dot's not moving away. It will suck that we can't hang out at the Old Mill anymore."

"Yeah. I don't see why we wouldn't come back," Noah said, and he hoped this wasn't just a dream he'd concocted in his mind. That somehow, this trip had changed things for him and his mom and that it wouldn't be another five years or whatever until they came for Christmas again. "It's a shame too." He chuckled. "I was just starting to like that place."

"Like" may not have been the best word to describe how he felt about the Old Mill. He wasn't even sure there was a word he knew of that could satisfy his feelings about it all. Baking and cooking, just making food and seeing what it did for the people in his life, he knew this was something he wanted to do forever. He only wished he had more time to learn.

"Wait!" An idea popped into Noah's head. It was wild but maybe given everything that was going on, maybe it wasn't too far out of the box.

"What is it?" Cally asked, her feet kicking off the ground so she could sway softly in the air.

"I think I might have an idea. But I could use some help," he said, raising his brows and looking at Cally's cool expression.

"Argh, fine. But only because you're likely to mess up whatever plan you think you have without me."

"Thanks! I think," he said before leaning in conspiratorially.

37

Dot

December 24th was always one of Dot's favourite days in the store, since it usually signalled the end of her year and it was one of the few times she was able to work in the front and just focus on visiting with the people without thinking about the four hundred other odds and ends she needed to get done when she found the time.

Plus, this year, with both Tia and Charlotte available in the kitchen to not just help finish up the baking but also clean everything down, it meant Dot was able to be out front for even longer.

Although she didn't necessarily need the help, she had decided to invite Riley, Cally and Noah to work as well. She would surely be losing money on the staffing but since they were going to be shutting their doors for good, she thought, like her, they might all want to say their goodbyes as well.

At least she supposed they did, though every time she caught sight of Cally and Noah talking quietly to one another, their eyes were darting periodically in her direction. Dot pretended not to notice and perhaps these kids were good at many things

307

but secrecy was not one of them.

"Morning, Dot," a familiar voice said from across the counter and Dot moved with delight around it to give Betty a warm hug.

"Betty!" Dot said, surprised at the various emotions she was beginning to feel at her presence. It wasn't as if she wasn't ever going to see her again, but she supposed this was the end of a particularly nice era in her life in which Betty had played such a huge part. "You're not working at the bookstore today?"

"Just a couple of hours this afternoon. A few pick-ups, I'm told." She smiled warmly. "Figured I'd get my own errands done early. Fondue with Emily and her family tonight at their place." Emily was Betty's daughter, who lived in another town just a short drive away, while her son, Nico, was overseas. Where exactly he was, Dot didn't know since he often moved around with his work.

"That sounds lovely. Here is your apple galette. I hope it's okay," Dot said, handing her a wrapped-up box with a warm caramel apple pastry inside. "And this one is on me," Dot said with a wink. Normally, she never made a habit of giving things away for free since she was in a small town and sooner or later, everyone started to feel like a friend, but there was something about the store closing that was making her feel a tad sentimental.

"No, no, I will be paying for my own galette today, Dot," Betty said, reaching into her purse to fish out her wallet.

Dot put a hand on hers to stop her. "Please. I want to," she said, and her tone must have swayed Betty to not argue.

"Fine," she said, her long arms wrapped tightly around Dot. "Aww, so it's really happening then. In the paper and everything. How are you feeling?"

Dot didn't need any explanation as to what Betty was referring to. It had been the talk of the town all morning. Everyone in some capacity had learned that after Christmas, the doors of the Old Mill would not be opening again.

She knew a part of her should be relieved that it was finally out in the open and she no longer had to keep the secret or ask others to keep her secret for her. She knew that had been hard on all of them.

Although for some reason, the weight of it all didn't float away like she had hoped. Certainly, she was excited by this new chapter in her life but also, it was hard to say goodbye to something she'd spent the better part of two decades building. She was not naive in believing it would be easy, but perhaps she wasn't entirely sure just how hard it was going to be.

"Good," Dot said before her silence threatened to stir up a much more difficult conversation. One she'd had on her own thousands of times. "I've booked my trip to France for January. Although, with everything going on with Bear, this might change slightly. At least I'll have the time to sort it all out. In a perfect world, he'll be alright, and I'll have twenty days on the French Riviera drinking wine and eating cheese, which should be just the start I am looking for," Dot said with a grin.

"Sounds horrific." Betty laughed. "I am sorry to hear about Bear, but I hear he is making a good recovery."

"He is." Dot didn't know whether she was ready to face reality or not, but sooner or later, the Old Mill wouldn't be the only change in her life. Although Bear would be a bitter pill to swallow. The only thing keeping her spirits up was the knowledge that she'd done everything she could for him and hoped that she managed to give him the best life a dog could have. And more of the finest cheeses than any dog ever truly needed to eat. "He is the best friend a girl could ask for." Dot was surprised when Betty pulled her in for another hug, which was ended quickly by Dot, who wasn't feeling as though she was ready to start crying about anything just yet. She would save that for her own time.

"Well, while you're off gallivanting around the French Riviera, I'll be here paying one of the neighbour boys to shovel out the hellish snow we are inevitably going to get," Betty said, and Dot was thankful for her friend's ability to know what she needed without being told. And right now, that was continuous distraction.

"Sounds horrific," Dot said. "You could always join me? There is a second bedroom."

"Please," Betty said, "and miss all of the excitement here? I think not. Besides, Nico has invited me to join him in Germany for a bit next month, so I'll be saving my trip for that."

"That sounds wonderful, Betty," and Dot couldn't help but feel like she was saying goodbye. Despite knowing she was going to be back, she knew that when she returned things would be different. *Yes, you will have more time to see your friend,* Dot thought.

"Well, if you decide to sneak away, I will have room for you."

"Thank you, love," Betty said. "Enjoy today, and Merry Christmas. I'll see you before you leave, though I suppose we will have to find a new café to go to," she said, her brows raised. "Change is happening everywhere."

"Indeed," Dot said. "Merry Christmas, Betty. I'll see you soon."

The rest of Dot's morning was filled with Merry Christmases and Happy Holidays as various residents of St Martins stopped in for one final goodie.

Perhaps whoever purchased the building from her would continue with a store of their own. The only thing she'd told herself was that she wasn't prepared to just sell it to the highest bidder. Too often, people stormed into little towns buying up buildings or store fronts and raising the rent on them to make a quick buck, capitalizing on the quaint atmosphere without caring about the town itself. She refused to be the next person to do this, knowing that she really wanted to sell to someone who would like to add to the town, like she'd hoped she had.

*

"What a day," Riley said taking a deep breath, quivering slightly as she let it out.

The last box had been picked up and the store had been cleaned and ready to be closed until it was time for Dot to come in and empty all the shelves. Something she would do later in her own time. One last big clean before she ventured off into the world of retirement, a big glass of rosé in her hand and the sun on her face. It was the reward she'd always dreamed of.

"I think people are going to miss this place," Tia said as she picked up a knapsack filled with various clothes and stuff left in the office over the years. Dot knew there was little chance she could have fit everything in that bag, but she would make sure she got her things to her eventually. Today wasn't about clearing out the store. It was just about saying goodbye.

"I know I am," Cally said her little cheeks lined with tears as she looked around the main room of the Old Mill. Riley's hand reached around her sister and pulled her close as the room fell silent, each of them looking around at the stacked-up chairs and tables, the large Christmas tree in the corner, the lights wrapped around it, highlighting all of the tiny ornaments made by the kids in town.

"I don't think you're the only one, Cally," Charlotte said, walking over to the tree and pulling off one of the ornaments from its branches.

"What do you mean?" Dot asked.

"Well, after you announced you were closing that night, some of the kids and parents started writing thank yous on the backs of the ornaments," Charlotte said, turning the wooden Santa in her hands that had been decently coloured by who she hoped was a child. "We're going to miss your butter tarts," Charlotte read. "Fair enough." She laughed.

Riley and Cally walked over and each picked one up.

"Thank you for the extra whipped cream," Cally read.

"The seasonal loaves," Riley read.

"The lemon squares," Noah said, picking one off the tree.

"This one just asks if you'll be releasing your recipes." Tia laughed before looking at Dot with a curious look. "You're not? Are you?"

Dot shrugged. "I hadn't planned on it." She chuckled, looking up at the tree and seeing all the different ornaments and messages on them. She picked one off the tree and read it to herself. "I hope Bear makes a speedy recovery." Dot sniffled, smiling at the tiny ornament in her hand and pulling it to her chest. "That's nice."

When Dot had set out on this little endeavour, all she had wanted was to create a place that was a part of the community, and looking up and reading all of the kind messages, she suddenly realized that through all of her years of feeling a half-step out of the community, having been from away, she hadn't even realized the moment she was all the way in. That moment when people started to care. *I did it.*

"You okay, Dot?" She heard Charlotte's voice as she wiped a tear from her cheek.

"Never better, love," she said, softly placing the ornament back on the tree as she knelt down and pressed the button to turn off the lights. "Let's go home," she said, turning around, placing one hand over Charlotte's shoulder and the other around Tia's and before she knew it, Cally and Noah were pressed into her at the waist and Riley squeezed in for a big hug.

No one said a word, though she could hear the soft weeping from each of them as she tried to keep it all together. Her head tilted back, and she saw the ugly old calico flour bags Eli had found shoved into the walls as makeshift insulation. She still remembered the day he found them crumpled up in the walls. She'd wanted to toss the old things, but instead, one afternoon, when she'd come back from lunch, she'd found them nailed to the ceiling, draped with some synthetic garland.

She remembered trying to get Eli to take them down but he refused, telling her it was important to remember what this old building had been. The labels on the bags looked down at her now, the small windmill at its centre with the words *The Flour Mill at St Martins* at its centre. Dot could still hear Eli's voice saying, *this old building has a history. You should embrace it. A part of it will always be the Old Mill.* And so she had.

Thank you, Eli.

And for the first time since he passed away, Dot allowed herself to cry.

*

"Henry?" Dot approached the tall man who must have only just arrived, as she could see a small amount of snow still on his head, as he stood helping himself to a drink at her kitchen island.

It hadn't been her idea to have the people from the shop over, though now that everyone was around, Dot had to admit, she was enjoying the company. It gave her less time to think about everything that had happened. And although she was exhausted she knew there was little chance of her falling asleep. At least not right away, even if her eyes were starting to droop.

"I hope you don't mind," Henry said, moving in to embrace her. It was unexpected but she had to admit, all the hugs were making her feel better. "Charlotte said I could come by if I had time, and since I wasn't planning on leaving until tomorrow morning to visit my son, I thought…"

"Your son?"

"Yeah. It's… Let's just say I got some good advice."

"That's wonderful, Henry, and I'm happy you're here. Very happy," she placed a hand on his.

"I also have someone else who will be very happy to see you," Henry said with a big grin. "Charlotte thought he might be more comfortable in the truck, and I got him all set up by the fi—"

"Bear!" Noah shouted as Dot watched him run over to the stove, stopping just before a little bed that Henry had set up. Bear laid nestled in, his tail wagging as all the attention turned to him, as shoes were kicked off and jackets hung up on hooks.

"Bear," Dot said, pressing a hand against her chest as a pressure that had lived there the past four days eased away. She wasn't willing to admit this to anyone, including herself, but Bear's collapse hit her much harder than anyone knew. With Henry's arm around her and seeing Bear wagging his tail as Noah softly stroked the back of his neck, she felt a sense of ease wash over her.

"Thank you for bringing him home," she said looking up at the big man, who surprised her by poking his head in for a kiss. She quickly pulled away.

"Sorry. I just got—" Henry began, stopping when Dot pressed a finger to his lips and pulled the big man over slightly, ignoring the curious expression on Charlotte's face, before gesturing up to the ceiling where some mistletoe hung.

"We shouldn't let it go to waste," she said, standing up on her tiptoes to give him a kiss herself. "Merry Christmas, Henry," she said softly.

"Merry Christmas, Dot," he said, pressing his forehead affectionately against hers before whispering, "I was thinking, I'm not sure if you're still thinking of going to France next month, what with everything going on and all, but I was thinking that… I don't know, maybe… well, it's just, I have some time off, you know… people don't usually need Christmas trees in January."

"What are you saying, Henry?" Dot asked, knowing exactly what he was trying to say but very much enjoying watching him fumble.

"Well, if you wanted some company. Maybe I could join you?"

"Join me in France?" Dot asked, feigning surprise.

"Only if you… I mean… yeah. If you would like that. Maybe?" he said, his face turning a particular Christmassy shade of red that made Dot's heart leap a little. She hadn't felt this kind of playfulness in a long time. She'd almost forgotten how wonderful it was.

"I would love that," she said reaching for his hand and giving it a squeeze. "I would love that a lot."

*

As the night settled down and everyone returned home, Dot sat by the fire, scratching the back of Bear's ears, looking up at the tree Henry and Noah had cut down, which they had all decorated. All month, she had been dreading what this day would feel like. The last day working at the store and the first day of what was about to become the rest of her life. She'd thought of all the possibilities in her mind, fear that she'd be making the worst mistake of her life, or that she was running away again.

Maybe it was the wine, or the fire, or just having spent the day with everyone she loved, which left Dot with a contentedness that she hadn't felt in a long time. Sure, she wasn't without her fears and worries, but she supposed that was the privilege of being alive. *Only we get to determine how these feelings affect us.*

"Open it," Dot said to Charlotte, whose head was resting against the edge of the chair as she stared at the tree. Everyone had left and Noah was tucked in under a blanket on the couch asleep, after he had refused to be the first one in the house to go to bed.

"What?" Charlotte asked, snapping out of her daze to glance over toward Dot.

"Eli's letter," Dot said, knowing from the grimace Charlotte was giving her that she knew what she was talking about even before she said it.

"I will," Charlotte said.

"What's stopping you?"

"Nothi—" She stopped before the word came out, knowing it was a lie that neither of them believed. "It's his last one," she said softly. "You know he never even liked writing them. Only did it because he knew I loved it. He would write them for my birthday and Christmas and our anniversary. So when he died, he… umm… he wrote one last letter for each, and I thought they were done but—" She gestured to the letter in the tree.

"And you're afraid to finish them."

"Sure. Afraid, maybe sad, angry, I don't know what I feel anymore. Just empty most of the time."

"And you think not reading that letter is going to fix that?"

"No. But even the idea of hope is better than nothing, I think. It's ironic, really." Charlotte chuckled as she wiped a tear away.

"Why's that?"

"I hate surprises, and this was a pretty big one. Hiding it in my stocking. What a dick." She choked out a laugh. "It's the last one I will ever get from him." Charlotte sipped her wine and stood up, walking over to the tree and looking at the letter tucked into the branches.

"Sounds like a pretty good reason to read it."

"Then it's over. I'm not sure I'm ready for it all to be over."

"It will never be over, Charlotte," Dot said, giving Bear a kiss on the head as she climbed up to her feet. "Who knows, maybe there is a reason you're finding it now."

"You mean the universe giving me a sign or something."

"Or something." Dot shrugged. "All I know is that a letter is only a letter if you read it." She moved over to give Charlotte a kiss on the cheek. "Right now, it's just a piece of paper," she said softly. "Goodnight, love."

Dot moved to give Noah a kiss on the head, leaving Charlotte to stare at the card. From the corner of her eye, she could see Charlotte pick it up and turn it over in her hand. As she left the living room, she turned to glance back at Charlotte, watching with a smile as she peeled the back of the letter open.

38

Eli

To my darling love,

"Merry Christmas!" he said, pretending he wasn't about to sit down to write one of the most difficult letters of his life.

I suppose it is so difficult because I don't know when you will actually open this letter. You will have noticed I hid this one in your stocking, which means you could open it up this year or many years after I've died. This leaves me in a difficult position.

Well, not really, I suppose. Since these letters have always been a way for me to express how I feel about you in ways you never truly believed. At least I hope they have.

Despite being your biggest fan and supporter, I believed there was always a small morsel of your brain that thought I was only saying those things because I had to, because that is what partners are supposed to say to each other. But it was never like that for me, and nothing could be further from the truth.

Right now, I hope you're sitting down with a nice glass of mulled wine, or one of those ridiculous Christmas spiced cocktails we would whip up together, staring up at a decorated tree and thinking about all the incredible memories you and I shared together at Christmas over the years.

I hope you get to walk in the snow, listen to Michael Bublé's Christmas album and dance around with Noah, trying to tire him out before bed. I choose to believe you're doing this, because the alternative is you moping around in tears, dreading the holiday season, and admittedly, nothing would kill me faster than ruining Christmas for you forever. Although I appreciate your heart may need time to mend, please don't let this be a time that lacks magic and hope for you and Noah.

I write this not knowing how much time I have left, but having the time to sit and write these letters has reminded me of how special our life together has been. Twenty-one years together is a remarkable gift we got to share, and although not all of it has been easy, I know in my heart that there's not a single person on this earth I would have rather done this with.

The opportunity to fall asleep with you beside me and wake up with you next to me is my crowning achievement. Please don't tell Noah, although soon enough, it will be on you to explain to him that those two ingredients tend to go hand in hand when making a baby. Good luck with that.

But I'm rambling, because I don't want this to be over. Even though I know sooner or later, things have to end, although not always when we want them to.

There's no easy way to go about saying anything I am about to say or write to you, I guess. So, here it goes. A section I'm calling "Eli's final request". Maybe "request" isn't the right term, but wish? A list of things for you to consider moving forward. Get on with it, Eli! I know that's what you're thinking. Because you asked.

Don't overthink everything. You are far more capable than you give yourself credit for. Try not to sweat the small stuff. Things always have a way of working out. I hear the irony in this since if you're reading this, I'm dead, but maybe that was just the journey I was on. Maybe I was here for a great time, not a long time.

You are beautiful inside and out.

Not everything is going to work out the way you want it to. That doesn't mean it didn't work out.

You are a brilliant mother.

Noah is going to be whoever he is going to be and honestly, all we have ever had to do is support him. You have always been great at just being there and showing up, and I'm sure at some point, you may feel like you're letting him down or failing him because you, my love, are a perfectionist. But you're not failing him. Just show up and give it time. It will all work out.

You have a capacity for love that is beyond anything you give yourself credit for—hell, you loved me for two decades. You should get a medal.

Most of all, I'm sorry. I'm sorry I can't be there to help you with Noah. To see him grow up, or to grow old with you like we'd always planned. I'm sorry you have to be the mom and the dad, be the good and the bad parent. None of this is fair to you. I should be there to play with him when he wants to try something new, and discipline him when he messes up. Which he will, because he is our kid and man, did we do our fair share of messing up.

You mean the world to me. Not figuratively—truly, you

are my world. I have loved you since the moment I saw you. I know how much you enjoy asking me why I love you, then you get upset with my responses. Telling you how you can always make me laugh, or how brilliant you are and effortlessly beautiful. Mostly, you just get mad when I tell you that there is no one on this earth I would rather spend my time with than you, although I stand behind this being the most important quality in a relationship. You are my best friend, and if that's lame then fine. I'm lame.

The depth of the love I have for you is greater than anything I could ever truly express. How do you tell someone they make up a part of you you never knew you had? To have existed in a world where I got to bask in your presence every day for so much of my life has been beyond anything I could have ever dreamed of. From the moment we met, all I have ever wanted to do was to be worthy of your love, to have the capacity to love, and be loved by you.

I know this life didn't pan out like you always wanted. I told you I would be with you forever. We just didn't realize then, we were talking about my forever. No doubt there is a part of you that doesn't think you can handle this, and I suppose that's why I'm writing this to you. Because I need you to know that you, love of my life, are capable of handling so much more than you have ever given yourself credit for. You're a brilliant mother and the kindest person I know. You don't need me to be these things—you never have. You just need a little faith that you are enough, and you have always been enough.

I don't want this to end. This letter. This life. But if I have learned anything going through all of this, it is that sooner or later, everything has to end, whether we are ready for it or not.

I will miss you so much.
To the moon and back,
Eli xoxo

P. S. If it's not too much trouble, could you please look out for my mom? I worry about her in the middle of nowhere.

39

Charlotte

"Merry Christmas!" Charlotte said as she stepped into the kitchen wearing a set of red pajamas with Christmas trees and tiny Rudolph's on them.

"Merry Christmas!" Noah said, wearing a matching set of pajamas which secretly made Charlotte happier than she would have ever admitted to her son. "You certainly took your time getting up," he said, rolling his eyes.

"It's six in the morning, Noah," Charlotte said, shaking her head.

"So, you thought you would just sleep in?" His tone was playful, though from the way he looked at her, she believed there was more than a hint of truth in his tone.

"Easy, you. I don't see Dot up," Charlotte said, regretting it the moment she said it since she knew there was no chance she would be up before her mother-in-law. Even if she couldn't see her, the smell of cinnamon bread coming from the oven should have been enough to tell her that not only was she up, she'd already baked something.

"She's in the—"

"Forget it." Charlotte tossed her hands in the air. "I'm up now. Let's try to focus on the positives, shall we?" She moved over to the island where she found a half-filled French press and decided to pour herself a cup.

"Can I go into the living room now?" Noah asked. "Nana told me I had to wait for everyone to be up before I could go in," he said, his eyes fixed on Charlotte.

Charlotte had forgotten about Dot's rules, which Eli had always said were his favourite worst part of Christmas. He said his dad would purposefully sit in the bedroom for hours just to make him wait and knowing Eli's father, it was likely to be true. Though Charlotte hoped she wasn't Eli's father in this particular instance.

"Yes, of course. Sorry for making you wai—"

"Awesome!" Noah said, hopping off the stool before Charlotte finished her thought and running into the living room, which was when Charlotte noticed for the first time, and to her surprise, how many presents were tucked under the tree. It was far more than there had been when she'd gone to bed the night before and certainly a lot more than she had picked up herself.

"Merry Christmas, love," Dot said, walking into the kitchen and pouring herself the last of the coffee. "I'll make more," she added with a wink.

"Merry Christmas, Dot," Charlotte said. "Looks like you've been busy this morning," her voice quiet as she tilted her head toward the stove and the tree.

"The cinnamon bun is a tradition, you know that love," Dot said, flicking on the light of the oven to have a glance inside. "And you prep it the night before, so it is hardly any work at all." She must have been satisfied with the buns, opening the oven as steam billowed out. Using the two cloths she kept in her apron, she pulled the tin out of the oven and immediately turned it upside down onto a wooden cutting board.

It didn't seem possible for the house to smell any better but somehow, the sweet aroma of sugar, cinnamon and spices filled the air.

"My God," Charlotte said, her eyes closing as she inhaled deeply. Already, her mouth was salivating at the thought of biting into the sticky bun.

"Good, cause there's a lot." Dot smiled as she tapped the top of the tin and using her cloths, slowly eased the tin up, letting the bun fall out as melted sugar oozed out the sides.

"You don't have to tell me twice."

"Smells delicious, Nana!" Noah said from the living room where he was examining the tree, while he glanced up at his stocking, murmuring things to Bear, who was happily wagging his tail by the fire. Charlotte wondered if the old boy had been there the entire night.

"How's he doing?" Charlotte asked.

"If you mean Noah, he's been impatiently waiting for you, though I refused to let him wake you before six, because I thought that was fair. And if you mean Bear." Dot sucked in a deep breath and looked over at her furry companion of over twelve years before sighing. "I think he's doing me a kindness." Her smile was genuine, but Charlotte could see the pain in the woman's eyes and understood what she meant.

"He's with us now," Charlotte said, standing up to wrap an arm around her mother-in-law.

"Yes, he is," she said softly.

Charlotte looked around for something but when she didn't see it, she moved to one of the cupboards and pulled out a bottle of Irish cream liquor from inside. "Shall we spice up this coffee a little?" she asked, her brows raising.

"You cheeky little girl," Dot said, sliding her cup over to Charlotte and pinching her fingers together signalling for a tiny bit.

"How in the world did you have time for any of that?" Charlotte said, trying to keep her eyes on the pour while her head nodded toward the surprisingly full tree. "I've been trying to keep my head above water this month and you managed to pull this off? What are you, a witch?" She chuckled as she poured a little liquor into the coffee cups.

"I don't know what you're talking about." Dot shrugged, tapping her glass as if to say, *A little more.* The two women laughed. "You can keep your secrets then."

"How was…?" Dot nodded to the tree, and it didn't take a genius to know she was referring to the letter Eli had written. Charlotte had managed to read and re-read the letter a dozen or so times before she finally fell asleep, and even though it would be the last letter she ever received from him, there was a sense of contentment, and perhaps a little sadness, with it as well.

"I think it was what I needed," Charlotte said, feeling as though it would be hard to ever explain just what she was feeling to anyone, but hopefully, that would suffice.

If Dot wanted more, she certainly didn't ask for it.

"You know he wrote me a letter," Dot said, sipping her coffee.

"He did?" Charlotte asked, surprised. She had no idea that he had done it for anyone else other than her, but she was happy that he had.

"He did. And I suppose I have you to thank for that," she

said, "since writing letters was never something we did. But it was… I was grateful."

Charlotte understood exactly what she meant. She may never know what it was Eli said to Dot but whatever it was she knew would be special—as all of the letters she received from him were.

"To Eli," Charlotte said, holding her coffee up.

"To Eli," Dot said, tapping her mug against Charlotte as the two women sipped their spiked coffees.

Charlotte took a moment to think about Eli and all the wonderful things that he had meant to her, feeling lucky that even now, with him gone, he and his family were still such an important part of her and Noah's life. She particularly thought about the last month and what coming here had meant. Sure, she might have messed things up a little, but she hoped that moving forward, she and Noah would have a relationship they could build on, and for the first time since Eli's death, she didn't feel utterly alone. She had Dot, and friends, and even though Eli wasn't there, she knew she had him with her too. Most importantly, she had Noah, even though he may get in trouble and scare the living bejesus out of her at times. He was a good, smart, compassionate kid, and at the end of the day, what else could she ask for?

She looked over at him now sorting through his presents and petting Bear. The room smelled of Christmas and her coffee was strong. It truly was a magical morning. Charlotte pulled off a piece of the sticky bun and bit into it, letting the sweet, gooey, spiced bread warm her up from the inside, while imagining Eli ripping into it the way he always did. It was the one time of year he was unapologetically childlike. The thought made her smile.

"I suppose we should get in there before he starts barking orders," Charlotte said, shoving the rest of the bun in her mouth.

"I suppose we should." Dot smiled as she tore off a piece of paper towel from a roll on the table and handed it to Charlotte, causing Charlotte to nearly choke on her bun as she began to laugh.

*

"Last one." Charlotte clapped her hands together excitedly, before finishing off her coffee. Successful may have been an understatement considering Charlotte had absolutely no idea how Dot had managed to pull any of this off. Each of them seemed to have an endless stream of presents to open and certainly more than any of them needed.

But even Charlotte had to admit that after the last couple of years and everything they had all gone through, the act of watching the surprise and the joy as they opened a gift was a generous change from the sadness of the year before. Charlotte had believed at one point that it would be hard to feel good again after losing Eli, or that it would feel like they were betraying him in some way.

But as they all sat there laughing and sharing stories, eating his favourite sticky buns, everything felt like they were trying to remember him for who he was rather than remind themselves that he was no longer there.

Sure, under all of the laughter, there was a continuous feeling of loss. But Charlotte was beginning to accept that was never going to leave her. It would remain a part of her identity, a part of each of their identities, for the rest of their lives. But that didn't mean that it needed to rule over them. There was no one way of feeling, and maybe that was a good thing.

"Wow!" Noah said, ripping the wrapping paper off the large hard-covered copy of *The Food Lab*.

"I figured you might find this one more appealing. The author is a scientist turned chef and, well, he certainly takes food science to a whole new level. At least in my opinion. Plus, I enjoy his food," Dot said, her legs crossed in her chair as she sipped on her coffee. "I hope you like it."

"I love it!" Noah said, standing up to give Dot a hug. "Thanks, Nana."

"You're welcome, love."

"Looks like we're all done," Charlotte said, looking around and picking up the wrapping paper from the floor, balling it up in her hand before opening the stove door and tossing it into the fire. "Should we take some of those recipes and maybe cook up a brunch?" she turned back to find both Noah and Dot staring at her.

"This," Charlotte said, pointing a finger at the pair, "is creepy."

"Go on, Nana," Noah said, which received a whack in the arm from Dot.

"What?" Charlotte asked, feeling on the outside of a joke for some reason.

"Well, I do have one more gift for you. But it comes with a stipulation."

"I think we got enough gifts," Charlotte joked, but no one else laughed.

"Don't be lame, Mom!" Noah said.

"Okay. So, what's this stipulation then?" Charlotte sighed, feeling utterly confused about what was happening right now.

Dot reached into her robe pocket, pulled out a little box and handed it to Charlotte.

"Here," she said, though it felt very ceremonial for some reason.

Noah was practically vibrating off the walls, trying to contain his excitement.

"You know what it is?" Charlotte asked and he nodded profusely, likely because he didn't seem capable of saying anything for fear of shouting out whatever this surprise was.

"It was actually his idea." Dot shook her head, appearing less excited than Noah by the gift. "Go on. Open it."

With some hesitation, Charlotte pulled the top off the box and inside were a set of keys, which only added to Charlotte's confusion.

"I didn't really have time to do anything special, but the keys are more of a symbol, I guess," Dot said.

"A symbol of what?"

"The Old Mill," Noah said, clapping, and Charlotte couldn't help herself from laughing, although she was unsure why she was since she still didn't really have any idea of what in the world was happening. She felt silly, the keys dangling in her finger, and Noah still clapping. But for the life of her, she had no idea why Dot was handing her the keys to—

Reality sank in, at least she thought it had but the idea was so foreign to her, she couldn't comprehend it.

"No. You mean…?"

"Yes," Dot said. "Only if you want to."

"I can't."

"Why not?" Noah asked. "You don't have a job, remember? You got fired."

"I prefer let go," Charlotte said, unsure why she felt the need to clarify any of this. "And we have a life and a home in

Toronto. Your school." Charlotte was just absently naming things now as the idea slowly started to sink in. "We can't—"

"You said it yourself. We might have to move anyways. Why not move here? Why not run the Old Mill?" Noah asked.

"You want to move here?" Charlotte asked Noah. "What about this place being stupid?"

"I may have been a little angry when I said that," Noah said, his face flushing red. "But if I have to change schools anyways, why not come here?"

"Noah, this is a big deal. You're talking about—"

"I know."

"It is," Dot said, jumping in, "which is why you have no obligation to say yes. The news is out there already, and I haven't told Tia or Riley and for all I know, they've already made plans to move on."

"I can't do it on my own." Charlotte said.

"I know," Dot said, "which is why I have been thinking I would stick around, part-time," she held up a finger, "just to make sure you're okay. Get you situated and everything. I have a new life to start after all."

"You would do that?" Charlotte asked, once again feeling an emotion wash over her that threatened to kick up the tears she'd been working so hard all morning to bury.

"I think I could manage it," Dot said with a shrug, "but only if this is something you want. And obviously, there would be some things we would have to work out, logistically, but I don't see why we couldn't make it work."

For days now, Charlotte had been trying to figure out what their life would look like going back to the city and moving on. She knew things would have to change and she didn't entirely know how.

But never in her wildest dream did she imagine herself moving to St Martins or taking over the Old Mill. Perhaps she thought that maybe Noah would never want to leave the city, or maybe it was her who could never really believe that leaving was an option. Where else would she feel comfortable starting over? Could she ever have the life she imagined here? Considering the life she had always imagined was already gone, perhaps it was time to rethink what she believed was possible.

"What do you think, Mom?" Noah asked, his little smile beaming, and the joy in his eyes reminding her so much of his father, it hurt.

"I know this is a big decision, Charlotte, so please don't feel like you have to answer now. You can think about it," Dot said.

"You want this, Noah?" Charlotte asked.

"Ye—I mean… only if you want it," he said, glancing at Dot, and it was suddenly clear to Charlotte Dot must have coached him a little in what to say as to not make Charlotte feel any pressure. Or maybe he was just being courteous. Charlotte didn't know what to think.

She sat staring at the keys for what felt like a lifetime. She tried to imagine what life would be like. Was the past month just some fairy tale that she would ruin by moving here? Would they destroy everything that made it all great? She had no idea, but eventually, her eyes found Dot and Noah as she desperately tried to process it all.

"Can I think about it?"

40

Noah

Noah's heart sank. He'd hoped his mom would be as excited by the idea as he was. Maybe he wasn't clear just how okay he was with staying. But one of his promises to Nana, which took far less convincing than Noah would have imagined and he hope that was because she secretly loved the idea, was that he wouldn't pressure mom into it. If she was going to make this decision, she had to do it on her own.

He tried not to let his disappointment show on his face, but it was hard. Until she suddenly began to laugh, hard. It was a laugh he wasn't sure he'd ever heard in his life but it seemed like raw joy.

"What's wrong?" Noah asked.

"Just something your father said to me," she said, shaking her head. "Yes," she said after looking at the keys again in her hand and gripping them tightly.

"What?" Noah said, trying to understand the emotional backflips twisting his gut now.

"I'm in, Noah. No overthinking it. My answer is yes."

THE END - BONUS

"Sending Love"

Music and Lyrics by Hilary Adams
Wherever you may be, I hope you enjoy this holiday tune.

Acknowledgements

Dear Reader,

I want to thank you for reading this story. For those of you who have read my work in the past, this one takes a slightly different approach to storytelling than my previous books. And for those of you who are giving my work a chance for the first time, I hope you enjoyed it enough to read another.

When I first came up with this story, I worked in my hometown at a fantastic market store called The Flour Mill, which, like the Old Mill, is in an actual old flour mill. There, I got to work with some amazing women making incredible food. If you ever find yourself in the small town of St. Marys, ON, I hope you can swing by and give it a try.

One of the things I have been trying to do with some of my stories is capture what it is like to live in a small town, and honestly, as a kid, I'll admit I spent most of my life trying to get out of it, move to the city and do something bigger than myself. Now, as I get older and return home, I begin to see just how special it was to live in a community like St. Marys. Even then, when it was much smaller than today, the life it provided me was priceless. So, I hope I captured some of the joy of a small town in this story, along with the joys of cooking and eating good, homemade food.

As always, this book took more than a few hands to make

it all happen. I would first like to thank my parents. My Dad continues to be one of the most supportive people in my life, without whom I wouldn't be able to do what I do. His support and understanding while I develop my work is a relief that I can't be more thankful for. As for my Mum, any of this, would not have been possible without her. She is the first to read all my work, my first and last editor, and though she loves me, she always will provide feedback, even if it isn't what I want to hear. Through this, she challenges me to be a better writer and storyteller. I am forever grateful for her and her support.

I would like to thank my family, who read my stories even when those books may not be in the genre they enjoy. I couldn't have asked for a better support system, and being lucky enough to have all these people in my life is incredible. Love to you all! GJJSHLRDJLAHBKALLNGKGRHTHDPG RJHKC

Along with my Mum and my partner, Hilary. I would like to thank Emily for helping edit the Old Mill. It was my first time working with Emily, and I appreciated some of her insights to help cut and make the story tighter.

My cover artist, Calder Campbell, a talented artist based in St. Marys, was gracious enough to put together a beautiful cover for me. One of my favourite things about writing a book is giving my very vague descriptions to an artist about the tone and style of the book and seeing what they come up with. Calder did not disappoint. What she created captured my vision, and I couldn't be more thrilled with the final product. She has been wonderful to work with, and I hope we can collaborate again!

Unlike other books, I will be pairing this one, for the first time, with an Audiobook. For the time being it will be offered on my website www.jonnyonthepage.com. I'm excited to enter this new adventure, and I feel truly grateful for the team I got to work with for making this happen. So, a huge thank you to Ian Sherwood, who recorded, engineered and produced this project. Ian is a talented musician and a friend, and I was so grateful for his support and expertise on this endeavour. Having never done something like this before, it was such a kindness to have a reliable friend there with me. Thank you, Ian.

If you listened to the Audiobook, you will have heard my partner, best friend, and narrator, Hilary Adams. When I thought of this story being read aloud, there was no one I trusted more than her to pull it off. I feel so grateful to have the chance to work with her on this. I hope she will accept doing it again soon with another book! Though she played a very real part in the Audiobook, Hilary's guiding hand can be felt across all my work. Her support and love are unwavering, and I truly can't thank her enough for everything she does for me. Also, thank you for allowing me to use your song at the end of the book, scan the QR code on the bonus page, to hear *Sending Love* by Hilary Adams, which was also produced by Ian Sherwood.

And this is the part where I finally say goodbye to you, the reader. I appreciate you coming on this journey with me, and I hope we do it again soon. I have other books, perhaps not the same mood as this one, but entertaining, I hope, in their own way, and you can find those at the end of the book. If you liked this one, please email me at Jonny@jonnyonthepage.com. I love to get feedback. Perhaps you have found some errors, or would just love to share your thoughts, both are helpful. But also, if you enjoyed it, let me know. I have a few more stories like this, and I would like to work on them one day. Knowing people are enjoying them may be the push I need. In the meantime, thank you all for your support, it means a lot, and please have yourself a Merry Christmas and a very Happy Holiday season, whatever that means to you. Thank you for reading!

Very best wishes,

Jonny Thompson

About the Author

Jonny Thompson is an award-winning writer living in Ponamogoatitjg/Dartmouth, NS with his partner Hilary and their dog Henry. Jonny was born in England and grew up in the traditional lands of the Anishinabewaki and Attiwonderonk nations now St. Marys, Ontario.

Jonny attended Dalhousie University, where he received a BA in Theatre. He's worked professionally in stage and film for over thirteen years, including five extremely exciting years travelling the world as a puppeteer.

Jonny's debut novel *Ash and Sun* was released in October 2022. His novels Atlantis and the Limestone Manor were released in 2023, while Firefly: Book two of the Ash and Sun trilogy was release in 2024. His most resent book *Murder at Winkleberry Farm: A Limestone Manor Mystery* was released in 2025. He has written various novels, novellas and short stories which can be found on his website.

He is continuously working through new projects and looks forward to sharing them with you soon. Thank you for reading!

You can connect with me on:

🌐 https://www.jonnyonthepage.com
📘 https://www.facebook.com/Jonnyonthepage
🔗 https://www.instagram.com/jonnythompson.author

Also by Jonny Thompson

Ash and Sun

After a 200-day suspension, all Senior Agent Adam Jennings wanted was a win on his return to the Global Investigation Bureau (GIB). But when a simple warehouse fire begins to look more like a homicide investigation, he is forced to watch as the entire case begins to unravel, slowly revealing the dark underbelly of a world that should not exist.

Firefly: Book 2 of the Ash and Sun Trilogy

Senior Agent Adam Jennings is ready to leave the past behind and move on. But when his partner Ali is kidnapped, Jens' hand is forced as lives suddenly hang in the balance. Unwelcomed truths are revealed, leaving Jens isolated, no longer knowing who he can trust or what he should believe.

THE LIMESTONE MANOR

When retired police detective Clifford Shaw hesitantly steps off the train in his former hometown of St. Marys, Ontario, the last thing he expects to greet him is a murder. The only thing worse than being inadvertently roped into the investigation is the surprise he receives when the too-good-to-be-true room rental from his lifelong friend Hans has one massive catch. It's in a shared house with six other retirees. Already hesitant about returning to the town he swore he never would, Cliff has one week to figure out if he wants to refuse the room or give his old town one last chance. All this while he helps unravel a mystery to save 'The Town Worth Living In'.

Murder At Winkleberry Farm: A Limestone Manor Mystery

When the residents of Limestone Manor head to the 75th anniversary celebration at Winkleberry Farm, it promises to be a joyful outing. But when the farm's beloved owner, Pieter VanWinkle, longtime friend of Hans, is found dead, the festivities take a dark turn. Pieter's daughter quickly becomes the prime suspect, but Hans is convinced there's more to the story. With Cliff and the rest of their housemates on the case, long-buried secrets begin to surface. Betrayals, old grudges, and family truths some would rather keep hidden threaten to derail the investigation, leaving the gang, and the police, racing to uncover the truth before it's too late.

Atlantis

In a high-stakes race against time, Master Sailor Clive Davis has only twenty-eight days to locate a world-altering weapon hidden in the technologically advanced city of Atlantis. Disguised as a deep-sea welder, he delves into the mysterious depths, determined to thwart billionaire Grace Alice's sinister plan. As Clive unravels the city's secrets, he grapples with his purpose and must race against the clock to separate truth from fiction. Time is ticking, secrets are unravelling, and Clive is our last hope. Will he save the world, or will Atlantis be its undoing?

www.ingramcontent.com/pod-product-compliance
Lightning Source LLC
Chambersburg PA
CBHW072202130726
47910CB00011B/1781